PRESENTING MISS LETITIA

Once a Wallflower
Book One

Maggi Andersen

Books from Dragonblade Publishing

Dangerous Lords Series by Maggi Andersen
The Baron's Betrothal
Seducing the Earl
The Viscount's Widowed Lady
Governess to the Duke's Heir

Once a Wallflower Series by Maggi Andersen
Presenting Miss Letitia

Also from Maggi Andersen
The Marquess Meets His Match

The St. Clairs Series by Alexa Aston
Devoted to the Duke
Midnight with the Marquess
Embracing the Earl

Knights of Honor Series by Alexa Aston
Word of Honor
Marked by Honor
Code of Honor
Journey to Honor
Heart of Honor
Bold in Honor
Love and Honor
Gift of Honor
Path to Honor
Return to Honor

The King's Cousins Series by Alexa Aston
The Pawn
The Heir
The Bastard

Queen of Thieves Series by Andy Peloquin
Child of the Night Guild
Thief of the Night Guild
Queen of the Night Guild

The Book of Love Series by Meara Platt
The Look of Love
The Touch of Love
The Taste of Love

Dark Gardens Series by Meara Platt
Garden of Shadows
Garden of Light
Garden of Dragons
Garden of Destiny

Rulers of the Sky Series by Paula Quinn
Scorched
Ember
White Hot

Hearts of the Highlands Series by Paula Quinn
Heart of Ashes
Heart of Shadows
Heart of Stone

Highlands Forever Series by Violetta Rand
Unbreakable
Undeniable
Unyielding

Viking's Fury Series by Violetta Rand
Love's Fury
Desire's Fury
Passion's Fury

CHAPTER ONE

Hawkshead Village, Cumbria
February 1816

UNCLE ALFORD REPLACED his quill in the standish and looked up at Letty from his desk and the neat pile of letters concerning vicarage affairs. "I have received a letter from your Aunt Edith." He leaned back in his chair and formed a steeple with his fingers while his serious gaze rested on her.

"Have you, Uncle?" Letty bit her lip as her heart began to beat faster. Were her prayers to be answered? She wished her uncle wouldn't pontificate. He was very sweet really, and she was terribly fond of him, but he sometimes made her want to scream in frustration. She tamped down the urge to hurry him along, impatiently yearning to hear if an exciting life beyond this small, slow-moving village awaited her.

He cleared his throat. "You know my feelings about this matter, Letitia. I would prefer you to remain here and marry someone from the village. What about the squire's son, young Geoffrey, up at the Grange? You seem to be as thick as thieves. You've known him most of your life. No nasty surprises there."

"Geoffrey isn't much older than I am. He has no wish to marry for years. And it will certainly not be to me!"

"Men marry young in these parts," her uncle persisted with that mulish look he wore when some parishioner failed to listen to his advice. "A good life awaits you here. Why throw it away for a little glitter? London is not as marvelous as you seem to think it is, for—"

"Uncle?"

"Yes?"

"Does this mean that Aunt Edith has offered to chaperone me? For the whole Season?" The last words ended in a squeak. She clutched her hands together and counted to ten.

"It seems so." He raised a shaggy gray eyebrow. "It appears from the look in your eyes, you are determined to go. I must say that I am disappointed."

She smiled at him across the desk. "It is just for one Season. I'll be home again in a few months. I've wanted to go to London since I turned eighteen, and I'm almost nineteen now. Before you know it, I will be too old!"

"What nonsense!" He pushed his spectacles up his nose and picked up Aunt Edith's letter, perusing it. "Apparently, you will require a new wardrobe. Your aunt believes it should be purchased in London. I would have thought the seamstress in the village, Mrs. Millichamp, would be more than capable of making you a few gowns."

Letty laughed. "No, it won't do. I shall need many items one can only purchase in London, a ball gown, evening gown, and day wear, hats, gloves and shoes…" When he raised a hand to shush her, she came around the desk to kiss his cheek. "Surely you want me to look smart? Not like a country mouse?"

Her uncle coughed and waved her away. "Now, now, none of that. You won't get around me with your feminine ways. But well…naturally…" He reached for his pipe and took several minutes to fill it. Then, he sat back and puffed thoughtfully as the air filled with his favorite blend of tobacco, while she hovered, her stomach doing flips. "Very well, I can see you are set on the idea. I don't see why we can't spare a little from your inheritance, which I've invested for your future. I accept you shall want to appear quite the thing."

Letty gasped. "Uncle Alford! Thank you!"

"I shall write to my sister immediately and advise her that if the weather permits safe travel, we will be arriving in three weeks. Naturally, I shall accompany you. I must book tickets on the stage-coach."

"There is no need, Uncle. I am perfectly able to go alone."

"Nonsense. The curate will take over while I'm gone. A change is as good as a holiday they say."

Letty left him to his letters and climbed the stairs to her bedchamber. She put on her sturdiest half-boots, warm pelisse, scarf, and a velvet bonnet, then pulled on woolen gloves. Outside in the garden, snow covered the path and piled up against the fence. She walked down the path to the vicarage front gate, opened it, and picked her way over the hard ground through a copse of trees, taking a shortcut she often used.

The front gates of the Grange, the home of Squire Varney, was a mile farther on by road. Walking briskly, her breath misting in the still air, she climbed a fence. The Grange appeared in the distance, a long two-story brick dwelling with ivy growing over the walls. Smoke rose from its four chimneys. Letty took the well-worn path to the stables. Despite what her uncle believed, there had never been anything remotely romantic between her and Geoffrey Verney. They had been friends since she came here at the age of seven after her parents died. Geoffrey was five years older than her. He had taught her to ride, as his father, who was master of the hunt, had many fine animals in his stables. She was confident Geoffrey would be as excited as she was by her news.

She trudged along, head down, traversing deep, ice-covered pot-holes. Her uncle's opinion of London was exaggerated. Why, everyone flocked there to visit the theatre and the opera and the parks.

Her close friend, Jane Ormsby, told her all about it after her trip two years ago. But she had not found a husband there. She had returned to the village and married Gordon, the local solicitor.

Uncle Alford had not visited London for years, so he might well have the wrong idea entirely. Letty hadn't traveled far from Hawkshead village since she came here to live, but she was sure, as long as one learned where one might go, and where one shouldn't, the city would prove to be most exhilarating.

She reached the large stable block. Horses hung their heads over the top of their boxes to neigh a greeting, their breaths misting the air. The resident goat darted across to butt its head into her hand.

"Oh, I am sorry, Julia. I've brought nothing for you," Letty said regretfully.

"Your hat will do." Geoffrey looked up but continued forking hay, moving steadily, his stocky body making light of the work. Finally, he threw down the fork and smiled a welcome. "What's brought you out into the cold and away from the fire?"

Her excited breath drew in the familiar smells of dusty hay, feed, and manure. "I am going to London! My Aunt Edith is to chaperone me for the whole Season!"

He wiped his brow with his forearm. "Oh? You'll be finding a husband then."

She sidestepped Julia as the goat tried to push Letty off her feet. "I might. And I might not."

"That's what these Seasons are for, isn't that so? It's a marriage market. They get a look at you, and you get a gander at them."

She stared at him, dismayed by his critical tone. "It's not because of that. There are balls, and dances, admittedly, but I will also see the London sights, the Tower, and Astley's Amphitheatre. I am to be presented to the queen!" After Julia gave up and wandered away, Letty picked up a piece of straw and shredded it with her fingers, watching Geoffrey out of the corner of her eye. "We are so far away from everything here. I am rusticated!"

He nodded at her. "I daresay."

She frowned. "Aren't you happy for me? I always wanted to ride in Rotten Row."

He smoothed back his fair hair. "Of course. If it's what you want, Letty. But I don't think any place would come close to living here. Not for me at any rate."

"I love it here, but it's so quiet nothing ever happens."

"The Thompson's just had twins."

She laughed. "Exactly! But I was not born here as you were, Geoffrey. As you know, my parents came from Richmond in Surrey, which is quite close to London." She watched as he worked for some sign he understood. "And my great-great-aunt fell in love with a pirate!"

"I'm familiar with the tale." He grinned and shook his head, then picked up the fork again. "Then I hope you enjoy London. A little excitement is good, I'll wager. But it's a dangerous place, and you can't wander about on your own as you do here. Take care."

She put her hands on her hips. "You sound like my uncle!"

"Aye. He's a wise one," Geoffrey said annoyingly.

Letty huffed and turned to leave.

"Won't take a minute to hitch up the gig. I'll drive you home," he said with a glance at the sky beyond the doorway. "More snow's coming."

"It's hours off." She walked outside.

"Have it your own way," he called after her. "You always do." He appeared at the stable doorway. "By the way, they won't let you gallop in Rotten Row, you know!"

Disappointed that he hadn't welcomed the exciting news, she stomped out across the meadow, the grass crackling beneath her feet. She refused to allow him to put a damper on her trip. It wasn't that she wished to marry a prince, or a duke, or really, to marry at all—at least not for years. She merely wanted to have an adventure. As did her

Aunt Lydia, whose incredible life in the early years of the last century had been recorded in her diaries.

Letty returned to them again and again, for they had struck a chord in her, the pages filled with adventure and danger on the high seas, reaching out to her from the past. While she didn't aspire to a swashbuckling romance, she did wish her life to be as thrilling as Lydia's. A portrait of her was once hung in the gallery at her parent's home. As Uncle Alford had no love for such things, it must be stored away somewhere. She had dark hair, and Letty imagined herself to be a little like her.

The birdcalls and the bleating of sheep became muffled as flurries of snow began to fall, icy upon her face. Annoyed that Geoffrey had been proven right, she put her head down and began to run.

The snowfall grew heavier, covering the road and the trees in a blanket of white, and threatening to blind her. Shivering, she picked her way over the ground, visualizing hot coffee and muffins. The vicarage gate appeared at last. Her face numb with cold, she hurried up the icy path to the door. Entering the warm vicarage, the thought of a new wardrobe made her smile as she sat and pulled off her wet boots.

"Is that you Letitia?" Her uncle stuck his head out of the study.

"Yes, Uncle."

"You should not have gone out. I told you it would snow."

"Mm, Geoffrey said the same."

"Well he would. He's a sensible fellow."

Letty shook her head and climbed the stairs.

THE AFTERNOON BEFORE they left for London, Letty called in to Jane's home to say goodbye.

In her modest parlor, Jane placed a cup and saucer before Letty on the table. She sat and passed Letty the plate of gingerbread. "It is my dear hope that you meet the love of your life."

Letty smiled at her as she took a piece. "I am looking forward to the experience, but if I come home without a husband, I shan't be too disappointed."

Jane laughed. "I returned to Cumbria without one and found the love of my life right here in the village. Perhaps you will, too?"

"That isn't likely to happen to me," Letty said.

Jane raised her auburn eyebrows above quizzical green eyes. "So, not Geoffrey?"

"No. Although Uncle Alford wishes me to marry him."

"Don't marry anyone you don't feel passion for, Letty. Life would be too long and dreary without feeling that way about your husband." Jane's freckled cheeks flushed.

"I couldn't wish for a better marriage than yours and Gordon's." It was wonderful to see how much they cared for each other. Letty smiled and took a bite of the gingerbread, a little envious.

"Please write when you can. I want to hear all the thrilling news," Jane said, pouring them another cup.

"If I have something thrilling to write about," Letty said with a deep breath.

"Of course you will! Just think, Letty, the balls! And all those handsome gentlemen waltzing you around the floor!"

Letty giggled and leapt up to perform a deep curtsey. "And don't forget my curtsey to Queen Charlotte!"

Jane's green eyes danced. "And you so pretty in your fashionable new gown."

THREE WEEKS ALMOST to the day, Letty and her uncle arrived weary and disheveled, at the Golden Cross Inn, a huge and thriving establishment in the village of Charing Cross, after an exhausting trip which required several overnight stops at uncomfortable coaching inns along the route.

Under lowering clouds, the streets were crammed with wagons, coaches, and pedestrians either seeking to travel or with that lost look of having just arrived, as she supposed she and her uncle did. Letty wrinkled her nose at the chimneys belching dark smoke into the gray air, and the piles of steaming horse dung, but couldn't tamp down the thrill of being here at last. She glanced at her uncle, knowing he was already affirming his poor opinion of the city, as he went to hail a hackney carriage to take them to her aunt's townhouse in Mayfair. Letty was a little nervous at the thought of spending a whole Season in her company. She hadn't met Aunt Edith who'd never visited Cumbria after Letty came to live with her uncle.

In Mount Street, Aunt Edith's narrow townhouse with black iron railings in front, was one of a row of identical two-story buildings of warm brick. As they alighted from the cab, a man selling pies wandered past them, calling in a loud voice. He paused to offer one to her uncle, who dismissed him with a sharp shake of his head.

A maid with a white apron and mob cap greeted them in the gloomy hall and led them to the parlor where Aunt Edith, close in age to her brother, dressed in a dark gray cambric with a lace collar and cuffs, rose from the sofa, a book held against her chest as if she regretted having to close it.

"My dear Edith, how very good to see you." Uncle Alford hurried across to kiss her cheek. "But I don't know how you can bear to live in this noisy metropolis."

"One becomes accustomed to the noise. Better by far than the bleating of sheep. Goodness, Alford, how white your hair has become." She turned to Letty. "And this is Letitia." As Letty rushed to hug her, Aunt Edith held out her hand. Letty had no recourse but to shake it.

"How do you do, my dear." Aunt Edith gazed at her myopically. "You are nothing like your dear mother. She was fair with blue eyes. It seems you favor your father. Well, never mind, we shall make do."

"Letitia is quite pretty, Edith," Uncle Alfred said with a frown.

For a moment, Letty feared an argument would ensue. She had visions of being carried off back to Cumbria. But Aunt Edith tapped Letty's chin. "Well yes, I now see a little of your mother in your features, and you get your dark hair and eyes from your father. A pity, when fair hair and blue eyes are so fashionable." She turned to the young maid. "Mary? Don't stand there as if you're frozen to the spot! Bring in the tea tray. Alford, I'm sure you and Letitia would care for tea? Good. Shall we sit? Don't tell me you came in a hired chaise? So extravagant."

Letty sat beside her aunt while Uncle Alford chose the overstuffed armchair. "No, we took the stage, and I must say…"

As they conversed, Letty sank back against an embroidered cushion. The room was old fashioned with big heavy pieces of furniture not in the modern style at all, the walls papered in dark green which made the room quite dark, even with the matching velvet curtains drawn aside. Outside the window was the brick wall of the house next door. She wished she didn't feel so flat. With a sigh, she acknowledged the trip had left her weary. She remained confident that tomorrow, after a good night's sleep, everything would look a great deal better.

THE COAL FIRE sent flickering lights over the Turkey carpet of Fraser Willard's cozy library, the walls covered in mahogany bookshelves stacked with tomes. A branch of candles, the only other light in the room, perched on the table beside a crystal decanter.

A whiskey in his hand, Brandon Cartwright lounged in the leather wing chair, his legs stretched out over the crimson rug as he blew a cloud of smoke from the cheroot he held between his long fingers. "So, I'm to find out all I can about Lord Ambrose Fraughton?"

"Become his shadow." The firelight warmed Willard's gray-streaked, fair hair. Brandon's superior at the Home Office, seated opposite him, took a pinch of snuff from an enamel box. "Whatever ball or soiree Fraughton attends, you attend. We want to know who he meets, and if possible, what is said." He sniffed delicately. "This mission is eminently suited to you, because as Sir Richard Cartwright's heir, you can inveigle an invite to any affair."

Brandon stubbed out his cheroot in the dish. "I've met his wife, but I don't know Fraughton. If I'm to be of service, I'll need to learn more about him."

"There's a scheme afoot to rescue the Comte de Lavalette from the prison of the Conciergerie, before he is executed," Willard responded. "As I'm sure you realize, to aid a French subject in escaping his country's justice is a sensitive matter. It must be kept under a cloak of absolute secrecy. Difficult, when we have the problem of a group of monarchists wishing to make an example of him. Blood runs high after the deposing of a king, and these men are looking for someone to punish."

"Who is this Lavalette, may I inquire?"

"It's a very interesting story," Willard said. "The Comte was Napoleon's postmaster and at one time, his *aide-de-campe*. He was appointed to the position so he could open, read, and then reseal suspicious mail on the grounds of intelligence gathering. The real purpose was to identify threats to Napoleon from the monarchists as well as others. Lavalette's wife, by the way, is the niece of the former empress, Josephine."

"And what is Fraughton's interest in this affair?"

"He is one of those who are determined to see Lavalette dead."

"What is the government's interest in Lavalette?"

"We are informed he has information vital to the interests of the British government."

Brandon took a deep sip of the smooth whiskey. "Why not arrest Fraughton, keep him out of the way until the business is done?"

"Can't do that. We have to wait to see what information Lavalette has passed on to his wife," Willard said, returning his snuff box to his pocket. "We also need to learn what it is these monarchists are planning."

"So, I'm to hide in the rooms where they gather," Brandon said dryly, pushing back his dark hair with an impatient hand. "Under the sofa?"

"I'll leave that to you. They are unlikely to view you as a threat. You've worked hard to create the image of a harmless rake." Willard's lips twitched. "You have quite a reputation with the ladies, not to mention your much talked about affair with Lady Mary Stanhope." He cast an eye over Brandon's snugly fitted, dark blue coat which spoke of the expertise of Schweitzer & Davison who enjoyed the patronage of the Prince of Wales. "You are known to be a dab hand at the reins since you won that curricle race to Brighton some few years ago. You strip well at Jackson's boxing salon and are an excellent judge of horseflesh at Tattersalls."

Brandon laughed at what he considered an unflattering description of his talents. "Exhausting work, but it befalls me to make the sacrifice."

Willard smiled. "I'm sure. Especially your well-earned reputation with the fairer sex. These men will not know about the work you performed for foreign affairs in Madrid during the war, or the other undercover operations for Whitehall you've been involved with. By the way, Princess de Vaudémont has requested we recruit you."

Brandon raised his eyebrows at that. The princess was a political plotter par excellence. He had always admired her intellect. "Did she indeed? Then I can hardly refuse, can I?"

CHAPTER TWO

FORTUNATELY, UNCLE ALFORD departed for the country on the morning following their arrival in London, after declaring himself a trifle uneasy about leaving Letty in a place where scoundrels lurked on every corner. He declared that Letty was an intelligent young woman, but of a spirited nature and not always prudent. Therefore, he demanded his sister write to him every week to assure him everything went well. Until the hackney took him away, Letty was on tenterhooks, fearing he'd demand she come with him.

Letty's first day at the modiste's disappointed her. It seemed that her aunt, who had never married, had quite conservative views about dress. And worse, the modiste, Mrs. Crotchet, a lady in her fifties, tended to agree with her. They decided that Letty must be seen to be a demure young lady, and it appeared that even her ball dress would lack glamor. No fripperies were to be indulged in. Letty's dreams of fur muffs, feathered, high-crowned bonnets, and military-styled pelisses, faded while practical styles were discussed in serviceable colors such as nankeen, snuff, and drab.

Because Letty's father had been the second son of a baron, she was to be presented. Young ladies were allowed to wear more color on this occasion. She dreamed of ruby velvet with point lace like the one she'd seen in the *Belle Assembly* fashion periodical, or a gown bordered in gold and adorned with tassels, but she didn't hold out much hope for either of these. Fortunately, the presentation was some weeks away and gave her time to practice her curtsey.

Now, all her hopes lay with the Kirkwood's ball held on the Saturday of the following week.

Letty's days were taken up with accompanying her aunt about. Many hours were spent in Hatchards Booksellers in Piccadilly, and Minerva Press on Leadenhall Street, where her aunt searched for a particular book. Aunt Edith's penchant for gothic fiction surprised her. On the way home, they often stopped for an ice at Gunter's, another of her aunt's indulgences.

Toward the end of her second week, two of Letty's gowns arrived from the modiste. She rushed to open the boxes. Once untied, and the gowns spread out over her bed, her heart sank. The morning gown was acceptable, although quite plain and of a serviceable material, but the ball gown! It was as bad as she had feared.

Aunt Edith came into the room. "Perfect for a modest young lady," she declared, looking pleased.

Letty stood before the mirror. The modest style wouldn't be hideous on an older lady, she thought bleakly. The sprigged muslin was undeniably pretty, but the green of the sash not a good color for her, and the frill around the neck made her think of an African lizard she had seen pictures of in a book.

On the night of the ball, Mary, Aunt Edith's maid, arranged Letty's hair, and struggled to create the style she wished for. The overall effect was uninspired, for her locks, as straight as a broom handle, resisted the curling tongs, and the green ribbon looked drab against her dark hair which had not a hint of gold.

"How nice you look, Letitia," her aunt declared, while handing her a velvet box. "You shall wear my pearls."

"Thank you, Aunt." Letty clasped the strand around her neck, her reluctant fingers fumbling with the catch. As the necklace rested against the high neck of the gown, the pearls tended to look more cluttered than glamorous, but at least the pearl earrings were pretty. She turned her head, enjoying the way they danced against her neck. If only she could take her scissors to the gown and cut a scoop neck and replace the horrid flat green ribbon with white. She was good with a needle, it wouldn't take more than an afternoon to create pretty puff sleeves. But of course, she couldn't. She would have to wear it and cringed at the thought.

On Saturday evening, a hand to her nervous stomach, Letty sat stiffly upright as the carriage took them through the streets to St. James's Square. They stepped down before the imposing Kirkwood mansion, ablaze with what must be a thousand candles. It was all so terribly grand, Lettie caught her breath. Admitted by a footman, they moved through the reception rooms like Aladdin's cave, crammed with guests decked out in fabulous jewels. Their names were announced in the ballroom by the expressionless butler to the seemingly disinterested guests, few of whom paused to glance at them.

Huge crystal chandeliers hung from a ceiling edged in gilt and painted with landscapes and putto. Swathes of gold silk damask dressed the long windows and banks of colorful blooms clustered around marble columns. It didn't matter to Letty that the long room was noisy, smoky, overly perfumed, and too warm, for the atmosphere was electric.

Aunt Edith introduced Letty to a couple of her friends, one a lady of similar age, and an elderly gentleman. They sat on a sofa placed amongst the potted ferns. Aunt Edith fanned herself and talked to them, while Letty, who could hardly hear for the voices swirling around them, watched the ladies mill about in their finery, and the gentlemen, so impressive in their evening wear and crisp white cravats, gather in groups. The *haute ton* were all here, and Letty was sure there would be intrigue and scandal on everyone's lips. A self-confessed snoop, she would have loved to wander among them and eavesdrop.

A quadrille was announced, and couples formed sets as the orchestra struck up. Not one gentleman approached Letty. She seemed to be invisible. Her aunt barely noticed being deep in conversation with the lady beside her. The elderly gentleman rose and limped away. No help in that quarter. Letty was even prepared to dance with him had he asked her.

When the footman appeared with a tray, Letty took a glass of lemonade, which she sipped to ease her dry throat. She trembled with humiliation and nerves when, following the announcement of a country dance, she again failed to attract a single man's attention. She might have a sign on her head declaring her a wallflower. Seated near her, were two young debutantes in their white muslins. Their wide-eyed gazes met hers briefly and then they quickly looked away. As if whatever kept the gentlemen at bay might be contagious.

Another hour passed while Letty became convinced that the whole ballroom had become aware of her discomfort. Gentlemen bypassed her with barely a glance, seeking the fashionably dressed women in their elegant finery. When the master of ceremonies called a waltz and the dance floor filled again with twirling dancers, Letty could bear it no more. She stood. "I must go to the ladies' withdrawing room, Aunt."

Aunt Edith cast her a glance that was faintly sympathetic. "Very well, Letitia. Come straight back."

Letty threaded her way through the crowd. Those not dancing stood drinking champagne together, either in deep discussion or laughing at some seemingly droll on-dit. Everyone seemed to know everyone else, which made her feel worse. She located the withdrawing room and hovered before the mirror. With the fear that she appeared desperate, Letty fiddled with her hair, but there was little she could do with it. She was tempted to pull the offending ribbon off, but then it would be like being naked, with every lady's head dressed so lavishly with flowers and pearls and feathers, so she let it be.

As she pinched her cheeks and bit her lips, two women of a similar age to her, entered the withdrawing room, talking together. They appeared like fairies in their fragile gauze and white satin gowns, bordered around the hem with embroidery and silk flowers. Their scoop-necked gowns displayed a tasteful amount of décolletage, and a few inches of skin between the small-capped sleeves and their long white gloves. Letty glanced at them enviously. She smoothed her long sleeves and smiled at the brunette the other girl had called Miss Somersby as she stood beside Letty at the mirror.

"It's quite a crush, isn't it?" Letty said.

Miss Somersby leaned closer to the mirror and patted a perfectly ordered curl by her ear. "Yes, the Kirkwood's always is, of course, being the first ball of the Season." She turned away and addressed the blonde girl with pink roses in her hair who came to join her. "Did you see Annabelle Freemont? If she had another feather in her headdress, she might fly off."

"And the jewels Lady Meredith Neave wore!" The blonde girl tittered. "I declare it hurt my eyes to look at her."

"Some badly dressed people here tonight," Miss Somersby observed, turning to view the elegant fall of her gown from over her shoulder.

Without another glance at Letty, they left the withdrawing room. Letty followed as they walked away through the crowd, arm in arm.

One look at the daunting crush of beautifully dressed, indifferent people, and she couldn't bear to face them. She turned and hurried away down a deserted corridor.

Entering through the first door she came to, she found herself in a library where a coal fire smoldered in the fireplace, despite the vast room being unoccupied. With a gasp of relief, she scurried across to ease the cold knot in her chest before the flames. The mirror above the marble mantel reflected her anguished face. How long before her aunt wished to leave? How long might she stay here until her absence was noted?

Hearing voices, Letty spun around. She spied an elaborate screen in the far corner, painted with a beautiful rustic scene. She'd just slipped behind it when the door opened. Not daring to risk a peek, she stood with her hands to her cheeks, trying to breathe quietly.

"Good, we can talk freely here," a woman said.

"Lord, Susan! What is this? Your husband will be looking for you," a man responded.

"He is busy, ensconced with his colleagues. And I wanted to see you privately, Marston," she said, sounding flirtatious. "I thought we might..." Her voice lowered into a whisper.

"A quick tumble here in the library? You may be that reckless, madam, but I am not."

Letty put a hand to her mouth to stop from gasping. How foolish of her not to make herself known to them and leave. But it was too late now. She was trapped!

"Where might we meet then?"

"We won't. Not until your husband has breathed his last. It's too perilous."

"I'll be too old," she said in a sulky voice.

He chuckled. "It won't be long by the look of him. Fraughton doesn't seem to be in the best of health. One never knows..."

She gasped. "You wouldn't! Surely not, Marston?"

"You have a vivid imagination, Susan. Or do you wish I would?" There was a pause where Letty strained to hear. "Can you be fond of him?"

"We barely see each other from day to day. He dines with his cronies and is never there at breakfast. I had no say in the marriage. Father insisted. He wished me to be well settled."

"And so you are. The man's as wealthy as Croesus. Give me a kiss then."

The kissing seemed to go on rather long. Letty wished she had a chair. When moans and groans reached her, her face heated, and she wanted to block her ears. What if they discovered her? But they seemed caught up with each other. So much so, she feared they might be there for hours. Finally, amid rustling noises and the lady's giggles, they left the room.

After waiting a moment to be sure, Letty slipped from her hiding place. She cautiously opened the library door and peered out. Without chancing discovery, she darted down the empty corridor to the door leading to the ball room.

"There you are, Letitia." Aunt Edith gathered up her shawl and reticule. "I thought I must have missed you on the dance floor." She frowned. "You cannot dance with just anyone, you know. You must first be introduced."

"I wasn't dancing, Aunt. And I don't see how I can be introduced when no one wishes to meet me."

Her aunt looked exasperated. "Where were you then? Surely not in the withdrawing room all this time?"

"I... tore my hem and had to pin it."

"Oh, your lovely dress. What a shame. I do hope you haven't ruined it. Give it to Mary to mend and launder. I found no one here tonight who might ask you to dance. But never fear, I'm sure more of my acquaintances will attend the next social event. It's still early in the Season, and many remain at their country estates." She smiled at Letty. "But it was your first ball, and you looked very well and behaved prettily. Did you enjoy yourself?"

Letty failed to imagine how crammed the ballrooms would become once the *ton* had all returned to London. "I did, Aunt. I found it most...enlightening."

"Good. Quite different to life in the country, is it not?" She put a gloved hand to her mouth. "I declare, I am ready for my bed. I haven't been out so late in years."

Letty had to stifle a yawn herself. She hadn't yet grown used to city hours, and her lowered spirits made her tired. Her anticipation of a wonderful Season waned a little. As they left the ballroom to wait for their carriage to be brought around, Letty stared about her at the milling guests, wondering what the man and woman in the library looked like. She knew only their names, Lord Fraughton's wife, Susan, and the man with the low seductive voice, Marston.

"Do you know of a man called Marston, Aunt Edith?" she asked when they'd settled in their carriage.

"Marston?" Her aunt frowned. "I hope *he* did not approach you."

"No, I heard his name mentioned, that's all."

"Robert Marston is a rake. You must have nothing to do with him!"

So, that was a rake. *My goodness!* Letty had read about them, but in all her eighteen years, had never met one. She thought again of the couple in the library, kissing, obviously, and whatever else—her imagination failed to fill in the details. Although such an experience had hardly been what she wished for, for they were not nice people, the episode had stirred something in her, an excitement and a curiosity. It was, after all, the beginning of her adventure. Once she got home, she would put pen to paper and tell Jane all about it. She frowned. Well, perhaps not all of it. She didn't want her dear friend worried about her.

BRANDON DISLIKED MISSIONS such as these. He would prefer to be in Paris, working actively in some way to serve the Crown. Not skulking behind pillars like some miscreant. He'd thus far had no success with Fraughton either, who seemed to be more interested in what was occurring in England among his peers, than anything to do with the man about to be beheaded in France. The whole affair seemed odd to him. He wondered if his spymaster had the right of it. But Willard was not one to be mistaken.

As he strolled through the ballroom, pausing to chat to those he knew, he nodded to Lady Fraughton. She smiled beguilingly at him from where she sat sipping champagne. He wandered over to her. "Alone, my lady?"

She pouted prettily. "As you see."

"Extraordinary! Where are your devoted admirers? Your husband?"

She shrugged her slender shoulders in her blue dress and waved her painted fan to the left while her gaze remained on Brandon. "Fraughton is amongst the group surrounding the Duke of Wellington."

"So he is," he said, quite well aware of where Fraughton was, hanging onto the great man's words, and being of no value to Brandon at all.

The Master of Ceremonies called from the dais as the musicians took their places.

"Ah, a waltz. Would you favor me with a dance, Lady Fraughton?"

She rose. "Delighted, sir."

Susan was young enough to be Fraughton's daughter, and he obviously neglected her. A mistake in Brandon's opinion, for it drove her into the arms of that nasty piece of work, Marston. Would Fraughton condone their affair? He rather doubted it. The man did not wear his anger on his sleeve, it simmered beneath the surface and was all the more dangerous for it. From what Brandon had learned this morning at the man's stables, Fraughton had taken a whip to his stable boy and thrashed him within an inch of his young life.

Brandon put a hand on her waist as the orchestra began to play Mozart. As he guided her over the floor, she gazed up at him coquettishly. "Why have you not married, Cartwright?"

"Must everyone be married, madam?"

"It seems the best of both worlds."

"Does it? Or do you wish to see me suffer the same constraints as you do?"

"Ha! What constraints do men ever suffer? The world is their oyster." She frowned. "A woman has not the same opportunities."

He swirled her around, leaving her breathless. "I suspect you make the most of your circumstances. But is it wise?"

Her hand tensed in his. "What do you mean, sir?"

"Some men you can read like a book. Fraughton is not one of them."

She gave him an arch look. "You are offering me advice, then?"

"Your husband, madam, may not be as compliant as you believe."

"I declare, you speak in riddles tonight," she said waspishly. "You are usually more entertaining."

He bowed his head. "Then I apologize."

They danced the rest of the waltz in silence. As Brandon led her back to her chair, her hand squeezed his arm. "If you wish to explain those cryptic comments, sir, you know where I live."

He raised his eyebrows. "Come to your home? I think not."

"Then send me a note. We shall meet."

He bowed and left her.

Lady Fraughton might prove the perfect source for the information he required. If he could charm her into providing it. Not an easy task with Marston lurking. No doubt the man, who found himself short of funds after succumbing to the betting tables, might have some plan afoot. At the very least, Brandon imagined Marston would find the fair-haired Susan a most appealing diversion.

As Brandon moved through the crush, Fraughton left Wellington's side and headed away down the corridor. With a pull on his cuffs, Brandon casually followed.

CHAPTER THREE

L ETTY WAS FORCED to wear the frumpy gown to their next ball, which was held at Lord and Lady Driscoll's in Grosvenor Square. She feared that had another garment been made at her request, she might like it even less.

This time, her aunt introduced her to more of her acquaintances. Letty danced a quadrille with Mr. Montague, who was of a similar age to her aunt, but quite sprightly. She'd begun to suspect Aunt Edith knew no one under the age of sixty, and again, after sitting for several hours watching the dancers merrily performing their steps, she took herself off to the withdrawing room. Her frowning face stared back at her from the mirror.

She really should be grateful. Here she was in London at a fabulous ball. She should not expect too much too soon. Things would surely improve. But when she left the withdrawing room, Miss Somersby, in yet another beautiful gown, stood in Letty's path while talking to a woman in emerald green. The humiliation was too much. The need to compose herself drove Letty from the ballroom in search of a quiet corner. Surely, this enormous house would have a library, which might be unoccupied, and the chance of overhearing lovers again seemed remote.

Letty soon discovered the library with its high, coffered ceiling, the walls covered in shelves of tightly packed gilt-edged books, and sighed with relief to find it empty. She sat in a brocade armchair and toasted herself by the fire. She would just stay for a few minutes, then return to her aunt. By then, Miss Somersby might be on the dance floor.

Letty enjoyed the quiet room, the scent of old books and leather and the crackle of the fire, so soothing, but at the sound of footsteps outside in the corridor, she leapt up.

Having anticipated this possibility, she'd located a hiding place before she sat down. The cloak cupboard in the wainscoting was roomy enough for her to be comfortable until she could leave again. Letty darted inside and shut the door.

The library door opened and closed, then footsteps crossed the carpet. With a gasp, Letty stiffened and edged back into the corner. A moment later, the cupboard door was pulled open, and the smell of tobacco and spicy cologne wafted into the space along with a large body, who closed the door after him.

In the total darkness, Letty tried not to breathe and to remain as still as death. But apparently not still enough. A deep voice cursed, and a heavy hand settled on her shoulder. Letty jumped and fought not to squeak.

"Violets," came a surprised comment as a big hand moved down to wrap strong fingers tightly around her arm.

The door opened, and she was pulled unceremoniously into the light.

A tall, dark-haired gentleman stood staring down at her. His dark eyebrows arched over angry blue eyes. "What the devil…"

At the sound of men's voices outside the door, without a word, the gentleman rudely pushed her back inside the cupboard again.

Letty opened her mouth to complain, but a hand smothered her words. "Shush," came a fierce whisper.

Affronted, she wanted to protest, but he pushed her down onto her bottom on the floor. A hard, masculine shoulder settled against hers. Considering it wise to obey him, she sat mutely, drawing in his sharp cologne with each anxious breath.

Outside their hiding place, a conversation had begun which appeared this man was intent on hearing.

From what she could gather, there were two gentlemen. The Englishman said something about France. Letty couldn't make head nor tail of it. Then the gentleman with a French accent, who sounded younger, raised his voice.

"*Mon Dieu,* Fraughton. We must act to find that cursed *Journal Noir.*"

"It was supposed to come to me, but never arrived. Lavalette intercepted it," Fraughton said.

"If he survives the guillotine," the Frenchman said, "he must be relieved of it and then silenced before he can give away too many secrets. Unless you wish to hang as a traitor!"

Laughter drifted in from the corridor outside the library.

"Quiet, Pierse!" the older man urged. "I fully understand the urgency. This was not a good idea. We might be overheard."

He must have risen quickly for something heavy fell to the floor with a clatter. "Hell's teeth! Pick up that table. You French have such short fuses. We cannot speak here. Whitehall could be closing in on us. We shall meet somewhere more discreet. The Anchor Tavern at the docks at eight Friday evening. No one will know us there."

"But it's a most unsavory area," the Frenchman complained. "Filled with cutthroats with a deep-seated hatred of the French! I could end up with a knife in my ribs."

"Come armed then."

"*Mon Dieu!* You think I wouldn't be?" A voluble string of French peppered with unfamiliar words followed the older man from the room. The door closed.

Silence fell. Letty had managed to control her breathing and attempted to climb to her feet.

"Sit still," the gentleman ordered.

"I beg your pardon?"

"You're English then. Who the devil are you? Who do you work for?"

"I don't work for anyone. This is my first trip to London. It's my come-out."

"Don't give me that! Debutantes don't hide in library cupboards." The man's voice might be pleasant if he wasn't so accusatory.

It was odd, but she wasn't a bit afraid of him. Perhaps the mellow tones of his voice misled her? Murdered in a library cupboard by a very well-spoken, well-dressed gentleman who smelled delightful? It seemed unlikely. "Well this one does," she snapped. "I didn't expect to share the cupboard with anyone. And I'm beginning to feel suffocated. Can we please leave?"

He opened the door, carefully looking out as candlelight flooded in. Then he reached down to help her up.

Letty ignored his outstretched hand. Gaining her feet, she left the stifling small space with relief. "I have told you the truth. Whether you choose to believe it or not is your affair." She shook out her muslin skirts. "I must return to my aunt."

She turned to go.

His hard grasp circled her arm again. "Not so fast. Who are you? And who is this aunt of yours?"

"I am Letitia Bromley, and Miss Edith Bromley is my aunt and chaperone."

"Well, if she is your chaperone, she has her work cut out." His blue eyes widened. "You're either who you say you are, or a very clever spy, to dress in that prim fashion."

"Prim?" She frowned.

"Rather like a...er, never mind." He gave her a little push. "Best we leave here before someone comes and accuses us of a liaison."

The prospect was obviously extremely distasteful to him. Was she so terribly unattractive? She caught sight of herself in the mirror. Her white face looked slightly green. It was probably the ribbon!

He opened the door and waited for her to pass through. Instead, Letty turned to face him, finding herself so close she breathed in his sharp fresh smell again. She dropped her gaze to his mouth; his sculptured lips were firm. At an inexplicable and annoying sense of attraction, she almost stepped back. She narrowed her eyes. "Who are you? And why were *you* in the cupboard?"

He grinned with a flash of even, white teeth. "None of your affair. But I shall escort you to the ballroom, Miss Bromley. And will be watching you. So be very careful. Say nothing about this to anyone."

"As if I would! No one would believe me!"

Letty's heart thudded. He was snooping on those men. Was he a spy? Goodness, but London had suddenly become rather too exciting for comfort.

She did not intend for him to escort her and hurried down the corridor, aware the gentleman followed. His long strides kept him close. If she wished to lose him, she would have to break into a run!

As if he guessed her thoughts, he paused at the door. "Forget what you heard tonight." With a small bow, he walked away.

Relieved, Letty entered the ballroom, comforted by the rush of heat and noise and laughter, patently aware that anything to do with spies was dangerous. But what alternative did she have? She was not about to scurry back to Cumbria! Well, she wouldn't hide away again, although uppermost in her thoughts was the man's criticism of her dress.

Letty gathered up the skirts of the offending gown and made her way to her aunt. Across the ballroom sat the two miserable looking debutantes. Perhaps they could get together, cheer each other up. Letty smiled at the red-haired girl, who quickly averted her gaze. Perhaps not. The Season must improve, she remained hopeful. Might she have a quiet talk with her aunt? Point out what the other girls wore and suggest another gown? But would a new gown change anything?

She hurried over to where her aunt sat frowning at her.

"Letitia, Mr. Montague expressed a wish to dance with you again. Where on earth did you get to?"

Letty trembled as she sat down. "I find the crowd a little alarming, Aunt. But I'm getting more accustomed to it."

Aunt Edith clucked sympathetically and patted her hand. "My dear girl. It is very different to the country assemblies, is it not? But I assure you, there is nothing to fear. No thieves and rascals here! This is the *haute ton*! Decent law-abiding people, every one!"

Letty nodded and managed a smile. Now that she was safely ensconced with her aunt, she could relive the experience without alarm. But at that moment, she chanced to look up. The dark-haired gentleman, tall and broad-shouldered in his midnight blue evening coat and crisp white linen, his hair artfully tousled in that popular style that was so attractive, leaned against a column not far away, his thoughtful gaze resting on her.

"Ah, here comes Mr. Montague wishing to dance with you," her aunt said as the elderly gentleman pushed his way through the crowd with a look of intent. "I believe a waltz is to be called. I'm sure he has that in mind."

"May I dance the waltz, Aunt?" Letty hoped desperately that her aunt would refuse.

"But of course. This is a private ball, not Almack's. I can foresee no objection."

Letty's heart sank, but before Mr. Montague could reach them, her partner in crime beat him by a whisker. He bent over her aunt's hand. "Brandon Cartwright, Miss Bromley. I believe we met last Season. The Cuthbert's rout, was it not? How nice to see you again." He turned to Letty who was aware that her mouth hung open. "And this young lady? She is your sister?"

Letty glared at him. How corny! Her aunt wouldn't fall for that!

But to her surprise, her aunt tittered, grew pink and fiddled with her shawl. "My niece, Mr. Cartwright. I can't recall our meeting, but I did attend that function. A sad crush, so perhaps you'll forgive my lapse of memory." Her aunt looked unconvinced, for no woman in her right mind would forget meeting Mr. Cartwright. But Aunt Edith recovered her manners beautifully and introduced Letty. While Mr. Montague hovered a few steps away, a scowl on his face, the spy invited her to waltz.

Her aunt had told her that if she refused a gentleman's request, she could not dance again during the evening. While relieved at escaping Mr. Montague, she still expected a further grilling from Mr. Cartwright. Letty rose and bobbed, offering him a smile which she hoped hid her disquiet from her aunt. "Delighted, sir."

Her hand resting on his arm, they crossed to the dance floor. "How well you charmed my aunt, Mr. Cartwright!"

He cast her a quizzical glance. "Ah, so I am charming, Miss Bromley?"

"Charm is only to be applauded when it is sincere," she said as they took their places on the dance floor.

"Shame on you, Miss Bromley. You don't feel your aunt warranted my attention?"

Letty could only frown and shake her head at him as he took her in his arms.

BRANDON GAZED DOWN at the young lady's face as he swung her into the waltz. He hadn't quite taken note of her in the library as the implications of Fraughton's conversation flittered through his mind. As he'd expected, there was more to what Willard had told him. He needed to attend their next encounter at the docks and discover who this Frenchman was. A dashed intriguing business this, it had sparked his interest.

But now he had Miss Letitia Bromley to deal with. She had also listened to Fraughton. It appeared she was what she claimed, and now in the better light, he could see she was very young. She'd shown spirit, but her large, rather lovely brown eyes studied him as if he was about to tackle her to the floor, rather than lead her in the dance.

"I am not about to badger you, Miss Bromley," he said, pleasantly, "But I would like to know what caused you to hide in the cupboard."

She bit her lip and gazed somewhere over his right shoulder. "I was escaping."

He raised his eyebrows. "Oh? Has a gentleman displayed an unattractive interest in you?"

She shook her head, a glossy dark lock escaping its ribbon. "No, of course not."

When she glanced down, he suddenly understood. "Your dress? It's a little fussy, but not ugly, you know. And does not detract from your charms."

A flush warmed her cheeks. "There's really no need to flatter me."

"I don't believe I was. But we shall speak no more about it."

A moment passed while he reversed her as the music swelled. She was slim and light on her feet, and he realized he was enjoying the dance, when he often didn't.

"Have I your promise that you'll never mention what you heard Lord Fraughton and the Frenchman speak of, Miss Bromley?"

"Of course I won't. But I am rather curious about it," she admitted, her eyes brightening. "The Frenchman spoke too quickly for me. French was never one of my best subjects."

"I believe that's just as well," he said dryly, recalling the man's fulsome curses. "I have no idea what they spoke of either. Best we forget it, mm?" He turned her again and enjoyed seeing her breath quicken and her cheeks flush as she followed him through the steps.

"You have a lovely smile. You should use it. You'll find the gentlemen queuing up."

She glared at him. "I find you patronizing, sir."

"I beg your pardon. I fancy I shan't see your smile then, Miss Bromley. Pity."

The dance ended, and he led her back to her aunt. "A pleasure," he said with a bow and left them.

It must be overwhelming for a young country lass to come to London for the Season. But he was confident that Miss Bromley would soon take, that was the expression used, he believed. Better dressed she would do well. She was tall and slender, and he suspected she had a good deal of saucy charm, which would emerge when she gained confidence. A man could drown in those beautiful brown eyes. It would not be him, however, he had work to do and could safely anticipate that he and the young lady would not cross paths again.

CHAPTER FOUR

LETTY AWOKE THE next morning and lay thinking of her encounter with Mr. Cartwright. How she'd felt in his strong arms as he'd swept her around the floor in the waltz. It would have been thrilling had she not been struggling to hide her embarrassment at him not only finding her in the cupboard, but discovering the reason she was hiding there. She cringed. Did he pity her? She could almost accept anything but pity. What would happen should they meet again? And more important still, why was *he* hiding in the library? He'd brushed her off smartly when she'd asked him.

She sat up. It was not to be borne! Never again would she go to a ball wearing that gown. She would have to tackle her aunt. She'd explain how upset she was about the style, because it was different to the other debutante's, and offer to alter it herself. Surely her aunt, who was not unkind, wouldn't expect her to continue to feel so uncomfortable!

In the afternoon, they were to embark on a shopping expedition in Bond Street to purchase those things Letty still required. She would be forced to wear her one decent carriage dress, along with her old, chip straw hat. Mrs. Crotchet had yet to make the rest of her clothes, which Letty remained in two minds about. Although they were sorely needed, she dreaded their arrival.

She dressed quickly and went down to the breakfast room. Apart from Mary setting the table, the room was empty, although Aunt Edith was generally an early riser.

"Is my aunt up yet, Mary?"

"No, Miss Bromley. I went in to draw back the curtains, and she asked me to leave them closed. She complained of a headache."

"Oh, poor Aunt Edith. Can I take something up to her? A tisane? Or a hot drink?"

"I have given her feverfew, and she has gone back to sleep."

Letty breakfasted alone, her appetite deserting her. After a piece of toast and strawberry jam and a cup of tea, she rose to wander the bookroom. She searched for something interesting to read, but her aunt's collection had nothing to tempt her. Two hours later, she was sent for.

She entered her aunt's darkened room. "Are you feeling better, Aunt?"

"No, regrettably. I've sent for the physician. I am sorry, Letitia. How dull it must be for you."

"Please don't worry. I am happy to read. I only hope the physician can make you feel more the thing."

"You're a dear girl, Letitia," her aunt said in a faint voice. "I think I'll sleep awhile."

Letty went downstairs, concerned. How kind of her aunt to think of her when she was so ill.

The physician, Mr. Phillips, a man of middle years with a brisk, confident manner, arrived within the hour and went up to her aunt while Letty waited in the parlor, nervously thumbing through periodicals.

When he came down, she offered him a cup of tea.

"Thank you, Miss Bromley, but I have another patient to see. I'm afraid your aunt has had a relapse of an old ailment."

"Oh dear! Is it very serious?"

"Not life threatening. Miss Edith will recover given time, but I have advised her to leave the city as soon as she is well enough to travel. The smoky London air is exceedingly bad for her."

After he left, Letty plunged into despair. It appeared her Season had come to an abrupt end before it even began.

AFTER SPENDING SEVERAL long, drawn out days where Letty found herself thrust into deep gloom, her aunt was well enough to make preparations for their journey the following Friday to Cumbria, where she would convalesce at the vicarage with Uncle Alford.

There was no alternative, Letty must accompany her. The orders for gowns placed with Mrs. Crotchet were cancelled, and Letty's shopping list relegated to the wastepaper basket. Letty feared that once her uncle had her back in Cumbria, he would never allow her to return to London.

With a heavy heart, she began to pack her trunk.

On Wednesday morning, Letty took a cup of tea and the post to her aunt.

"Thank you, my dear." Aunt Edith's face was a better color as she leaned back against the pillows and opened a letter. "You look despondent, I am so very sorry." She dropped her gaze to the words on the page. "Oh, this is good news!"

"What is, Aunt?"

"I so regretted not to be able to present you, that I wrote to a distant cousin of your mother's, Lady Arietta Kendall, on the off chance she might agree to take my place."

Letty held her breath. "What has she replied, Aunt?"

"She is in London for the Season and will be happy to chaperone you."

Letty gasped. "Oh my goodness! I've heard of her, of course. She married Sir Gareth Kendall."

"Yes, she is now a widow. Her husband died last year." Aunt Edith's hands trembled, and she seemed unsure when she looked up from the page. "I do hope I've done the right thing! Arietta is a society lady. She and Kendall were part of the Prince's smart set, and once the subject of gossip, although I was unable to discover what it was all about. But without her husband's influence, I can only trust she has sobered in her middle years, and will guide you safely through your Season." She put down the letter and picked up her teacup. "I hope Alford will not be cross with me for arranging it."

"Of course, he won't, Aunt. He will be happy for me," Letty added hastily. Her letters home would reassure them both as she would do nothing to cause any concern. She had no idea what lay ahead for her under Lady Kendall's aegis, but how wonderful not to have to leave London.

Her aunt took a sip of tea. "You have yet to acquire a suitable wardrobe, as Mrs. Crotchet has been busy and is behind with her orders."

"Such a pity," Letty said, forcing her features into an expression of regret.

"Yes, indeed. But Arietta has promised to oversee it." She looked worried as she replaced the cup in the saucer and handed them to Letty. "Unless you'd rather return home with me, dear? I am not entirely sure you enjoy London."

"Oh, but I do! I've seen so little, Aunt. There's the Tower, and the Egyptian Hall in Piccadilly, and well... so many places I have yet to visit! I should like very much to stay for the Season."

"Very well." Her aunt moved her shoulders in a nervous gesture. "But you must write to your uncle every week and tell him how you go on. Any sign of trouble, and he will come and get you."

"I will, Aunt. You are not to worry. You must rest and regain your strength."

"It is my wish for you to find a decent man to marry, Letitia. Do not be swayed by rakes, I beg of you. I'm not entirely sure that Arietta…well, never mind. I shall rely on your commonsense."

"What are rakes like, Aunt? How will I know if I meet one?"

"Mm. They're excessively charming, often handsome. Have quite a way with words and their manners." She shook her head with a faint sigh and said, "Are faultless."

Letty thought they sounded rather nice. Although handsome, apparently Mr. Cartwright was not one. For indeed, he had not been charming, and his manners left much to be desired.

Her aunt narrowed her eyes. "But rakes are intent on something a young lady must never give them."

"What is that?" Letty asked. "I shouldn't think I have much to offer. I am hardly an heiress."

"Your virtue," Aunt Edith said, firming her lips. "And that's all I will say on the subject."

BRANDON MET FRASER Willard in a coffee house and passed on the information he'd overheard. "So, it concerns this *Journal Noir*. It appears Fraughton's interest in seeing Lavalette dead is not entirely related to his Bourbon sympathies." Brandon sipped his ale. "It certainly is intriguing, is it not? Could this be what Lavalette believes will be of interest to the British government?

His spymaster looked pensive. "We aren't sure what the comtesse is offering. She approached us for help with the promise we will not be disappointed. Once she has our agreement, she'll reveal what it is. It could be a ploy on her part to help get her husband safely out of France. But if we can help save him, I'm sure he'll be eager to show his gratitude. And with Napoleon gone to cool his heels on Saint Helena, he has only his own hide to care about."

Brandon glanced at the meeting taking place at the next table where three men argued over some venture. "I gather you have accepted her offer?"

"We have. Should the plan be successful, we will send someone to France to furnish Lavalette with a passport and escort him over the Belgian border."

Brandon put down his coffee cup. "He hopes to escape the Conciergerie? Seems a bit farfetched. How might that come about?"

"His wife has something in mind, but she's keeping it to herself until she's sure of us. Let us put that aside for a moment. Our interest must remain on Fraughton. Go to the Anchor Tavern and find out what you can from that pair of conspirators."

"And if I learn nothing?"

Willard raised his eyebrows. "Is it possible that Lady Fraughton might render assistance?"

"I doubt she knows anything," Brandon said. "She appears disinterested in her husband's activities. And he in hers, which is a sore point with her. That might work in our favor. I will pursue it."

It was past dusk, and the candles were alight when Brandon arrived at his house to change his clothes. His valet, Hove, had ordered a trunk to be brought down from the attic. It now sat on the carpet in Brandon's bedchamber. Brandon opened the lid and rifled through it.

"Shall you require burnt cork or ash, sir?" Hove inquired.

"Both, I imagine." Pulling out several items, Brandon began to change his clothes.

When he'd dressed, he stood before the mirror. A shabby shirt open at the neck, a brown coat that had never been of good cloth, breeches, and scuffed boots. Nodding approval, he sat while Hove applied the burnt cork to his whiskered jaw, where he had foregone shaving and his new beard sprouted. Ash was ground into the back of his hands and under his fingernails. He pulled a faded hat low over his expensive haircut.

"Look the part do I, Hove?" Brandon slipped a knife into his boot and pocketed his pistol. Outside the window, the sky was relatively clear of clouds and lit by a mistrustfully serene moon.

"Indeed yes, sir." The valet grinned. "Would think twice before I gave you any lip."

Brandon left his townhouse via the mews behind. Keeping to the shadows, he walked to the busy thoroughfare where he hailed a hackney. The jarvey pulled up and eyed him, unsure whether to drive on. Brandon held up a small, fat leather bag of coins. "The Anchor Tavern at London Dock."

"Don't go down there at night, guv'nor," the jarvey said, studying the bag as if to assess the weight of it. "Not worth the risk."

"Your decision." Brandon went to place it in his pocket.

"Tell yer what. I'll drop yer at the top of Pennington Street. It is located near the northern edge of the dock."

"Agreed." Brandon opened the bag and tipped out half of it. "You'll get the other half if you come back for me in two hours."

"Right you are, sir."

Brandon opened the door and climbed inside. His soiled clothes might carry a whiff of horse, but the smells emanating from the dirty squabs surpassed him. He sat back in the corner where he was less likely to be noticed as the jarvey urged the horse on.

CHAPTER FIVE

TWO DAYS BEFORE Aunt Edith departed for Cumbria, they received a visitor. Lady Arietta Kendall entered their parlor like a whirlwind, brightening the dreary room. Letty tried not to stare, while her aunt, reclining on the sofa, raised herself from the cushions. "Oh, it is you, Arietta," she said faintly.

"'Tis I, Edith. And this must be Letitia. How do you do?"

Lady Arietta was lovely with creamy skin and fine features. A dark straw bonnet, adorned with curling feathers, covered her golden locks. She wore a purple velvet spencer which featured cream epilates, over a lilac walking dress with an elaborately patterned hem. Extracting a small hand encased in lilac kid from a huge cream muff, she offered it to Letty.

Letty dipped the slightest curtsey as excitement gripped her, and she shook the lady's hand. "How good of you to sponsor me, Lady Arietta."

The lady, somewhere close to forty years in age, but might be older, looked Letty over quizzically with intelligent, bright blue eyes. "Mm, we have much to do," she said with a wave of her hand. She sat on a chair near her aunt. "I am sorry to find you unwell, my dear. I do hope that the long journey north won't be too fatiguing?"

"I shall endure," Aunt Edith said. A crease marred her forehead. "I trust you will take very good care of my niece. Letitia is new to

London."

"We must all begin somewhere," Lady Arietta said. "There is nothing like experience to teach one."

"I hope it will be an enjoyable experience, but also one where Letitia will learn how to conduct herself in society." Her aunt plucked at her shawl. "I have no option but to leave her with you, with the hope you will be instrumental in finding Letitia a good husband. I know she is in safe hands," she added, more out of politeness, Letty felt, rather than a firm conviction.

"I shall do my very best." Lady Arietta smiled at Letty. "Fortunately, this young lady shows great promise. Best we begin this very afternoon. Are you prepared to leave, Letitia?"

"Yes, all packed, Lady Arietta." Letty had no idea what her new sponsor had in mind, but she was eager to find out.

"I will send for tea." Her aunt reached for the small bell on the occasional table beside her.

Lady Arietta stood and shook out her skirts. "No thank you, Edith. We must go." She bent to kiss Aunt Edith's cheek. "I'm sure the country air will soon restore you to health. I'll tell my footman to fetch Letitia's trunk."

Letty was grateful to Aunt Edith. She had done her best, but had no understanding of nineteenth century ways. When she bent to hug her aunt, Letty became entangled in the lavender-scented shawl over her shoulders and the lorgnette hanging around her neck. "I promise to write to you and Uncle Alford," she said, extracting herself. "I pray you will soon feel better."

She'd barely said her goodbyes, when Lady Arietta ushered her through the door. Outside in the street, a stylish town chaise the color of chocolate, drawn by a pair of grays, awaited them.

They were assisted inside, then Letty's trunk was strapped to the back by the groom. He leapt up to join the coachman who told the horses to walk on.

"We shall visit my modiste," Lady Arietta said as they turned toward Piccadilly. "We have no time to lose to fit you out with a proper wardrobe, as the Season will soon be in full swing." She cocked her head, her observant blue eyes twinkling. "And I suspect there is nothing in that trunk of yours worthy of our consideration. I do look forward to dressing you. I always wished for a daughter, but it was not to be."

Letty wondered briefly what befell her husband for Aunt Edith had made no mention of it, but she did not like to ask. As the carriage drew up in the street outside the dressmaker's establishment, Letty had great hopes that any gowns Madame Rochette produced would be a far cry from Mrs. Crotchet's. After all, the modiste had dressed Lady Arietta, whose outfit was in the first stare of fashion. Letty smiled at her benefactress, hardly able to believe her good fortune.

Some hours later, Letty felt as limp as a wet glove when they left Madame Rochette's salon. It was as she'd guessed, a far cry from Mrs. Crotchet's establishment with the reception room walls covered in enormous gilt-framed mirrors and curtained areas in which to change. Seated on velvet couches, they'd sipped coffee while exquisite fabrics, furs, feathers, beading, and braid were brought for their consideration. Both the modiste and Lady Arietta seemed in accord. Their knowledgeable discussion of styles and fabrics made Letty's head whirl.

Lady Arietta's carriage deposited them at her London townhouse, an elegant dwelling that overlooked Hyde Park. Footmen assisted them from the carriage before it was whisked away to the stables. Lady Arietta, talking all the time, led her through the impressive entrance hall, across a floor of marble tiles like a checkerboard, and up the sweeping staircase. They sat on a cream and gilt satin sofa in the elegant small salon while a footman brought glasses of madeira and placed a plate of wafer biscuits on the table before them.

"We shall stay in tonight," Lady Arietta announced. "You must be fatigued, Letitia. It's been quite a day, hasn't it, being pulled this way and that?" She lifted her slender shoulders. "Unless you have something suitable to wear to Mrs. Fountain's musicale?"

"I'm afraid not." Letty wished she could answer in the affirmative. Regretfully, nothing she had was stylish enough for a musicale, which she imagined would be an elegant affair.

"I would lend you a gown if you were not taller than me." Lady Arietta patted her hand. "Best we don't go. Even though you've attended two balls, no one is likely to remember you. And you must make a suitably dramatic entrance. It's a pity there's no time to organize your come-out ball. But we shall do nicely. The streets are beginning to fill with carriages. Everyone who is anyone returns to London." She smiled at Letty. "We have the Longtree's ball on Saturday, and Madame Rochette has promised to have your gown ready."

Letty hoped Lady Arietta was right that no one would remember her; although a certain gentleman might. Of all the fabrics and styles finally settled upon, the ball gown stood out in her mind. It promised to be very different to the one she'd been wearing. "I can't wait to see it!"

"I promise you, it will be beautiful. Gentlemen will be lining up to dance with you, my dear."

Letty rather doubted it, but she smiled and hoped it was true. It would be thrilling, but more than that, she was eager to justify all the time and effort this kind lady was prepared to spend on her.

"And tomorrow, we simply must shop the day away. You have need of a great many accessories to go with your new clothes."

Letty bit her lip. "The expense, Lady Arietta..."

"Call me Arietta, Letitia, please. You have no need to concern yourself. Your aunt has given me a bank draft which will cover expenses."

"But that cannot be enough," Letty said.

A small frown creased Arietta's smooth pale forehead. "It is quite generous!" She cocked her head again, a golden ringlet trembling against her ear. "You have a handsome dowry, my dear, did you not know?"

Letty stared. "No…I didn't."

"No doubt your uncle properly chose not to concern you with money. So vulgar, isn't it! Whilst you are no heiress, you are not without the means to attract a suitable gentleman." Arietta picked up her wineglass. She raised it. "Let us toast your Season, my dear!"

While Letty couldn't help wondering how much her dowry was, and why her uncle hadn't seen fit to tell her, she grinned and raised her glass. It was all so terribly thrilling. She was sure she wouldn't sleep a wink.

BRANDON ENTERED THE tavern which smelled strongly of male sweat and hops. He recognized the tall, thin man with graying hair at a table in the corner. *Fraughton.* Seated with him was the Frenchman, Pierse, who was shorter and younger by some years, speaking volubly, his dark head close to Fraughton's.

After he purchased a frothy tankard of ale, Brandon sat at a table out of their line of vision but still near enough to overhear them.

With a furtive glance in his direction, they continued to talk, their voices low and urgent.

"Would he have hidden it in his apartment?" Pierse asked.

"It was searched but nothing was found," Fraughton said.

"What about Lavalette's chateau in the Loire?"

"That will be the next place we look, and we'll have to search the apartment again. But it's impossible to escape the Conciergerie. He'll go to the guillotine, sure as hell."

"*Oui!* Then that will be the end of the matter."

Fraughton grunted. "Such careless thinking could get you hanged." He glanced around again at Brandon who appeared interested in the two dock laborers arguing in the opposite corner. "What does it matter if Lavalette dies? The journal could still fall into the wrong hands. We must not give up until it's found."

Brandon's gaze flickered over them. Fraughton scowled, and Pierse looked close to unravelling.

"What do you want me to do then?" Pierse asked with a surly look.

"You must return to France..."

Suddenly, the disagreement between the two dock laborers turned into a fight. A table was upset, spilling ale over the flagstones. The tavern owner, a burly fellow, moved to separate them by grabbing them both by their coat collars and heaving them outside.

Just then, two more laborers, laughing at a ribald joke which Brandon caught the tail end of, came in.

Fraughton muttered something to Pierse that Brandon failed to catch. The tall Englishman stood and left the tavern with the Frenchman casting an intense glance around at Brandon before following in his wake.

One of the laborers also eyed Brandon with interest. He nudged the other man, saying something in his ear. A new face around the docks could cause speculation. Jobs were few and highly sought. Brandon drank the last of his ale, slammed down the tankard, and wiped his mouth with the back of his hand. He rose and strolled out, only to see Fraughton and Pierse climb into a carriage.

The weather had changed. A stiffening breeze thinned and cleared the clouds. Moonlight reflected in the harbor waters, and rats scuttled across the road. Brandon set out to walk to where his carriage should be. He hoped the promise of a healthy purse would ensure the jarvey's return.

He dug his hands into the pockets of his coat, reassured by the touch of cold steel. It was dangerous to walk about alone here at night even if he looked as if he had little more than a farthing to his name.

Brandon turned at the sound of footsteps approaching behind him. The two laborers advanced purposely toward him. Swiveling, he faced them, while he cursed himself for his carelessness. He should have insisted the jarvey come down to meet him.

Sly grins stretched their mouths, their coarse faces filled with intent.

"What d'yer want?" Brandon demanded.

"We 'aven't seen the likes of you round 'ere." The shorter of the two, a thick-set fellow, shuffled closer.

Brandon preferred not to use his gun. A gunshot would bring people running to investigate, and it wasn't wise to have himself talked about.

The biggest of the two began to circle, a knife in his hand. Brandon took purchase on the road, pivoted, and delivered a well-placed kick to the man's knee before the fellow could conceive such a thing might happen. He fell to the ground screaming in agony, the knife flying out of reach. With a sideways twist, Brandon raised his fists as the other thief charged him. A blow glanced off Brandon's ear. His left jab landed on the thief's jaw with a satisfying crunch, then he followed up with a right to the man's stomach. The thief swayed, his eyes rolling back. Transferring his weight, Brandon stepped in and hooked a leg at the back of the man's knee and pushed hard. With a scream, he went down. Brandon stepped in and stomped on his knee to make a thorough job of it.

Both men lay groaning, as Brandon, taking no chances, took off at a fast run to where he'd arranged to meet the jarvey. *If he came.*

And there he was. Brandon heaved a relieved sigh, his ear throbbing.

"In a hurry, guv?" the man inquired, checking out the street behind him.

"You might say that." Brandon ripped open the carriage door. "Back to where you picked me up, there's a good fellow. And hurry."

"Right you are. Move on, Sally!" The jarvey cracked his whip, and the horse, for all its worn-out appearance, went forward at a clip. "Knows her feedbag and dry stall awaits," the jarvey called out, chuckling.

Brandon was deposited on the road near his house. He paid the jarvey and entered through the back gate. No sense in scaring Cook half to death, he checked through the window. The kitchen was empty, the staff having retired, so he quietly climbed the servants' stairs.

When he slipped unnoticed into his bedchamber, Hove was waiting. "I expect you'll be wanting a bath and a shave, sir," the valet said with a grin.

Brandon ran a hand over his prickly jaw. His grazed knuckles stung. "You have the right of it, Hove."

With nothing to impart to Willard, Brandon would need to pursue Lady Fraughton, which could prove difficult with the rake, Robert Marston, hanging around her.

Some twenty minutes later, Brandon stepped from the hip bath and toweled himself. He was yet to discover just what Marston was after, apart from seducing Lady Fraughton. Once a rake had succeeded in their aims, and Brandon suspected Marston had, they usually moved on to another conquest. Brandon understood the rake's mentality only too well. While he didn't place himself in that category, because he had too much respect for women to treat them in that fashion, he didn't place much faith in love, either.

Chapter Six

LETTY SIGHED WITH pure joy. She turned full circle before the Cheval mirror in the elegant bedchamber assigned to her. The scoop-necked, sleek white satin underdress glowed beneath net as delicate as a spider's web. The pale pink satin sash under the bust that she considered a clever touch, was echoed in the pink and silver, silk embroidery on the capped sleeves and around the hem. Her hair had been dressed by Arietta's skillful French lady's maid, Adele, who coaxed curls to frame Letty's face, then tucked tiny fresh white flowers into the coiffure. Pearls, a parting gift from her aunt, dressed her ears and circled her throat. She wore embroidered white satin shoes and long white gloves, and tucked her handkerchief, a small bottle of perfume, comb, and needle and thread into her reticule with the silver tassels.

"How pretty you look! As I knew you would!" Arietta exclaimed coming into the bedchamber. "The right gown and accessories do much for a woman's charms, my dear."

Letty knew she wasn't a diamond of the first water who would set London on fire, but she was delighted with the result. She complimented Arietta, who certainly had been all that when she was younger, and was still lovely, in a low-cut lavender silk gown, diamonds at her throat and ears. As Arietta's mourning period had passed, Letty wondered why she did not appear interested in remarrying, when so many widows did.

Arietta tucked her hand through Letty's arm. "Shall we go and set the gentlemen on their ears?"

Letty grinned and tried not to feel guilty about poor Aunt Edith ensconced in Cumbria. Her aunt disliked the country, and Uncle Alford might not be so pleased with her. She would write tomorrow and tell them all her news. It was sure to cheer her aunt up.

The chaise took them to the Duke and Duchess of Dunstan's home in Grosvenor Square. Entering the grand mansion, they climbed the staircase to the reception areas which had been thrown open to create a splendid ballroom where a line of footmen in puce and gold livery waited to serve them. The elegantly dressed guests gathered beneath three splendid Italian crystal chandeliers. Around the walls, seating was placed amid ferns and pots of oranges. The lofty ballroom resonated with chatter and laughter while a discordant sound came from the orchestra on the dais as they tuned their instruments for the next dance.

As they were announced, their entrance caused quite a stir. Letty was glad of Arietta's company when women halted in conversation to appraise her. The frank stares of some gentlemen made her shy, one reaching for his pince-nez to better view her.

Arietta's many acquaintances came to greet them. Letty was introduced to so many she doubted she would remember their names.

A gentleman claimed Letty's hand for the next dance, a quadrille, and they joined the dancers on the floor. When she returned, pleased that she'd performed reasonably well, she learned that most of her nine dances remaining had been claimed.

The two debutantes Letty had spied at her first ball, sat together. Letty smiled at them. When they both returned the smile, she went to introduce herself. Miss Arabella Blake explained that she had come from Devon to stay with her grandmother who was bringing her out. Miss Jennifer Wallace, who lived in Ham, was under her married sister's chaperonage. Now more at ease, they chatted for several minutes, until the quadrille was called, and Arietta beckoned. They parted, promising to meet again.

While the ball was not quite as wildly exciting as she'd hoped, the evening passed pleasantly. Some men she danced with said nothing beyond the merest pleasantries, others expressed an interest in her life in Cumbria, when the movements of the dance permitted. All failed to cause any quickening of her pulse. Letty was engaged for the supper dance with a Mr. Boyce, a tall, studious gentleman just down from Oxford.

Mr. Boyce led her into supper. He earnestly filled her plate and brought her a glass of ratafia. Letty soon discovered the best way to deal with him was to ask him a lot of questions about literature. While he answered, she sat and listened politely to him speak solemnly about Horace and Cicero. She nibbled the tasty food and allowed her gaze to roam the surrounding guests. Miss Somersby, having ignored her before, and whom Letty envied for appearing so at ease in Society, passed by on a gentleman's arm. She deigned to acknowledge Letty with a regal nod. Letty, glad to be no longer invisible at least, inclined her head. Perhaps they might become better acquainted, although she rather doubted it.

At a lady's peal of laughter, Letty turned and found none other than Mr. Cartwright, talking to a pretty blonde woman. The lady coyly tapped him on the arm with her fan. She fluttered it open and leaned forward to whisper to him from behind the painted ivory sticks.

Her comment must have been droll, for Cartwright chuckled.

"I believe I might have met that lady in blue," Letty said to Mr. Boyce with a nod in their direction.

"Eh? Lady Fraughton?" Mr. Boyce paused in his glowing description of a work by Virgil. "She has captured the interest of that rakehell, Cartwright, I see."

"Oh. No. I must be mistaken," Letty murmured. *Was Cartwright a rake? Otherwise, why was he flirting with the wife of that gentleman they had overheard in the library?*

Boyce took her empty plate and handed it to a waiter. "Might I interest you in a dish of nuts or some trifle, Miss Bromley?"

"You are most kind, Mr. Boyce. I have been admiring that towering confection in the center of the table. Is it an ice?"

"You are correct. An artistic arrangement, is it not? Might I fetch you some?"

"If you would be so good. Thank you."

Her escort rose and hurried over to the long tables set with crisp white linen cloths and sparkling silverware. It was laden with sumptuous dishes: platters of lobster patties, chicken, thinly sliced ham, poached salmon, fruits, a selection of cheeses, and cake.

"Good evening, Miss Bromley." Letty glanced up at the deep voice. Cartwright's amused blue eyes smiled down at her.

Letty's heart began a strange thumping, which quite unsettled her. "I hope you have not left the lady disappointed, Mr. Cartwright. She seemed enamored of your conversation."

He smiled. "You noticed?"

She smoothed her skirts over her knees and eyed him. "Lord Fraughton's wife, was it not?"

He cocked a brow. "I believe we had an agreement to forget about that business in the library, Miss Bromley."

"Our agreement? You made the rules, Mr. Cartwright. You need not fear I will break them."

He nodded. "I merely wished to tell you how charming you look tonight." His blue eyes danced. "The dress is quite lovely."

She raised her eyebrows. "If you plan to refer to my previous attire, I beg that you do not."

The smile lifted a corner of his mouth. "I would be quite beyond the pale to do so."

"You would indeed," she agreed. "But still, I fear you might succumb to it."

"You have such a poor opinion of me," he said in that manner she distrusted. "I should like to know what I have done to deserve it."

"As good manners prevent me from telling you, I fear you must remain in the dark, sir."

Mr. Boyce was shouldering his way through those clustered around the table, carrying a plate of ice cream. A frown furrowed his brow.

Cartwright glanced at him. "Here comes your eager beau."

"He is not my beau," Letty said quickly.

"I believe he has that in mind."

Mr. Boyce stood before them. Letty was forced to introduce them.

"Good evening, sir." Cartwright's clipped tone suggested no polite conversation would ensue. Indeed, Mr. Boyce, still holding the plate, hardly seemed to welcome any. Cartwright bowed. "I trust your evening will be enjoyable, Miss Bromley."

He walked away before she could respond, and as Mr. Boyce now pressed his offering upon her, she could only smile and thank him.

"You are acquainted with Mr. Cartwright?" he asked, unhappiness in his tone.

"Through my aunt," Letty said vaguely. "This looks delicious. Are you not to have some, too?"

Boyce shook his head. "I don't possess a sweet tooth. But I shall enjoy watching you eat it."

Letty took up the spoon, wishing he wouldn't. Out of the corner of her eye, she saw Cartwright's broad back disappear through the door leading into the ballroom. She should be pleased that he'd come to compliment her, but wasn't, for everything he said to her seemed tinged with amusement. The suspicion returned that he considered her youth and inexperience vastly entertaining. She narrowed her eyes, wishing she could show him how wrong he was, or at least, give him a set down, but she doubted the opportunity would arise to do either.

"Is the ice cream not to your liking, Miss Bromley?" Mr. Boyce asked, hovering over her.

Letty had almost forgotten it. She smiled and took a mouthful of the smooth sweet dessert. "It's delicious, Mr. Boyce. But so cold on the tongue!" She managed another two spoonfuls before she handed the plate to a footman and rose. "Shall we return to the ballroom?"

"Indeed. I hope you'll permit me another dance, Miss Bromley."

She took Boyce's proffered arm and sighed inwardly. It was to be hoped that Arietta, who had proved adroit at handling overeager bucks, would rescue her.

And thankfully, she did. Mr. Boyce was politely and firmly informed that the rest of Letty's dances had been promised.

"I shall call on you tomorrow," he said undaunted.

"Oh dear, what does that mean?" Letty asked Arietta after he'd gone.

"It is customary for him to call, my dear. I expect we shall receive morning calls from several gentlemen tomorrow. Boyce was not to your liking?"

When Letty shook her head, Arietta nodded. "That is not surprising. He is a little too staid for someone with your passion for life."

Letty was surprised Arietta thought that about her. But the same could not be leveled at Mr. Cartwright. He made her breath catch without any effort on his part. She did not expect a morning call from him, which was just as well as the man was precisely the sort her aunt warned her about, and a spy to boot. What might he be doing with Lady Fraughton? Was it merely rakish behavior, or something else? She would need to curb her curiosity, for he wasn't likely to tell her.

Her busy fingers smoothed her gloves to the elbow while she was forced to admit that Cartwright had a certain appeal. But if a rake, her virtue would be safe in his company as he showed no eagerness to pursue her. She was surprised by a twinge of disappointment. Rakes were dangerous, she could quite see that. They drew women to them like bees to honey, even sober Aunt Edith had grown pink at the mention of them. Letty firmed her shoulders. She would never succumb to a rake's charm. Forewarned was forearmed.

She danced the waltz with Lord Craven, a gentleman of some fifty years who had a tendency to count under his breath. As she stared vacantly over his shoulder, impatient for the music to end, Cartwright danced past with Lady Fraughton in his arms. When he turned the lady, her eyes met Letty's. Beneath furrowed brows, she stared daggers at her. Letty gasped. What had she done to deserve that?

BRANDON DANCED LADY Fraughton over the floor, but his mind was not on his partner. Instead, he was preoccupied with Miss Bromley, who looked extremely attractive tonight. Delicious in fact, with her creamy-skinned bosom and the slender column of her throat bared to his view in the low-cut gown. Her large eyes were like chocolate velvet, soft, except when she gazed critically at him, which she tended to do quite often. She was a good deal too interested in him, however, and that, he suspected, had nothing to do with his charm, although it did little for his ego to admit it. Brandon reminded himself of the job assigned him. He had no time for flirtations with young ladies. He'd made it plain amongst the marriage-mad mamas that he was not in the market for a wife. Getting too close to Miss Bromley would be a mistake. He gave himself a mental shake. These thoughts would hardly assist him to gain the information he needed from the lady in his arms, who seemed to welcome his interest. Recovering himself, he smiled down at her.

"I'm surprised that young, dark-haired debutante has come to your notice," Lady Fraughton said waspishly. "She is fresh from the country without an ounce of Town bronze."

"You have met Miss Bromley?"

"No. But debutantes are all from the same mold. They are too inexperienced for a man such as yourself. They don't know how to play the game as they are merely intent on finding a husband. Green girls are so dreadfully dull. And some will do almost anything to trap a man. The stories you hear!"

He looked over to where Miss Bromley, obviously bored stiff, danced with Craven, and stifled a chuckle. She wasn't at all dull. In fact, she was a good deal too bright. He hoped she would soon meet a man who held her interest, otherwise, his dealings might come under her scrutiny again. It was the last thing he needed.

The dance ended.

"The night is warm." He led the lady from the floor. "Shall we stroll on the terrace?"

She smiled. "It is fortunate that my husband isn't present tonight."

Nor her *nouvel amant*, Marston, Brandon thought. With a clear field he needed to act quickly. "Is Fraughton out of town?"

She cast him a coquettish grin. "Why do you ask?"

"I should feel uncomfortable with him breathing down my neck."

She laughed.

Outside, another couple stood at the far end of the terrace enjoying the night air. Brandon rested a hand on the balustrade, the stone cool through his glove. "Surprising for your husband to miss one of the most prominent balls of the Season."

She shrugged, her slim shoulders encased in blue silk and lace. "What Fraughton does is of no interest to me."

"And is what you do, madam, of no interest to him?"

"It would appear not," she said in an acerbic tone. "He is at a meeting at Lord Elford's home."

"He advised you of his direction?"

"No, he did not see fit to tell me. I discovered it for myself."

"Is this meeting a matter of great importance? Or was that beyond your powers of discovery?"

She cast him an arch look. "Nothing is, if it interests me enough. Apparently, one of his cohorts has just returned from France. A Mr. Descrier."

Brandon turned away to view the gardens. "The wealthy gentleman of commerce?"

"The same."

She stood beside him at the rail. "Why does this interest you? Or should I ask, does it interest you, Cartwright, more than I do?"

He chuckled. "I find you fascinating, my lady. As well you know. You are not only beautiful, you are clever. I admire that in women."

Slightly mollified, skepticism still hovered in her eyes. "And you wish to learn more."

"If you should like to tell me more."

"What do I get out of it?" She held her fan up to her face, her eyes alight with invitation. "Were we not to meet somewhere more convivial to discuss it?"

The other couple strolled back into the ballroom.

"I won't take you to bed, Susan," Brandon said softly. "Not that I don't very much want to."

"I never thought you a prude, Cartwright."

"I am not one, but I still cling to a few principles."

She frowned. "If I help you, might it bring Fraughton down?"

He hid his reaction to her cold-bloodedness. "I could not say."

"No, you would not. You keep your secrets close." She shrugged carelessly. "As I have not a shred of affection for my husband, I shall advise you of anything I discover. And don't be too sure we shall not become lovers."

Brandon reached out and grasped her shoulders, turning her toward him. He sought her gaze. "Do not trivialize your husband's power to hurt you. Remain very careful, my dear. Take no chances on my account."

She raised her eyebrows. "He barely notices me." She took his arm, and they strolled back to the ballroom.

CHAPTER SEVEN

A T TEN O'CLOCK the following morning, Letty was on her way to breakfast when she paused to sift through several gilt-edged cards piled on the silver tray on the half-moon table in the front hall.

"Do gentlemen rise this early?" she asked the butler, Thane, in surprise.

"Some ride in the park before breakfast, Miss Bromley."

Mr. Boyce and Lord Craven had left their cards as did two other gentlemen. None of whom she wished to see. With a sigh, she made her way to the breakfast room. She was hungry. It was several hours past her usual time to eat.

While Letty drank tea and ate buttered eggs, she went over the previous evening's events. Uppermost in her mind was her conversation with Cartwright. Annoyingly, the man seemed to diminish in stature all the other men she had met. It might be because of his brooding good looks, but she suspected it was most particularly the aura of mystery that clung to him.

She remained hopeful that Arietta, who never rose until late, might make an appearance and agree to a walk in Hyde Park before luncheon.

She had finished her eggs and was spreading jam over a second slice of toast when Arietta swept into the breakfast room. She was dressed in a cambric muslin negligee of pale blue flounced with French

trimming. The mob cap of Brussels lace over her hair had correspond-
ing bows of pale blue satin ribbon. While admiring Arietta, Letty
doubted she could ever be quite as stylish.

"Up early, my pet?" Arietta nodded at the footman who brought a
fresh pot of tea.

While Arietta sipped her tea, Letty told her about the morning
calls.

Arietta cradled the tea cup in her hands. "We must expect a busy
afternoon."

Letty suffered a stab of guilt. It was so good of her to be doing this.
It must surely be tedious. "Shall we go for a refreshing walk before
luncheon?"

Arietta yawned behind her hand. "I declare, you young things have
such energy. We did not get to bed until after three. Indeed, I am
surprised to find myself up at this hour. I awoke to the sound of a
hawker who made a dreadful racket beneath my window."

Arietta's sigh indicated that Letty had failed to hide her disappointment. "Very well. After I have attended to my letters, we shall
promenade through the park." She took a roll from the basket and
reached for the butter. "The *ton* don't generally make an appearance
until five o'clock, but you never know who you might meet."

When they set out an hour later, it was a lovely morning, the dew
still fresh beneath the trees and the air scented with damp foliage.
Letty angled her silk parasol to shade her face from the sun as they
walked along a path. She considered herself quite smart in her new
primrose sarsnet and brown linen spencer, her bonnet of straw-colored
satin dressed with a plume of feathers, tied at one side of her chin with
primrose ribbons. She chatted with Arietta about the previous
evening. The park was far from deserted with riders cantering along
Rotten Row. On the South Carriage drive, a landau and a cabriolet had
pulled up side by side to allow those inside to engage in conversation.
Two ladies greeted them on the path, and after Arietta introduced

Letty, they remained to discuss the opera program for this Season.

As their conversation didn't include her, Letty watched the equestrians. She wondered if Arietta rode. It was one thing she sorely missed since coming to London. How wonderful it would be to hire a hack and ride through the park.

As the two ladies said their goodbyes and walked on, a glossy chestnut stallion cantered smartly down the Row. Letty raised her parasol for a better look. It was! Cartwright, in a dark coat and riding breeches, glossy top boots, his black hat at a rakish angle. He had spied her and, reining in, walked the horse over to them.

"Good morning, ladies." He removed his hat and bowed from the saddle. "I would not have expected to see you out so early, Lady Arietta."

"Good morning, Mr. Cartwright," Arietta said, her smile tight. "I believe I was persuaded by Miss Bromley to rise early, but now find myself appreciating the fresh morning air. Allow me to introduce her to you. I am sponsoring Miss Bromley for the Season."

"Miss Bromley and I have met," Cartwright said, with a smile in Letty's direction. "Her aunt, Miss Edith Bromley, introduced us."

"My goodness. You are acquainted with Edith Bromley?" Arietta raised slender brows.

Cartwright flicked another glance at Letty. "Is there any reason why I should not be?"

Arietta's mouth twitched. "It is a little surprising, when one so often finds you in very different company."

"I enjoy a wide variety of acquaintances, Lady Arietta. As I sense you do."

"Not nearly as interesting as yours, Mr. Cartwright."

"But you are too modest! I am positive that you are wrong. But I should have to make their acquaintance to be sure of that."

"Which I fear is most unlikely," Arietta responded.

Letty, who had been following their conversation with interest, could only agree with Arietta. It seemed extremely unlikely that Cartwright would know her aunt. And of course, he didn't. But she found Arietta and Cartwright's conversation confusing. As if a covert one was going on underneath, which intrigued and puzzled her.

"Did you enjoy the ball, Miss Bromley?" When Cartwright suddenly turned his attention to Letty, she almost jumped.

"Very much, thank you."

"I imagine there will be morning callers beating a path to your door today."

Arietta nodded. "Yes, indeed Miss Bromley was a success. We have great expectations."

Cartwright settled his steely blue gaze on her. "I am pleased you are enjoying London, Miss Bromley. I hope, should we meet again, that you will save a dance for me."

"Miss Bromley's dances are quickly filled," Arietta said, rather rudely, Letty thought, disappointed. She would like to dance with him again. She might learn more about the intrigue he was involved in, but feared it was a faint hope.

The beautiful horse snorted and struck an impatient hoof on the ground. "You must excuse me." Cartwright patted the glossy neck of his mount. "As you see, my horse requires exercise. Good day."

He dropped the reins and rode away.

"Well." Arietta turned to Letty, her eyebrows raised. "We must have a talk after we return home. I am eager to discover how you and your aunt came to know Mr. Cartwright."

Letty watched Cartwright disappear down the Row. How at ease he was in the saddle. She was glad to have time to conjure up a story to alleviate Arietta's suspicions. Although she hated having to embellish the truth, she would keep her word to him.

After luncheon, their afternoon was spent with ladies and gentlemen paying their respects. Finally, the butler closed the door behind the last of them. Letty hadn't realized how much of the Season would be spent in such tedious pursuits.

Arietta poured herself and Letty another cup of tea. Handing Letty the painted cup and saucer, she leaned back and smiled. "Lord Craven is quite the fuddy-duddy, is he not?"

Letty giggled, pleased that Arietta was of the same opinion as she. "And Mr. Cornwallis has the most distracting habit of repeatedly sniffing."

Arietta laughed. "He does, doesn't he? Quite dreadful." She sobered. "And I'm aware that you haven't warmed to Boyce, so I gather none of these gentlemen appealed to you?"

"I'm afraid not." Letty grimaced. She wished she could like one of them, at least, for Arietta appeared so hopeful that she should.

"Never mind. The Season has only just begun." Arietta reached for a small triangle of bread and butter. She bit into it contemplatively. "So, tell me all about Cartwright. How did your aunt come to meet him?"

Letty took a sip of tea to clear her dry throat. "Apparently, Mr. Cartwright met Aunt Edith at a rout. He came and introduced himself to her at Lady Driscoll's ball and asked me to dance."

"There is more to this, Letitia," Arietta said with a frown. "I shall have the truth from you. What are you not telling me?"

Letty released a breath. Arietta's pale eyes seemed to bore into her, as if she could read her thoughts. "I ran into Mr. Cartwright when I was hiding in the library," she said, deciding a little more information was required before Arietta would be satisfied. After all, it was Fraughton of whom Cartwright asked her not to speak.

"Hiding in the library? Why on earth were you doing that?"

"I hated my dress. No one was asking me to dance. I was miserable."

"Oh, you poor child. But where did you hide?"

"In a cloak cupboard. It wasn't the first time. I hid behind a screen at my first ball."

Arietta laughed and her eyes lit up. "And how did Cartwright come to discover you in this cupboard?"

"I suppose he must have heard me," Letty said evasively. "He opened the door and found me there."

"Was anyone with him?

"No." Letty swallowed, wishing she could say more. "He was alone."

"What happened then?"

"Um. We talked…"

"Yes?"

"And then he escorted me back to the ballroom. He was quite annoyed."

"And yet he still danced with you?" Thoughtful, Arietta sipped her tea.

"Yes. I suppose he regretted his bad humor."

"How interesting," Arietta said vaguely. "We are to attend a soiree this evening. Your muslin with the yellow flowers is suitable."

"Yes, Arietta," Letty said with relief. The inquisition appeared to be over. She only hoped that would be the end of it, for it left her feeling shabby and ungrateful. How she hated telling untruths when she owed Arietta so much. She frowned. Cartwright should not have made her promise.

SOME HOURS LATER, they returned from the soiree where a small concert had been held to introduce a visiting violinist. He had performed several pieces with great expertise.

"There is something you can do for me," Arietta said, having invited Letty to her bedchamber to drink chocolate and discuss the evening.

"Of course. Anything," Letty said, eager to make amends.

"This ability you have to move about without being seen."

"But I was seen. Mr. Cartwright found me."

"Yes, on that occasion," Arietta said impatiently. "But I should like you to do it again, for me."

Letty widened her eyes. "Do what exactly?"

"Follow Mr. Cartwright. See what he does. Who he talks to."

"Oh, I don't see…"

Arietta raised a hand. "My husband, Sir Gareth Kendall, suspected Cartwright spied for France," she said. "But my dear Kendall could never prove it. In his attempts, he died under a cloud of suspicion. I should like him to be remembered with honor. His reputation restored."

"How dreadfully sad!" Letty felt torn. Her mind was racing. Although she had suspected Cartwright of spying, for him to be a traitor was so horrifying, she found it hard to believe. Had she made a promise to keep his secrets when it might ultimately harm Arietta? "But the war is over."

"Intrigue continues in peace time, Letty, don't think it doesn't. And what can be gleaned from it remains of vital importance to the government. You would wish to help your country, wouldn't you?"

"Yes, of course. But Mr. Cartwright is smart. I'll never fool him."

"You're clever, too. And what better cover than as a debutante. Most will think you're an unsophisticated country girl." She clasped Letty's hands in hers. "I know you want to enjoy your Season, have fun and fall in love, and that will all come to pass. I shall make sure of it." She gave Letty's hands a shake with an imploring smile. "But first, do this for me, please?"

Letty tried to think of a reason to refuse, but her mind went blank with distress. "Very well, Arietta," she said reluctantly. "But I'm not at all sure I can be of any help."

Arietta smiled. "Good girl. I knew I could depend on you."

BRANDON RODE BACK to his townhouse in Brook Street. So, Miss Bromley was now under Arietta's patronage. An unwelcome development to say the least. Arietta and her husband Sir Gareth had quite a history, which had at one point become entwined with his. A murky business concerning an act of thievery from the Foreign Office. Kendall had accused him of it and attempted to plant the evidence on him, but he had failed on both counts, for not only did the Home Office disbelieve him, they began to look into Kendall's activities. Brandon had little time to dwell on it. He was to rendezvous with Willard Fraser, who had interesting information to impart, since he'd been in contact with the Comtesse de Lavalette.

Once he'd changed from his riding clothes, Brandon made his way to a tavern he and Willard used on occasion.

Willard was waiting in the busy taproom, and he joined him at a table in a corner where they drank tankards of ale. "The French are vacillating on whether to send our French friend to his end, and his wife grows nervous," he said. "She has reported a break-in at their chateau."

"Was anything taken?"

"No. But she writes now of this *Journal Noir*. Lavalette had it secreted away. He entrusted it to her when he began to fear for his life."

"Does she say what the book contains?"

"She does not. Whether she wishes to keep an ace up her sleeve, or she genuinely doesn't understand the significance of what is in her possession, is moot."

Brandon put down his tankard. "Does her request to us still stand?"

"Yes. She is to put her plan in motion if Lavalette's appeal fails. I have sent Borrowdale to Paris with the passport. He will assist Lavalette over the border into Belgium if, and when he is freed."

"And in the unlikely event that this comes off, will the comtesse pass the journal on to us?"

"Lavalette will come to London and personally deliver it."

Brandon gave a doubtful shrug. "Is there a way we can get our hands on it should his escape bid fail?"

"None presents itself as yet. But I remain hopeful."

"What do you want me to do?"

"Continue to investigate Fraughton. Learn who his cronies are. It is urgent that we understand just what they are up to. Whatever is in that journal is of great importance to the government, otherwise these men would not be so fearful. If they discover that the comtesse plans an attempt to free Lavalette from the Conciergerie, they will stop her by violent means. And should she succeed, and her husband reaches England, these men will attempt to kill him before he sets foot in London."

"It appears that Lady Fraughton wishes to rid herself of her husband. She has agreed to assist me."

Willard nodded and put down his tankard. "We need to keep one step ahead of these men. It's not just about this smoky business they've been involved in, it's what they plan to do next."

They left the tavern and stood on the pavement waiting to hail a hackney.

"If Comtesse de Lavalette doesn't know what the journal contains, might you have any idea?" Brandon asked with no real expectation of Willard telling him.

"It would be pure conjecture on my part," Willard replied, never one to speculate.

"Then I hope it falls into our hands. I, for one, am consumed with curiosity."

Willard grinned. He raised his cane to hail a cab rattling down the road.

Uneasy, Brandon walked away down the street. How desperate were these men? He didn't trust Susan Fraughton's discretion. And he didn't like Fraughton. He didn't tell Willard, for the man would disapprove of letting a possible good source of information go, but he planned to put a stop to her involvement.

CHAPTER EIGHT

L ETTY SIPPED HER tea. Earlier, she had been toiling over a letter to Cumbria, finding it difficult when she had to exclude so much. If Uncle Alford learned the truth, he would be on the doorstep within days.

Arietta came into the breakfast room. "Tonight, we are to attend a rout in Hampstead at Lord and Lady Willcox's home. You are sure to enjoy it, Letitia."

Letty put down her teacup. "What is a rout?"

"A rout is a house party," Arietta said. "Guests fill the reception rooms to listen to music, discuss books and art, and enjoy a nice supper. There might also be card tables." She nodded to the footman who hurried to attend her. "Your jaconet muslin dinner dress with the embroidered roses will be perfect." She cocked her head. "Tell Adele to place a plume in your hair, they are *de rigueur.*"

That evening, their carriage traveled down a long driveway lit by flickering lanterns, to the stone mansion set amongst formal gardens. Letty stepped from the carriage with mixed emotions. While she hoped that Cartwright wouldn't be here, she admitted to the desire to see him again. Did he spy for the French? She remembered the Frenchman with Fraughton in the library whom Cartwright obviously hadn't met. But that told her nothing. How frustrating!

"There will be music but no dancing," Arietta said as they climbed the steps to the portico and the tall front doors. "A harp or pianoforte, perhaps."

Routs seemed an odd thing to Letty. To be crammed in a drawing room with so many people? Some of the behaviors and rules the *ton* lived by made little sense to her. The world her mother and father inhabited had never been hers. At seven years old, she had watched from the staircase as they left the house in their elegant clothes to go to a party. Her beautiful mother had looked like a fairy queen, and her father so handsome in his evening clothes. But during the night, a snowstorm hit, and they did not return. A bridge had given way, and their carriage plunged into the icy waters.

Letty was left crushed with loneliness. Uncle Alford tried to help, but having never married and therefore, no children of his own, he really didn't know quite what to do. His idea of comfort was to read the Bible and invite her to pray with him. It took her a long time to become content with her life in Cumbria. But she still yearned for something more. A sense of freedom, perhaps, to choose the life she wanted. And yes, the love of a good man. But she doubted marriage would provide what she sought. Wives were even more constrained by their husbands. Yet, what else was there for her but marriage?

Following Arietta's example, Letty handed her evening cloak to a footman, and they moved into the stuffy, overcrowded drawing room where guests stood shoulder to shoulder. The noise greeted them like a blow. A harpist played in a corner but could barely be heard. Even though the night wasn't cold, a fire crackled in the fireplace. The smoky air blended with the scents of warm bodies seemed to suck all the oxygen from the room. She was glad of the glass of wine a footman gave her. As she sipped, Letty studied those around her, searching for a familiar face.

Arietta whispered in her ear from behind her fan. "Cartwright is over in the corner talking to Lord Fleetwood. Watch him. I wish to know whom he seeks out this evening."

"But I don't know anyone's names." Letty turned to find Arietta had been swallowed up in the crowd.

With an eye on Cartwright, she gulped down her drink and placed it on a waiter's tray. Cartwright had left the gentleman he'd been talking to and purposefully made his way to a door. He disappeared through it.

Excusing herself left and right, Letty followed him out.

She found herself in a wide corridor, the walls hung with gilt-framed paintings and tapestries. Her heart beating fast, she crept along it, glad that her silk evening slippers made little sound on the hall runner. Voices reached her. She edged forward and paused at a doorway, then peeked into the room. In the small study, Lady Fraughton talked to Cartwright. She leaned back against an oak desk and laughed, running a hand over his waistcoat. "What has caused this change of heart?" she asked in a low seductive voice.

Cartwright caught her wrist. Letty couldn't catch his low reply.

Afraid he would turn, or Lady Fraughton would peel her eyes away from Cartwright's broad chest and see her, Letty pulled back. She checked the corridor, but thankfully no one had entered from the busy reception rooms beyond the door. Was Cartwright intent on some covert mission as Arietta suggested? Or was it a liaison? The way he whispered to the lady suggested they were on intimate terms. Letty's blood boiled to think he would have an affair with a married woman. She had thought better of him, though any reason why she should, escaped her, since she knew absolutely nothing about him.

She chanced another quick glance with the excuse of seeking the withdrawing room, should she be discovered. Lady Fraughton removed a letter from her reticule and handed it to Cartwright. He unfolded it and held it up to the candlelight. After a quick scan, he handed it to her. "Put it back where you found it, and quickly, before it is missed," he said in a sharp tone. "And let that be the end of it. I shall require no further assistance from you, Lady Fraughton."

"Have I not been helpful?" she murmured.

"You have. I am grateful."

"How grateful are you, Cartwright?"

Fearful of discovery, Letty reluctantly left them and hurried back to the drawing room. Whatever that letter contained had been of great interest to him. However, none of this meant he was working for the French. Arietta must be wrong. Letty realized she made excuses for him. She supposed she must be that naïve country miss Arietta said she was.

She waited for Cartwright's return by taking shelter behind the broad back of a portly gentleman who talked disparagingly of Lord Byron's recent marriage and his latest poem. She did not have long to wait. Cartwright walked into the room alone with a serious mien, but when a man clapped him on the back, his expression lightened, and he was drawn laughingly into a group. Letty admired his expertise. Such skill! So untrustworthy! With a polite smile, she edged away through the throng as erudite discussions swirled around her peppered with witticisms and laughter.

A few moments later, Lady Fraughton emerged. Without glancing at Cartwright, she joined an older man whom Letty assumed was her husband. Fraughton's long narrow face bore a humorless expression. He would be some thirty years older than her, tall and lean, his hair white, but with a kind of upright wiry strength, which gave the impression of a good deal of self-consequence. Might Lady Fraughton's interest in the younger, more handsome Cartwright merely be prompted by desire? Yet, she could not discount the letter. What did it contain? Lady Fraughton had replaced it in her reticule which now hung on her arm. Arietta would be interested to learn what it contained. Letty stared at the bag, hoping the woman might put it down somewhere.

As she considered this, Fraughton left his wife's side and walked out through the French doors leading to the gardens. Letty spun around to watch as Cartwright immediately excused himself and went after Fraughton.

Anxious to seize the opportunity to follow him and discover just what his interest was in this man, she hurried in his wake.

Outside, braziers burned along the terrace and the garden paths, their fiery glow casting light and shade over the manicured grounds. Neither Cartwright nor Fraughton were anywhere to be seen.

She walked along the path, taking deep breaths of the welcome fresh air scented with flowers and trees in their new spring green, the breeze cool on her face.

Men's voices drifted over the lawn from a gazebo along with a faint tang of cigar smoke. Was Cartwright there? As they may spot her if she ventured farther, she decided to stay where she was, in the hope they'd come her way. She might pick up enough of their conversation to relay to Arietta. She peered through the branches of a flowering tree while finding it difficult to keep her balance on the uneven ground.

Suddenly, a hard hand gripped her arm as if to steady her. Cartwright drew her around to face him, and not gently.

"Dash it all, Miss Bromley! What in God's name are you doing here?" He sounded as if he'd clamped his teeth.

Her heart beating hard, she shook herself free of his hand, determined not to let him see how rattled he made her. "I was enjoying the peace and the night air, until you came and spoiled it, sir. I planned to stroll over the lawns, but there are people in the gazebo, and I didn't wish to disturb them." She glared at him. "What gives you the right to manhandle me? And what might *you* be doing here, Mr. Cartwright?"

His face partly in shadow, enough light revealed his rigid jaw and deep scowl. "I knew you'd be trouble. I'm beginning to wonder if you are who you say you are."

"It would not be hard to find out all about me," Letty said. "I have no secrets. You, on the other hand...." She raised her eyebrows.

"You are entirely too inquisitive. I wonder why?" He gripped her sleeve again and pulled her into the deep purple shadow cast by a high hedge.

She tried to resist, not quite sure what he had in mind for her, her heart skipping a beat, but her slippers skidded over the grass and she was obliged to grab hold of his arm.

"Sir!" Once she'd regained her balance, Letty released him with a gasp of indignation.

He ignored her protest, his presence so close that she inhaled his familiar spicy cologne and was compelled to step back. She could feel the sharp prickles of the hedge against her spine through the thin fabric of her evening gown. "Ow! Do you mind?" She moved away, fearing her gown might rent.

"Be quiet. Explain, yourself. Why are you following me?"

"Do you want me to be quiet or explain that I'm not following you?" She glared at him. "I can hardly do both."

"Don't get cocky with me, miss," he said grittily.

"I wasn't aware the gardens were exclusively yours," she said smartly, fairly confident he would not hurt her.

He cursed under his breath. "What a minx you are, Miss Bromley."

"Please don't mind me," Letty said with a frown. "Curse all you like."

"Are you going to explain your presence here?" There was no trace of irony in Cartwright's voice now. He sounded very cross.

"The rooms are so crowded and hot," she said in a beseeching tone. Suddenly very conscious of being alone with him in the dark, she began to edge toward the welcome light flooding out the French doors. "But I believe I'll go inside."

She had gone two steps when Cartwright moved to block her way to the terrace. He arched an eyebrow and studied her for a moment. "An excellent idea, Miss Bromley." A hand against her arm, he gave her a gentle push. "Let's make sure you do. Please proceed. I shall see you safely inside."

"You are no gentleman, Mr. Cartwright," Letty said over her shoulder as she hurried up the path.

Outraged at his ordering her about in such a careless manner, her face hot with embarrassment, she reached the terrace, then turned, but he'd disappeared. Where had he gone? He was nothing better than a rake and mixed up in goodness knew what. But she would have to get better at this spying business, for she felt sure Arietta would expect her to continue.

Candlelight and chatter flooded out through the open doors. Bracing herself, she entered and searched over gentlemen's heads and the ladies' waving feather headdresses, then wended her way to the adjoining salon where guests played cards at tables set up for the purpose. What would she tell Arietta? Cartwright hadn't done much worth mentioning, except for his clandestine meeting with Fraughton's wife, and his obvious interest in Fraughton. He'd been defensive, too, and wanted her to stop following him. Perhaps Arietta would assume it was a romantic liaison. Should she mention the letter? It could be anything. Letty was torn with indecision, and struck by a puzzling sense of loyalty to Cartwright, who certainly didn't deserve it.

"There you are," Arietta linked arms with her and guided her into the supper room where a tasty array of food was served.

Letty discovered herself in need of sustenance. Shadowing Cartwright made her hungry, and she needed some strengthening before she faced Arietta's questions. She ate a portion of delicious tender chicken and sliced beef, and two rout cakes, which were sweet and richly flavored with fruit.

"I saw you follow our quarry into the corridor. You must tell me everything later," Arietta said, *sotto voche,* as they drank wine. "I hope it's something that will aid poor Kendall's memory," she said. "He wasn't buried in his family's crypt, you know." Her gaze over the rim of her glass looked desperately sad.

Letty caught her breath as the inner struggle to keep faith with both of them tightened her ribs.

"But the night is not yet over," Arietta continued. "You might discover something more. Come and meet my friends, and when it is prudent to do so, you can slip away."

The tart wine went down the wrong way, making Letty cough. "Yes, of course," she said feebly. Arietta had obviously not given up.

ONCE BRANDON MADE sure that Miss Bromley returned to the house, he entered the shrubbery. He circled the gazebo and came up behind it, hidden from view by the broad trunk of a chestnut while close enough to hear what was said. He feared he was too late to glean much. They had stamped out their cigars and were preparing to depart.

"Lavalette's wife might know more than we think," Fraughton said. "She could be persuaded to reveal it."

The other man, who was shorter and broader in stature, shook his head. "What? And then kill her? We might as well put a notice in *The Times*. Patience, Fraughton!"

"How can I be patient when you came back empty handed from Paris, Descrier? Lavalette has hidden it somewhere. It was his intention to blackmail us before he was thrown into prison, but he may well still intend to do so." There was a note of anguish in Fraughton's voice.

"Lavalette will soon face the guillotine. It changes the game, does it not? We shall have more time to find this *Journal Noir* at our leisure. And with luck on our side, it will never be found."

"There is an appeal to save him," Fraughton said.

"Lavalette was in service to Napoleon," Descrier said edgily. "He took over the Post Office for the General at the beginning of the

Hundred Days, when Louis XVIII had already left Paris. Despite a popular campaign to free Marshall Ney and others, they were executed. Lavalette doesn't have a chance."

"Will the others agree with you?"

"Robert Marston is impatient," Descrier said. "He lost a great deal of money this year at the gaming tables. The fact our market has grown considerably smaller has made him skittish. He is already planning to find a wealthy widow to marry."

"I'm afraid Marston's reputation precedes him. And there are not a lot of gullible, wealthy widows about," Descrier said dryly. He gave a heavy sigh. "It's a blow for all of us. What about Elford?"

"Distracted. His new bride is demanding. Elford doubts the journal will ever see the light of day, and if it does, it would be difficult to prove it is genuine."

"I believe it is written in Napoleon's hand," Fraughton said sharply.

"Hell and damnation," Descrier muttered. "Unfortunate. But still I think it wise to be patient. Lavalette could die within a matter of days. We shall decide what next to do at the meeting."

"Pierse is about to go to France and will visit the comtesse. He has ways of gaining information."

"He's a hot head and might kill her," Descrier snarled. "You must caution him against any rash action. It will stir up no end of trouble for us. And with no guarantee of success, for the woman may know nothing."

"As you have nothing better to offer, I shall do what I see fit," Fraughton growled.

They emerged from the gazebo and began to cross the lawn to the house. Brandon stepped farther into the deep shadows. The letter Susan Fraughton had shown him was to advise her husband of a meeting between the key players, the time, and the place. And Brandon intended to be there. As he watched them go, he mused over what he'd heard. He would have to pay Willard a visit at his home tonight. Word must be sent immediately to warn the comtesse.

He turned to make his way back along the circuitous route he'd come.

It came as a surprise that Robert Marston was party to this, but it explained a lot. The rake had been toying with Susan, no doubt with some ploy in mind. Should she be warned? Brandon dismissed it. There was scant reason for it yet, and he couldn't see how he'd manage it without giving too much away. The less she knew the better. It was possible that her interest in finding a new lover could mean her involvement with Marston had ended.

Brandon lit a cheroot and wandered toward a fountain centered in the closely shaved lawns. He rested a foot on the stone edge. It was an agreeable sight, the water cascading from a nymph's stone urn into the pool, and sending out ripples across the surface. Like the ripples Miss Bromley set in motion when she'd first appeared in that library. From their seemingly innocuous meeting, their paths continued to cross. What was she about? She kept turning up like a bad penny though he did admit she intrigued him. He had been convinced she was what she appeared to be, a young innocent. She certainly looked the part when her thickly-fringed brown eyes implored him. But he couldn't allow a girl to sway him. Too much was at stake. What was her involvement with Lady Arietta? He had thought after Kendall died the lady would let things be. Dangerous for her, and Letitia, surely, to get involved in this.

He flicked his cheroot away and headed back to the house. What to do about Miss Bromley? He suspected he wasn't done with her; his bully-boy tactics having failed. He must devise another strategy, he felt sure he would need it.

CHAPTER NINE

A S ARIETTA HAD promised, after supper, she introduced Letty to several gentlemen and two ladies with daughters making their Come-out. Most greeted her warmly, but one older lady raised her plucked eyebrows. "Cumbria? At least you do not have the country burr." Letty feared she expected her to chew on a hayseed. When Arietta gave her a subtle signal with her fan, Letty excused herself and left them.

Arietta's plea for information urged Letty to discover something more before the evening was over. It would be useless to shadow Cartwright; he would be watching for her. And she refused to subject herself to such embarrassment again. Not after the way he'd treated her in the garden. She didn't trust him after that clandestine meeting with Fraughton's wife and then lurking in the garden watching Fraughton. With such inexplicable behavior, he could not be a good man. If only she could get hold of that letter in Lady Fraughton's reticule. It might explain why Cartwright wished to see it.

After searching the reception rooms, she found the lady playing whist at a card table in the salon. But there was no sign of her reticule. Letty cast about but could not see it. She went to the drawing room. There it was! It must be hers. So unusual, shaped like a shell, with a shell clasp and decorated with gold beads. Lady Fraughton had left it on an occasional table, but unfortunately, her husband was not far away.

Letty was about to admit defeat when Fraughton suddenly left the room. Her heart thudding, she glanced around before approaching the table. She placed a hand on the glossy wooden surface, as if to steady herself, her fingers inches from the bag, when Lord Fraughton appeared at the door. He came over to the table and picked up the reticule, casting a glance at her. "Lady Fraughton's, I believe."

"Is it? It is very like my friend's. I was about to return it to her."

Fraughton nodded and left the room.

Letty remained where she was relieved that he hadn't sought to question her. She trembled at the expression in Fraughton's eyes. Could he suspect her? She tried to calm herself and order her thoughts.

A dark superfine sleeve appeared in the corner of her eye, and a low voice sounded in her ear. She jumped and glanced up. Cartwright, with that steely glint in his eyes. He had a habit of appearing out of nowhere. Had he been hiding behind the curtains? The question hovered on her tongue, but now others had come within earshot, so she clamped her lips together.

"Miss Bromley. How nice to see you again," he said politely. "How is your aunt?"

Letty swallowed, her throat horribly dry. "Aunt Edith is very well, thank you, Mr. Cartwright. She enjoys her stay in the country."

"Cumbria, wasn't it? I have often wished to visit the area and the beautiful lakes. You must tell me all about it. I daresay you are returning there very soon. How could one stay away?"

"No, I..."

He shepherded her away, a hand resting lightly on her back. While he barely touched her, she still felt the heat of his skin through the silk. "Shall we find a seat? I believe I saw one or two free in the salon."

She was effortlessly propelled from the room. Small groups in fervent discussion paused to nod at Cartwright as they passed. One gentleman murmured something to his companion. Did they think

Cartwright had made a conquest? She firmed her lips.

In the salon, Letty eased away from him. She put a gloved hand to her mouth to feign a yawn. "You must excuse me, sir. I am fatigued. I shall ask Lady Arietta if she is ready to leave."

"Quite so." Noting the resolute expression in his eyes, she had to look away. "I shall have to be patient to hear all your news at a better time, Miss Bromley. The hour does grow late."

With a bow he left her. Without moving beyond the bounds of propriety, he'd managed to inject a note of warning into his voice. She watched him disappear through the drawing room door. His cold blue eyes told her he had declared war. He wanted her to go back to Cumbria or at least, stay out of his way. Letty would not return to Cumbria, and Arietta would not agree to the latter. She wished sorely that she might utter some of his curses. It was clear he was now determined to thwart her.

Letty did not welcome their next meeting. She went in search of Arietta and finally found her in the withdrawing room.

Arietta turned from the mirror. "I can see you are tired, my dear. We shall say our goodbyes."

Letty, wishing she had more to offer her kind patroness, walked with Arietta through the reception rooms.

"I'm afraid we must go. Dear Miss Bromley is accustomed to country hours," Arietta cried gayly, in response to entreaties to stay. "Shall we meet again at the races, tomorrow? Who has a horse running?"

Two gentlemen spoke up.

"Then I shall cheer them both home," Arietta said warmly. "Come, Letitia, dear."

Letty followed slowly, beginning to droop while she wondered if Mr. Cartwright attended the races.

As they traveled home, Arietta turned to her. "Well? Did you discover anything of interest?"

She explained about the meeting between Cartwright and Lady Fraughton, and the letter.

Arietta frowned. "What happened? Did you see them embrace?"

"No. Although they seemed to be on comfortable terms. He told her to put the letter back where she found it."

"It would appear that Cartwright is spying on Lord Fraughton. I wonder why? Fraughton is an honorable gentleman. He should be warned."

"That would put an end to our endeavors and anything we may yet discover," Letty said quickly. She would hate to be responsible for what might occur if Fraughton was made aware of Cartwright's association with his wife. There was something mean about Fraughton. She saw it in his eyes. Although duels were illegal, they were fought for less reason, and inevitably, someone was badly wounded or killed. That it might be down to her made her tremble with horror. She waited, holding her breath as Arietta gave it some thought.

"Yes, you are right," Arietta said finally. "Though I would like to know the content of that letter," she mused.

"I did try to remove it from Lady Fraughton's reticule, but then her husband came to get it. Cartwright had his eye on me, so I gave the idea away."

Arietta placed an arm around Letty's shoulders. "But how interesting. This alone tells us a lot, Letty!" She gave her a squeeze. "We are onto something. I can feel it in my bones. You are doing far better than I anticipated. How very clever of you!"

"I wish I could do more, but Cartwright suspects me. I fear I may be unable to continue."

Arietta removed her arm from around Letty and took up her fan, employing it vigorously. "Nonsense! You have shown yourself to be remarkably skilled. I feel sure another chance will present itself. Be ready to grasp it with both hands. I don't mind telling you, my dear, that I am excited by this. There's some conspiracy afoot which will show Cartwright's true colors, and clear my dear husband's name."

Letty smiled weakly as she sank back onto the squabs.

BRANDON ENTERED WILLARD'S library. He repressed a chuckle. Willard had just returned from a soiree and wore a purple brocade dressing gown, patterned with snarling gold dragons, over his shirt and pantaloons.

"A Christmas present," Willard said in answer to Brandon's raised eyebrows. "From my mother."

"Very handsome," Brandon observed, tongue in cheek.

"*Enough.*" A smile lifted a corner of Willard's mouth as he waved him to a chair. "Brandy?"

"Please."

Willard went to the drinks tray and poured two snifters of brandy from the crystal decanter, returning to hand Brandon one. He took the chair opposite. "What have you uncovered that requires this visit?"

Brandon told him.

"A good evening's work. I shall alert the comtesse to the danger although she is well aware of it. The lady is intent on pursuing her plan at whatever cost. So, what is this market they speak of, I wonder? And how does it relate to the *Journal Noir?*"

Brandon felt the familiar kick of excitement tighten his chest. "I'll try to discover it without delay."

Willard nodded. "Yes. Time grows short. But now we have the gentlemen's names. Wealthy and powerful men who will be difficult to bring to justice. We must have proof, and until we get the journal, we need to catch them red-handed at something unlawful. However, the investigation shall continue. I trust you will be nearby when they attend that meeting?"

"Depend upon it." Brandon drained his glass and stood. "I shan't keep you from your bed, and I must confess, I am ready for mine."

As Willard saw him to the door, Brandon turned. "Remember that business with Sir Gareth Kendall? Killed himself when he came under a cloud of suspicion after he was accused of working for the French. He tried to make me the scapegoat, but failed when Whitehall took measures to silence him."

"Yes, agents paid him a visit and persuaded him to keep his mouth shut."

"Is there evidence that he was working for the French?"

"The Home Office had enough information to arrest him. He would have been hanged, knew it, of course, and beat them to the punch. If indeed it was suicide," he said after a thoughtful silence. "The postmortem was inconclusive. Some evidence of interference."

This was new to him. Brandon whistled silently. "What about his wife? Could she have been involved?"

"Lady Arietta? Nothing to suggest it. I felt rather sorry for her at the time. She fought tooth and nail for him. A loyal and loving wife, it would appear."

"Foolish. But love can blind one." He shrugged into his greatcoat.

"Eh?" Willard opened the door. "Rather late in the evening for such a deep philosophical thought, is it not? You aren't in love, by any chance?"

Brandon shook his head with a wry smile. "No. Spies have no business falling in love. Best we avoid the parson's mousetrap while in the business."

"You'll consider it one day, surely."

"I doubt I'm husband material."

"Don't sell yourself short, Brandon." Willard frowned. "I sometimes wonder if I did the right thing dragging you into this."

"You didn't drag me in, you rescued me," Brandon said as he

donned his hat. "Goodness knows where I might have ended up if you hadn't."

"You would have righted yourself." He rubbed at the beginnings of a beard on his jaw. "I should have resisted, perhaps. You were young, but I recognized your potential when you saved me from those footpads in Covent Garden. A handy piece of work." He nodded. "My judgement was on the money. About your potential, I mean."

"I don't regret it. I hope you don't."

Willard smiled. "That goes without saying. Just as long as you stay alive. I don't want your death on my conscience."

Brandon merely grinned and picked up his cane from the hall table. With a nod, he departed into the night in search of a hackney. It had been raining, the roads wet and not a carriage in sight. Sighing, his cane over his shoulder, he set off down the street. When would he toss it in? Did the reason he took this path no longer drive him? He had become involved in his early twenties. His father had cut him off, accused him of being a wastrel after he'd been sent down from Oxford in his final year. It was the result of a wild escapade that ended in tragedy.

After a night spent in the local pub drinking into the early hours, he and Freddie Maxwell emerged in their cups and decided to climb the church tower. He couldn't remember whose decision it was, and it didn't matter. The pain of what followed would have equal force either way when Freddie had lost his grip and fallen to his death.

His father's contempt for him was justified. For a while, Brandon made sure he lived up to it, carousing in London with a rowdy group of bucks, until he was approached by Willard and took up the offer to become an agent for the Crown. He'd gone into it back then because he agreed with his father's assessment of his character and didn't care if he lived or died. He continued to do it because he wanted to prove something to himself, that he wasn't that complete wastrel his father considered him, and because the work he performed was important to the nation's security.

Seven years later, his father, who was a respected member of parliament, still disapproved of him. Brandon rarely visited Fernborough Park, the family's country home in Surrey. His reception had not changed through the years, still the veiled criticism from his father, whom Brandon chose not to tell of his work for the Crown. And should he discover it, his father would put it down solely to his son's reckless need for excitement and danger. Then there was the constant urging from his mother to marry and provide her with grandchildren. As if that was the panacea for all ills. He had little to offer a wife. Far simpler to remain single.

As the rain started again, a jarvey pulled up his hackney and called to him. With a nod, Brandon gave him his direction and climbed inside. He removed his hat, shaking off the rainwater and smoothed his damp hair.

None of the young women his mother presented to him had stirred his interest. They were nervous, he supposed, when they repeated his opinions back at him and revealed none of their own. He frowned. Unlike Miss Bromley, who was decidedly opinionated. So, he had been correct about her determination. He needed to find out what drove her to follow him around like an insistent puppy. It appeared that Lady Arietta had set her onto him. Miss Bromley could find herself in very real danger should she persist. And he wasn't confident she'd let matters rest. He did not fancy having to break his cover to rescue her from these dangerous men who thought little about murdering a woman to save their hides. He must find a way to reason with her. Make her stop.

But how might he achieve it? That required some thought, and in the meantime, there were more pressing things he must do.

CHAPTER TEN

"I'VE BEEN TO race meets in the country, but nothing like this," Letty said to Arietta where they stood with a group of her friends viewing the races.

Ascot racecourse was surrounded by woodlands, with sheep and cattle roaming the pastures, but any similarity to the countryside vanished where thousands of patrons milled over the grounds, lining the barrier on both sides of the green turf where the horses raced. A deafening cheer or a chorus of groans went up each time the horses galloped past. Some gentlemen even stood atop their carriages to urge the horses on.

"Time for champagne." Lord Chumley topped off their glasses. He was full of good cheer; his horse having won a race.

Ladies in their flowery hats and gentlemen in their tailcoats and tall hats filled the cottage tent where afternoon tea was served while the tavern sold champagne, wine, and ale to the men.

Letty, fascinated by the sights, took a deep breath of the cool spring air laden with the pungent smells of humanity and horseflesh. On the other side of the course, many were not so beautifully attired. They ate pies and more simple fare, while enjoying the prize-fighting, the gaming tents, and a singer who sang ballads. A juggler balancing a dozen spinning plates caught her eye.

"I've seen Cartwright. Over there by the rail," Arietta said. "He's walking toward the Duke of Colchester's coach." She nudged Letty's arm. "Quick!"

Letty's heart sank. "I can't follow him. There are too many people. I'll get lost."

Arietta removed Letty's half-full champagne glass from her limp fingers. "Nonsense! You can easily find your way back to this tent. I shall stay here and wait for you, and then we'll have tea."

As she hurried after Cartwright, Letty was jostled by the large throng of people. She fixed her eye on his black silk top hat and the broad expanse of his back garbed in a pale gray tailcoat. Fortunately, he was taller than many around him. He made his way purposefully through the crowd. Was he on the scent of a group of conspirators? Or was he one of them? With a glance over his shoulder, he approached a tent and disappeared inside. Unable to follow, Letty hovered while angling her blush-pink parasol to hide her face, far enough away to be inconspicuous. Or so she thought.

Suddenly, when she raised her parasol, he was beside her.

He swept off his hat. "Miss Bromley. How surprising to find you here outside the gentleman's convenience."

"Was it?" Her face burned. "I...um, was looking for the ladies'."

He pointed to another tent some way off.

"Thank you." She turned to leave, but he continued to walk beside her.

"What are you doing?" Letty glared at him. "You can't accompany me there."

"No. But I shall wait outside. I have wanted to speak to you, and this seems the perfect time."

"I can't imagine what about."

"Can you not?"

She sneaked a glance at his patrician profile, noting the harsh set of his jaw. "I have nothing to say that might be of interest to you, sir," she said doggedly, finding little to say in her defense.

"Oh, I think you might." He stopped and nodded toward the tent. "Don't let me detain you."

Letty let down her parasol and hurried inside the large tent where screens were set up for the women's privacy. Finding another doorway toward the back, she gasped with relief and darted through it.

Cartwright waited outside, his arms folded.

She glared at him as she walked past, eager to escape him and return to Arietta.

Cartwright strolled beside her as if they were enjoying a promenade in the park. He seemed impervious to snubs.

"I am disappointed you refuse to talk to me, Miss Bromley," he said, his voice tinged with irony. "I fear I may be losing my charm."

"I shouldn't think so, sir. I am doubtful you ever had a surfeit of it." She bit her lip, now she was being most dreadfully impolite, what was it about this man? Really, Arietta did expect a lot of her.

He laughed. "That's not very polite. Don't they teach you manners in Cumbria?"

"In Cumbria…." She stopped to face him, surprised at the level of outrage that tightened her chest at the distressing rebuffs she'd received from some since she came here; most particularly Miss Somersby, who had made her spirits plummet. "We are nothing like the *ton*. Country folk are plain-speaking. We do not indulge in innuendo and veiled spite, not like some I have met since I came to London."

He nodded slowly as his blue gaze drifted over her. "Some members of the *ton* can be cruel. Has it been difficult?"

Surprised to find sympathy in his eyes, she bit her lip. She'd been moaning, what was wrong with her? For the most part, London had been wonderful. She cast him a quick glance. This change in Cartwright's demeanor was even more difficult to deal with. "*Au contraire.* I have been most fortunate. Lady Arietta is a generous, wonderful person. I am having a very enjoyable time."

"A Season can be a special time for a young lady," he agreed. "I wonder why you don't just do what the other ladies do, shop and attend dances, and so forth."

She caught her lip between her teeth again. She owed him an explanation, she supposed, but not if it betrayed Arietta.

"Why do you pursue me, Miss Bromley? Is it with a view to marriage?"

She drew in a horrified breath and stared at him. "Oh! Of course it isn't," she cried, incensed. The man was incorrigible. "I would never employ such tricks. Not if you were the last man in London."

"You have no need to make it so plain," he said with a wry lift of his eyebrow. "Tell me then please, what attracts you to me."

She opened her mouth. Then shut it again. "But you are mistaken, sir, I'm not," she said finally, horribly aware of how rude that sounded. *A bit of a lie, too.* Unable to meet his serious blue gaze, she looked down at her dusty half-boots.

His silence forced her to look up. "Much as I might enjoy a charming young woman's attention for whatever reason, please listen to me, Miss Bromley," he said, his voice lowered. "You are placing yourself in danger. If your patroness tells you to follow me, say no!"

Her eyes widened. *He knew!* All this time he knew Arietta was behind this. What was the truth of their association? She'd begun to feel like a pawn in some horrid game. Was it dangerous, or was he merely trying to scare her?

He offered her his arm. "Come with me and watch a race. My good friend, Lord Downing, has a horse called Sweet Minx running," he said. "Appropriate, I feel."

"Appropriate? I can't imagine why." She fought to resist his undeniably attractive smile. His behavior and quite possibly his morals were sadly lacking. Because it would be discourteous to refuse, and she remained curious about him, she took his arm and walked with him to the rail where the majestic thoroughbreds cantered past toward the starting line.

Once the horses were lined up, a man whom Cartwright called the starter, dropped the flag and the horses leapt forward.

Despite herself, excitement built. She cheered like those around them as the horses thundered around the final turn in a riot of colored jackets.

"Which is your friend's horse?" Letty called above the crescendo of sound.

He put his head close to hers, affording her a glimpse of a smoothly shaven, olive-toned cheek and a whiff of spicy cologne. "The roan ridden by the jockey in a yellow coat."

"But surely he rides too heavy!"

He chuckled. "That is my friend, Lord Downing. He always rides Sweet Minx."

"Does he ever win?"

"Not often, but by Jove, they're in front! Well, look at that!" he cried. "They are going to win!"

Caught up in the excitement, Letty began to cheer Sweet Minx on.

As the horses crossed the finishing line, Cartwright snatched her up with his hands at her waist and swung her around. "Sweet Minx won!"

Letty laughed with him.

He set her back on her feet, slightly giddy at his masculine strength and the warmth of his hands. *Heaven's!* What if anyone she knew saw them? She would be labelled a dreadful flirt, or worse!

Before she could object to his impertinence, he sobered, his gaze seeking hers. "Best return to your party. You will be missed. Don't forget my warning, Miss Bromley. It was heartfelt."

"I have nothing to fear whilst in Lady Arietta's care," Letty said firmly, despite her heart still fluttering.

"Are you sure?" Cartwright looked skeptical. His gaze wandered over her, taking her in from her white satin hat in the latest mode trimmed with white dyed ostrich feathers to match her spencer, down to her green kid boots. It wasn't an admiring glance, and a deep crease had formed between his dark brows.

Still slightly flustered, she raised her chin and smoothed the skirts of her French cambric dress. "Of course, I am sure."

"You should not be wandering around a place such as this on your own without even a duenna to accompany you," he said shortly. "This is not a *ton* ballroom or Almack's. Your patroness is not so caring in my opinion. What's her game, Miss Bromley? Are you sure it's a noble one? Think on it if you will."

With a brief bow, he left her.

Letty looked after him until he was swallowed up by the crowd. Then she hurried back to Arietta. Might whatever Cartwright was up to have some connection to Arietta's husband? It seemed unlikely when Kendall had been gone for over a year. Cartwright's criticism of Arietta might be justified, but until there was proof, she had to remain loyal to Arietta, after all she had done for her. No one could mistake the despair Arietta suffered concerning her husband's unfair treatment, which drove her to uncover the truth. And Letty was firmly committed to aiding her in any way she could.

Arietta waited outside the cottage tent. "Come and have a cup of tea," she said. "And tell me what you've discovered."

The tent was filled with patrons partaking of tea and the delicious selection of cakes, the air sweetly scented with lemon, honey, and spices. "There is nothing to tell. Cartwright is here to watch a friend's horse race."

"Oh? Well, no matter. There's always next time. Would you care for cake or a strawberry tart?"

Letty followed her to a vacant table with Cartwright's foreboding message ringing in her ears.

PRETTY MISS BROMLEY reminded him of early spring snowdrops. Fresh and new and filled with promise. He rather wished she didn't. She was bound to be hurt if she continued in this vein. And he seemed powerless to stop her, without approaching Lady Arietta directly, which would be unwise when he wasn't sure what that lady's motive was.

It appeared that Miss Bromley's loyalty to her knew no bounds. He doubted even his bald suggestion that she was attempting to snare him failed to deter her. She merely raised her chin at him and went on her merry way. Was this how they raised girls in Cumbria? It was his policy to avoid debutantes. If one for some unknown reason cast out a lure for him, he was always careful to distance himself without bruising their tender sensibilities. Miss Bromley was nothing like them, she cast no lures, and it appeared that she didn't bruise quite so easily.

He took out his pocket watch. Replacing it in his waistcoat pocket, he returned to the men's convenience, his intention disrupted by Miss Bromley's appearance. When he emerged again ten minutes later, he was dressed in a groom's garb. He entered the area where owners, trainers, grooms, and stable hands milled around the rows of horse stalls. The gentlemen he sought stood in front of the stall allocated to Dancer, Lord Elford's thoroughbred, which had just raced.

Brandon tugged his hat down and found a pitchfork in the empty stall next to theirs. Working swiftly, he ducked his head, breathing in the strong odors of horse manure, urine, and dusty straw, as he transferred hay to a corner where he could better hear their conversation.

"Do you know how the journal came into Lavalette's possession?" Elford asked.

"Not conclusively. After Waterloo, I asked for it to be sent to me for safe keeping, as our arrangement was at an end, because I feared it might fall into the wrong hands," Fraughton said in a pained voice. "I inquired after it failed to arrive. Couldn't get a definitive answer. Napoleon's man Bouvier assured me it was sent in a diplomatic bag. I finally concluded the only one who could have accessed it was Lavalette. It was he who examined the mail to ferret out any plots against the general." He sighed heavily. "He must have intercepted one of the mounted couriers and searched the bag. His loyalty to Napoleon prevented him from using it, I suppose, but then the game changed when Napoleon was incarcerated on St. Helena. Then Lavalette's blackmail letter arrived. I suppose he hoped it would finance his escape from France after others were put to death, and he began to fear for his life."

"His appeal will be denied, and he'll face the guillotine like the others," Marston said. "So, I fail to see why we should concern ourselves with this journal. We need to deal with the change in our arrangements, now that Napoleon is no longer able to support our venture. I'm told he's a spent force. I doubt he'll escape a second time."

A murmured consensus followed this statement.

"Certainly, changes need to be made," Descrier said. "We will need to think long and hard about it."

"I have sent Pierse to France," Fraughton said. "He will deal with the Comtesse Lavalette. If she has the journal in her possession, it shall not be for long."

"What? You sent that violent fool to attack her?" Lord Elford growled. "We already have a death on our hands which could lead authorities to us."

"Nonsense. That was some time ago. His death cannot implicate us. My instructions to Pierse were to make another search of her apartments," Fraughton said coolly. "Not to confront the comtesse."

"I had Lavalette's properties searched thoroughly," said Descrier.

"It is pointless and could well expose us. Pierse is about as reliable as a faulty pistol."

"We shall see." Fraughton said grittily. "No doubt you will stop complaining if Pierse returns with it."

Descrier groaned. "But we can't rely on it. We must come to a decision. We are like headless chickens. Let us talk again at the Moncrief's ball. We shall organize our journey to your Kent estate, Elford."

"Good, a decision of sorts at last," Marston growled.

"Very well, we'll go to Kent and deal with the problem there. But as there's not a lot we can do about this journal, I vote we do nothing. Just let the cards fall where they may. I have to be careful. The new Lady Elford is a wily woman." There was a cautious note in Elford's voice.

"Can't afford to wait," muttered Marston.

"Well, if that's it, gentlemen? I see this has been a complete waste of time, and I need to be elsewhere for the next race." Elford's voice faded as he strode away.

After several minutes of silence, Brandon tossed down the fork and emerged. The stall next door was empty. Outside, a groom raised his head from bandaging the legs of a glossy-coated chestnut. He glanced at Brandon with mild curiosity before going about his business.

Brandon walked swiftly away. The one thing he took from that meeting was the likelihood that these men were mixed up with smuggling. What interested him most was in what way they'd been in cahoots with Napoleon. It was no secret that Bonaparte turned a blind eye to smugglers. He had associations with some Englishmen, because he benefited from the information sent across to France during the war, which helped shore up his empire. It was a piece of the puzzle perhaps, but not the whole.

If these men incriminated themselves during the Moncrieff's masquerade, he'd alert Willard and organize the customs and excise men in Kent, and with a bit of luck, catch them red-handed.

CHAPTER ELEVEN

ARIETTA HAD HIRED costumes especially for the Moncrief's masked ball, to be held at their estate in Richmond. Letty in white and gold was Titania, Queen of the Fairies, from Shakespeare's play *A Midsummer Night's Dream*. Arietta in crimson and black, a lady from a fifteenth century Venice masked ball.

Letty turned before the mirror, admiring her flowing white gown, smoothing the long, full sleeves. A wide gold braid belt defined her waist, and narrow gold cord crossed over her bust. Artificial flowers and leaves of rose, gold, and green, decorated the low-cut bodice. Holding up the folds of the gown with a broad gold border at the hem, she slipped her feet into the gold sandals. More flowers circled her head, while wisps of her long hair framed her face, the rest was pinned loosely in a bun. She thought it a pity to cover such a lovely gown with the loose, hooded white cloak lined with yellow silk, called a domino. She stood ready, holding the cream and gold demi-mask which would tie at the back of her head.

"Titania!" Arietta greeted her at the foot of the stairs, dressed in her voluminous crimson gown revealing a slim waist and a dramatic black domino lined with crimson draped over her shoulders. Her crimson and black Venetian-styled mask looked exotic and mysterious.

When they entered the Moncrief's ballroom, Letty gasped with amazement at the swirling tableau of color, riotous noise, and heavily scented air. The atmosphere was unlike anything she had yet experienced, or indeed ever imagined. It appeared that the masks lent the guests a sense of freedom as decorum and manners seemed to have deserted many of them.

The dancing was less ordered, the laughter louder, and displays of boisterous behavior made Letty stare openmouthed. A woman dressed as Bo-peep, held a crook with a satin bow, and led a lamb by a blue ribbon. A man, his legs bare beneath a tunic, wore a knight's armor and a metal helmet which sported pink feathers. Another man in brightly colored silk trousers wore a turban on his head, and his slippers curled up oddly at the toes. There were several men in black dominoes, their masks like crows with elongated and fearsome beaks.

A man in green and gold with a high ruff around his neck in the manner of Shakespeare claimed her for the quadrille. "'Tis I, Miss Bromley," said Mr. Boyce, his eyes warm behind his green mask.

"Heavens, sir, I would never have guessed," Letty said. "How did you recognize me?"

"A mask does not hide your beauty, Miss Bromley, if I may be so bold," her faithful and undeterred suitor claimed, before they were parted by the steps of the dance.

Letty waltzed with a gentleman in purple hose and black satin, whose hands moved lower than they should on her back. His leg pressed between hers as he turned her. She attempted to ease away from him, but he gripped her tightly. Arietta was dancing with their host nearby but not close enough for Letty to gain her attention. Nor would she welcome it. Letty would have to deal with this herself. "You are crushing my hand, sir," she said loudly enough to be overheard by those around them.

"Beg pardon." He loosened his grasp, his eyes glittering through the slits in his mask. He made a point of bending his head to ogle her bosom in the low-cut dress.

When the music stopped, and he led her back to her chair, she was so affronted, she refused to thank him. Slightly tipsy, he wandered away, apparently failing to notice the snub. A masquerade, it appeared, was a license to engage in bad behavior.

Letty looked about for Cartwright amid the sea of colorful costumes though it was impossible to spot him. Had he not come tonight? Somehow, she sensed he would be here. What better opportunity for a spy than a masked ball? Arietta had told her to wander at will, and confident no one would object, with only the few gentlemen who appeared at her side at every entertainment likely to approach her, Letty fully intended to.

When the orchestra took a recess, she slipped from the ballroom. Her heart in her mouth, she peeked into the other reception rooms. In the library, three men smoked and drank spirits, chuckling over an anecdote; none of them tall enough to be Cartwright.

She continued her search, determined to find him. Pleased that the domino and mask afforded her some freedom to eavesdrop, she went out onto the terrace and down the steps into the gardens. The path ambled through the topiary illuminated by braziers.

A couple passed her. "Have you lost your paramour?" the gentleman asked. His companion laughed as they continued on to the house.

Letty walked on past an arbor of fragrant roses in full bloom. The path wound its way through the shrubbery. Laughter came from amongst the trees, but she was relieved not to meet anyone, aware of how difficult it would be to explain why she wandered about without an escort.

She emerged from the rhododendron walk onto the closely clipped lawns. An artistic array of rocks hung with creepers formed a grotto where a small waterfall fed into a pool.

Men's voices sounded nearby. Letty darted back in amongst the rhododendrons and crouched down, a purple flower tickling her chin. She peered through the branches, breathing in the honey-like aroma. Four gentlemen emerged from the side of the ruin, the hoods of their black dominoes pushed back, and their crow-like masks on top of their heads. Two of them smoked cigars, the smoke wafting toward her. As they gathered beside the pool, the moon cast off the fitful clouds and its rays alighted on a head of white hair. *Lord Fraughton.*

Surely Cartwright can't be far away? She didn't fancy him finding her as she'd chosen to ignore his somewhat sinister warning. Letty didn't mind fencing with him, in fact, she quite enjoyed it, but not when it would be so one-sided. Best keep to the shadows. She had no intention of missing this. It was an excellent opportunity to hear something of interest to convey to Arietta.

"I am informed our cargo was landed in the marsh wrapped in oilskin bags," a man said as he tossed his cigar into the pool. "It was then ferried up the creek on a moonless night to a waiting wagon, successfully avoiding the coastguard. The dragoons search all the houses and lands near the coast, but never venture as far as my estate. They won't accuse a lord of smuggling unless they've clear proof. Not if they know what's good for them."

"Unless the excisemen get wind of it," a familiar voice growled. "They might be waiting until they have that evidence."

"You are a dreary fellow these days, Marston," Fraughton said. He sounded quite jubilant. "Well done, Elford! Our first operation since we lost Napoleon's support has been a success."

"The goods will be brought to London through the usual channels," Elford said. "But the smugglers are asking for a larger cut of the profits."

"How much more?"

Letty could never forget Marston's deep voice. Not after she'd overheard him in the library with Fraughton's wife. It shocked her, he was the lady's lover, and they'd spoken, however frivolously, of wanting Fraughton out of the way. She wondered if Cartwright knew?

They showed no inclination to leave. A painful cramp in her calf forced Letty to straighten slowly and carefully from her crouched position. She peered through the branches.

"They want a cut of our profits," Elford said.

"Not a chance. Should we have them disposed of after the next batch arrives?" Fraughton asked.

Marston made a derogatory sound. "A watery grave seems fitting."

"You don't know who you are dealing with." There was a warning note in Elford's voice. "These men would slash your throat soon as look at you."

A chill down her spine made Letty shiver.

Something brushed against her leg; taken by surprise, she darted back with a muffled cry. A cat meowed in outrage.

"Someone's in those bushes," Marston barked.

She gasped at the click of a cocked pistol. Letty backed onto the path, turned, and proceeded to hurry away. A heavy-set man pushed through the bushes and stood in her path. "What are you doing wandering around alone?"

"A man's boorish behavior upset me on the dance floor," she said. "I wanted some peace and quiet."

"Well perhaps you should…"

"I know this young woman." Fraughton joined them. He reached over and tugged away the strings of her demi-mask which she'd hastily put back in place. "Ah! Miss Bromley, Lady Arietta is introducing her to society. Where is your patroness?"

"Lady Arietta Kendall?" Marston queried.

"She is dancing," Letty said.

"You stood suspiciously close to my wife's reticule at the rout. I got the impression you were about to take it."

"Do you think me a thief?" Letty hated how her voice squeaked.

"I don't like this," Marston said. Elford and Descrier joined them. "Sounds like too much of a coincidence to me."

"Are you not overacting?" Descrier asked.

"Here you are, my dear." Cartwright emerged from the dark, the folds of his cravat and waistcoat gleaming white, his domino pushed back over his shoulders and the narrow black mask dangling from his fingers. "Didn't I tell you to be discreet?" He sauntered toward them. "Gentlemen. What bad *ton*. You are interrupting our, er, stroll together in the moonlight."

Decrier laughed. "There's a lot of that going on tonight."

"I find that difficult to believe," Fraughton said.

"Really? I am but human." Cartwright chuckled. "And this young lady is quite comely, as you see."

Elford frowned. "Lighten up, Fraughton." He turned to Cartwright with a polite smile. "Please, sir, do not let us spoil your evening's entertainment."

They appeared to have accepted Cartwright's explanation. Greatly relieved, she slipped her hand through his arm. "I see I have made a terrible mistake. Kindly take me back, Mr. Cartwright."

"I tell you this young lady was snooping. She's in cahoots with him," Fraughton said in a hard voice. "Remember, Kendall warned us about Cartwright before he was...."

Elford turned to glare at Fraughton. "Shut up you fool!"

"Poor Kendall had lost his mind." Descrier shrugged in apology. "You are more likely to be in pursuit of a pretty lady, is that not right, Cartwright? You wouldn't wish to despoil that coat. Weston's, is it not?"

The four men stood shoulder to shoulder and observed her and Cartwright. Letty cast a smile of appeal at Descrier and Elford, the two more reasonable men.

Cartwright dusted a sleeve. "Indeed, I have a particular fondness for this coat." He took a firm hold of Letty's hand. "Now gentlemen, if you have had your fun, you must excuse us." He turned to draw her away.

Suddenly, Marston darted forward, pistol raised. With a flash, he brought the butt down on Cartwright's head.

Letty screamed as Cartwright crumpled to the ground. "You devil! You've killed him!"

"Will you never learn?" Elford shouted at Marston.

"Nothing for it now." Descrier groaned in disgust. "Grab her, Fraughton."

Fraughton spun Letty around, an arm across her chest, a surprisingly strong hand covering her mouth. She struggled to free herself. In a panic, she feared she would smother.

"Let her go," Marston said coldly.

Fraughton released his hold as Marston stepped close. Letty watched helplessly as he raised his fist.

A sharp blow to her chin, a shot of pain, and she sank into darkness.

BRANDON WOKE TO a rocking sensation. A throb of pain radiated from a sore spot at the back of his head. His mouth dry, he licked his lips, needing water. He eased his eyes open and looked upon two, perfectly shaped, pale breasts. He moaned. Miss Bromley, her body lying beside him on the coach seat. In the dim carriage light, her long dark lashes fluttered, but she breathed well. Relieved, he put up a hand to cover her chest with the domino, and discovered as her hand accompanied his, that their wrists were tightly shackled together with rope. The seat opposite them was empty; it appeared they traveled alone. The horses moving at a measured pace, the coach rolled through the night, he had no idea as to where they went, nor who held the reins.

The immediate question of escape was quickly dashed. Even supposing he managed to kick the door open, which would probably be locked, it would be impossible to act on it with any degree of safety while tied to Miss Bromley.

"Miss Bromley," he whispered, shaking her wrists gently.

She stirred. "Ohh." Her big brown eyes widened. "Cartwright! What happened? Where are we?"

"In a carriage." His concern for her warred with frustration. "I'm afraid we are in a nasty fix."

"I know, I…there was a cat."

He raised his eyebrows. "A cat?"

"Yes. It startled me, and I leapt out of the bushes."

"The bushes?"

"Where I was hiding," she explained, watching him carefully. "Then they found me."

"I gathered that."

"Are you all right? You have suffered a head injury. Your understanding may have been affected."

"My understanding is perfectly fine, thank you, Miss Bromley. Although I would prefer it to desert me at this point."

She tried to sit up and fell across him. "Oh my God! We are tied together!"

"So it would seem," he said dryly.

She attempted to ease her body away from his, a useless exercise on the narrow coach seat. "Your knee is touching my…are you doing that deliberately?"

"I am not." He eased his knee away from her thigh. "There, is that better?"

"I'm sorry, Cartwright, I have no right to scold you."

He saw the panic in her eyes. "Best conserve your energy," he said. "I give you my word, I'll not hurt you."

"The word of a spy? Is that supposed to reassure me?"

"I have no designs on your person, and even if I did, I doubt such an attempt would be successful." *No reason why he couldn't look, however.*

She peered up at him through a loosened lock of dark hair. "I seem to have got us into an awful pickle."

"You might say that."

She raised her hand and his with it, grimaced, and gingerly touched her chin. "I remember now. Marston struck you with his pistol butt. Then he punched me."

Cold fury filled his gut. *I'll get even with him for that. If it's the last thing I do.* He might not even get to do that if he couldn't find a way out of this. What did these ruthless men intend for them? They would not balk at murder.

"Can you undo this rope?" she asked. "It's very tight and hurts my wrists."

"I should love to. Do you have scissors?" he asked politely. He'd already had a good look at the knots.

"I did," she said bitterly, either missing or ignoring his sarcasm. "In my reticule. I always carry them, and needle and thread, to mend a tear, should a gentleman stand on my hem. But I must have dropped it in the garden."

"What a shame. I believe I have a loose button. We might spend the time with a little sewing."

She grimaced. "You are angry, of course."

"Let me see," he said, relenting. She held up her wrists. "The twine is tightly tied with professional looking knots. I doubt we'll even be able to loosen it." He tested the theory.

"Ow! Stop! That will never work. We can pound on the roof and make them pull up."

"Let's not encourage them to shoot us. Best wait until we arrive at our destination. Wherever that is."

"It might be Kent. Lord Elford's estate. I overheard them talking about smugglers."

"Tell me what they said."

Letitia explained, while he marveled at her self-control. He'd expected her to be in hysterics by now. "That explains a lot," he said.

"Pity I couldn't alert my superior."

"Will he know where to find us?"

"It's possible. He is very good at putting two and two together." Brandon tried to sound confident, but Willard would not expect to hear from him for up to forty-eight hours. Even if he grew suspicious, there was little for him to go on. "I have no idea where we are or how long we've been traveling, but I imagine a lengthy journey still awaits us."

"I expect so." She tried again to sit up, pulling him painfully with her. "Arietta! She'll be frantic. But if my reticule is found, she will alert Bow Street."

He had his doubts. "We need to rest while we can."

She flopped down again. "How can I rest, when I'm so uncomfortable, and…" her eyes widened "… so very frightened."

Her face was close to his. She was anxious, breathing too fast. He wished he could hold her. Impossible, and she might not welcome it. "You have a perfect right," he said. "If it helps, lean against me."

"I can't do anything *but* lean against you." Her sweet breath fanned his neck. "And it doesn't help at all."

It wasn't easy for him either, in quite a different way, when her constant wriggles brushing against his nether region caused a certain amount of friction, but he refrained from mentioning it.

"Once they stop, we'll find a way to escape," she murmured. "I'll poke Fraughton in the eye, then you can punch Marson in the stomach. *Hard,"* she added through her teeth.

"Sounds like an excellent plan." He grinned at her in admiration, despite his fear this would end badly. She had no conception of the ruthlessness of these men who had taken them prisoner. That she was such a game girl somehow made it worse.

He wanted to live through this not only to restore Letitia to her family, but to get his hands on Lady Arietta, if for nothing else than her careless attitude toward a girl in her care. He moved further over on his side to give her more room. "Cover yourself with the cape to keep warm." He needed to think of something else other than Miss Bromley's assets.

She settled beside him and closed her eyes without a murmur of protest, despite the position of their hands, now nestling beneath the rise of her breasts. The delicate folds of her white dress hugged her slim body and long legs, her lustrous dark hair, escaping its pins, scattered flowers over the floor. Breathing in her sweet feminine scent, mingled with soap and violets, a sharp anguished pain stabbed him in the gut at his inability to free her. This helpless feeling was entirely new to him. To have to care for someone else besides himself. He would fight to his last breath to save her.

He searched beyond the window, hoping for a sight of something he recognized, but the land lay in darkness. Would they pass through Canterbury? They would need to stop at a coaching inn somewhere to change horses. He'd have to remain on the alert.

At least the constant throb in his head would keep him awake.

CHAPTER TWELVE

CARTWRIGHT HAD BEEN quiet for some time. In the dim light, Letty studied him, taking in his features at close quarters. His face was narrow, his nose straight, his well-formed mouth in repose was softer. A shadow of a beard now painted his sharp jaw. His eyes were closed, but she was unsure if he slept or remained still to allow her to rest. *Rest?* How could she when the future looked so bleak? There was some comfort to be had by his large warm body beside her. The carriage jostled her, and her empty stomach churned with anxiety and guilt. Cartwright must hate her. This was all her fault. Although she still hoped he would find a way to save them, she feared those ruthless men intended they never returned to London. For what other reason had they whisked the two of them away from the ball?

Cartwright opened his eyes. "All right there?"

"Do you hate me. Cartwright?"

"No, of course, I don't, sweetheart. You should rest. They'll have to stop soon to change the horses."

But when they finally did stop, any chance of escape while the horses were changed was dashed when a ruffian pointed a gun at them. The four villains were not to be seen, and no other carriages pulled into the inn's stable yard while they were there. Were the men waiting for her and Cartwright like malevolent spiders, ready to draw them into their web of deceit? They must want something. Otherwise, why not just kill them?

Cartwright had asked the armed man to fetch a drink and some food for her. He'd offered a handsome payment if the fellow would let them go. The man just laughed.

That laugh had sent a chill rushing through her veins.

Once back on the road, she closed her eyes and breathed in Cartwright's clean, manly smell, which calmed her a little. If anyone could find a way out of this predicament they were in, it was he. She frowned, surprised by her blind acceptance of his prowess. She must find a way out of this herself. There was so much she didn't know about him. She wasn't about to die not knowing. Startled by a sudden thought, she inhaled sharply.

"What is it?" Cartwright asked, removing his hands from where they'd fallen onto her breasts. She rolled over to face him.

"Kendall! They mentioned Arietta's husband, Sir Gareth Kendall. Just before they hit you. Do you remember? They said he warned them about you."

"I remember."

"I should like you to explain all this to me, Cartwright. I can hardly repeat it to anyone, now can I? Not when I'm about to die."

"You don't know that, Letitia."

"I prefer Letty, and I'm still waiting. Was Kendall right about you?"

"Now's not the time for this. We will soon arrive at our destination. We passed through St Mary on the Marsh a few minutes ago."

"You are fobbing me off, Cartwright!"

"Brandon. And yes, I'm afraid I am."

"Brandon. I've a right to be told the truth, surely..." This new familiarity made it even more difficult to think, especially when she was so close to him. "Can we sit up?"

"We might, but it won't be easy."

She considered the logistics of it, then discounted it as something that would rob her of more energy. She bit her lip. "I expect you're right. You shall have to tell me while we are lying down."

He grunted. "Nice try, Letty. I don't intend to reveal government secrets while under duress."

"But this concerns Arietta! She may not be aware that her saintly husband was part of this band of smugglers."

"Perhaps not." His voice deepened. "These men have already committed murder, Letty. Please don't forget that. Don't be reckless. When we arrive, follow my direction."

"Who might they have killed, Cart... Brandon?"

"Kendall, possibly."

"Arietta's husband?" She twisted herself toward him, which proved a mistake. They were now almost nose to nose, and his hard body rested against hers in the most embarrassing places. She drew in a breath and made a valiant effort to ignore it. "But Arietta is sure he was wrongly accused." She glared at him and attempted to draw back, suspecting any action on her part would bounce off him like a pebble off a boulder. "Arietta told me you were to blame for him killing himself. She accused you of working for the French."

"I'm not, but I cannot say the same for Kendall. And I doubt his death was by his own hand. More likely he was murdered by these men."

Her throat tightened. "But why would they kill one of their own?" she asked. Her voice sounded high-pitched, and she swallowed desperately to calm herself.

"Because he had come under suspicion. Whitehall was about to arrest him. There was a danger, I suppose, that he would talk."

"Oh! These men are horrid."

"They are a good deal more than that," he said dryly. "They are frightened men. And frightened men are extremely dangerous."

She closed her eyes and went limp. "Then they will certainly murder us."

He gently shook her wrists. "Hey! I don't intend that to happen."

A small sliver of hope warmed her insides, spreading to her cramped, chilled limbs. "You have a plan?"

"Not exactly, but I'm working on it."

She gulped. "How comforting."

"Don't give up hope, sweetheart," Brandon said softly. "We are not lost yet."

"No, I suppose not… Brandon, please don't call me sweetheart." She feared it might render her completely undone.

"We have been in this position for some hours now," he said with a heavy sigh. "Have I given you any reason to suspect me of taking advantage?"

She didn't fear him taking advantage, she feared she would cling to him too much. What was that saying from Shakespeare's *Macbeth? But screw your courage to the sticking-place.* "You have been called a rake," she accused.

"A label bandied about far too loosely in my opinion. I believe my actions speak louder than words."

"Well, you are a man," she pointed out, warming to her theme.

"So, I am damned by my sex. No man, in your estimation, is worthy of higher thoughts whilst in this position."

"Not many, I imagine. But my Uncle Alford certainly." She gasped. "Oh, poor Uncle! And Aunt Edith! They will be so upset. I suppose they will bury me in the Hawkshead Village churchyard. I shall have a fine eulogy at least."

Brandon chuckled. "You're a game one, Letty."

"Am I?" She sniffed, wishing she had a handkerchief and the wherewithal to wipe her nose. "I don't feel very brave."

The horses slowed. The carriage proceeded between a pair of tall gateposts. "Quiet now," Brandon said in a steely tone. "Let me do the talking."

Letty felt hot and cold at once. She shivered as the carriage rattled along at a smart pace through an avenue of trees. They came to a turning circle where a large building loomed, ghostly in the moonlight. A few candles were alight in the lower floors. The carriage didn't stop; it swept around the mansion and pulled up at the stables.

BRANDON TENSED WHEN the same ruffian who had seen to the change of horses, appeared. But this time, he had an armed accomplice. He opened the carriage door and climbed inside. Looming over them, he held up a knife.

Letty squealed.

"No funny business," he growled. "Hold out yer hands."

"For God's sake, be careful." Brandon watched in trepidation as the evil smelling ruffian's knife sliced through the ropes. "You will annoy your bosses should you cut us."

"Don't be so sure." He continued to saw through the tight twine, coming perilously close to bare skin.

The ropes fell away. Letty sat up with a whimper and rubbed her wrists.

Brandon seethed with fury at the sight of her delicate skin rubbed raw. He clamped his teeth. This was no place for emotion. Ordinarily, he was good at remaining calm and thinking clearly under duress; it would have been far easier alone. He'd never had a young woman depending on him. It changed the game considerably. Any thoughts of overpowering these rogues became an insurmountable risk. Although he doubted these two had a decent brain between them, they were probably endowed with a good deal of animal cunning.

The ruffian Brandon longed to take his fists to, climbed out of the carriage. He stood beside the door and gestured with his pistol. "Out. And no tricks, or I'll shoot."

Brandon helped Letty down from the coach. He urged himself to be patient. It would be too risky to try to escape now. He could take one of them down easily enough, but the other might shoot Letty. The four men would be waiting inside the house. They'd be highly nervous; their plans having gone awry. They would want their questions answered. It was a weakness he intended to exploit.

One of the rogues prodded Brandon in the back with his gun. "Move. To the 'ouse. And no funny business."

Brandon took a firm hold of Letty's arm after she stumbled, her muscles most likely stiff after the long, cramped journey. The servant's quarters lay in darkness. He and Letty were urged along the drive to the southern front of the big house where the front hall, and a window on the floor above, were now illuminated by candles. So his guess was correct. An interrogation awaited them. He doubted these two would be invited into the room. That might give him and Letty a better chance.

"Follow my lead," he murmured to Letty.

Her eyes anxious, she nodded.

They climbed the steps of the brick mansion to the entrance, the windows along the front shuttered. One of the heavy oak doors stood open, spilling candlelight onto the porch. Inside, the entry hall was lit by wall sconces. There was no sign of servants as they were pushed up the staircase.

The rogue's pistol still at his back, they entered a drawing room where a fire burned in the marble fireplace. The four men stood around it with glasses of wine.

Her eyes wide with fear, Letty stepped closer to Brandon.

"Welcome to Elford Park," Lord Elford said, dismissing his two henchmen with a wave of his hand. "I must apologize for the uncomfortable journey. Unfortunately, Cartwright, you're a man I find difficult to trust."

Descrier, a man of considerable wealth and address, gave a mirthless chuckle, while Fraughton and Marston both glared.

Brandon coolly stared at each one in turn. He saw what he'd hoped to, the tension in their bodies despite them wishing to appear at ease, obvious in the way they stood, their spines too stiff, their eyes wary.

"You seem to have something against me, gentlemen, which has left me confused and more than a little angry. I am eager to discuss this reasonably, however. But this young lady is entirely innocent. Allow her to return to London. There is nothing she can do to hurt you."

"I think not, Cartwright," Marston said implacably.

"Her absence will be noted and stir up a host of questions," Brandon reasoned. "Which you most surely don't want."

"Bow Street has nothing on us," Fraughton said. "We carried you out through a gate into the back lane to the coach. Quiet place, Richmond. No one saw us."

"The Home Office is drawing up a detailed dossier on each of you, the contents of which I don't intend to reveal in front of the lady. I'm sure it would be of interest to you. Forewarned is forearmed, is it not?" Brandon smiled. "If you allow me to send Miss Bromley back to London in a hired chaise, I shall be happy to reveal it to you."

"You can't let her go," Marston snarled at Descrier, who seemed to be considering it. "Lady Arietta was watching us. This girl is in cahoots with her."

"Cahoots? What does that mean? I've no idea what you're talking about," Letty cried. "Lady Arietta is my chaperone for the Season."

"Maybe this young lady doesn't know anything," Descrier observed. "And even if she did, she wouldn't understand a word of it. No one would take any notice of a silly chit."

Elford shook his head. "What's wrong with you, Descrier? Second thoughts? She might have overheard something which could damn us whilst hiding in those bushes. We cannot take that chance. Much as I hate to say it."

"Return Miss Bromley to London, gentlemen. Or you will learn nothing helpful from me," Brandon growled.

"There is one thing I can tell you," Letty said. "Lord Fraughton, are you aware that Mr. Marston is having an affair with your wife?"

Brandon turned to stare at her as a stunned silence enveloped the room.

CHAPTER THIRTEEN

"THAT'S A LIE!" Marston smashed his wineglass into the fireplace and took a step toward her. With a gasp of fear, Letty backed away as Brandon moved to place himself between her and the seething man.

"Let's hear what she has to say, Marston," said Descrier coolly.

Fraughton had gone white with rage. "Yes, Miss Bromley. How do you know this?"

Letty's heart beat loud in the quiet menace that had fallen over the room. Brandon had taken a firm, reassuring hold of her arm. "It was at the Kirkwood's ball. Marston and Lady Fraughton weren't aware that I was in the library. I was hiding from someone behind a screen. Their behavior quite shocked me. They spoke of how they would be together when you were dead, Lord Fraughton."

"Did they indeed?" Fraughton cried. He reached inside his coat and pulled out a pistol.

"For God's sake, man." Brandon's hand slid down her arm to grip hers.

"Don't be a fool," Elford screamed. "A gunshot can be heard for miles over the marshes. It will bring the excisemen to our door. There are bales of opium remaining in the cellar awaiting shipment to London."

Fraughton dropped the gun and leapt at Marston. Marston was of a larger build, yet he still struggled with the older man. "She lies, I tell you," he cried feebly as Fraughton, showing more strength than Letty would have credited him with, placed his hands around the man's neck.

Marston gasped for air, his face turning purple.

"Be ready to run," Brandon whispered.

As Descrier rushed in to part them, Brandon tugged on her hand and they ran for the door.

"They're getting away, you idiots," came Elford's cry as Letty and Brandon sprinted down the stairs. He whipped open the front door and they ran outside. "Not the stables, those two rogues could be there."

They ran down through the gardens to a wicket gate in a black-thorn hedge, and then into the park. The moon played games with them as clouds scudded across the sky driven by a strong wind that whipped Letty's hair in her eyes.

"I think we're somewhere near Dymchurch. We'll head for the Hythe coast where we're more likely to run into the excisemen," Brandon said. "There's enough left of the night for them to still be around. But we don't have long. It will be daylight soon."

Letty managed to keep up with him, but his long legs would soon outpace her. Her sandals were never meant for this activity, and she couldn't see the ground clearly. A moment later, she stumbled into a ditch. A pain shot up her leg. "Ow!" She hopped on one foot.

Brandon bent over her. "Are you hurt?"

"I think I've twisted my ankle." She tried to put her weight on it, and the flash of pain made her gasp. "Go on without me. I'll hide here somewhere."

"Not a good idea." Brandon lifted her into his arms and set off again, stalking through the trees.

"I am slowing you down," she protested. "I am not a feather-weight."

"It can't be helped."

"You might have disagreed with me." She rested her head against his chest, his voice rumbling against her ear.

"I have not time nor breath to be charming. I do apologize."

It worried her that his breath was becoming labored, and the others would be in pursuit. "You're never charming, and you aren't carrying me properly."

"How many men have carried you? Or is that an impertinent question?" He grunted as he stopped to settle her better in his arms.

"I remember my father did when I was seven. I'd hurt my ankle then, too. It might be the same one."

He put her down before hefting her up again, this time over his shoulder. "Better?"

"Oomph! No, it's not!" Letty gritted her teeth and hung on to his coat. "And you can take your hand away. It's too near my derriere."

"Oh? I wasn't aware of it. I must apologize again." There was a deplorable lack of regret in his voice.

He shifted his hand farther down her legs, which was only marginally better. She sighed. This was no time to be pernickety. Indeed, if they escaped with their lives, he would have become familiar with a good deal of her.

They hadn't gone more than fifty yards when the moon disappeared, and complete darkness descended.

Brandon placed her on her feet.

Relieved, Letty sat on the grass.

Brandon cursed. "The sky is clouding over, and it feels like a storm brewing. They get pretty fierce ones down here." He sat beside her. "We might have to find shelter."

She spread her domino over her knees and battled to allay her fears. "My costume will be ruined. It was hired, you know."

"That's the least of our troubles."

"Do you think they'll come after us?"

"Listen."

The sound of horses thudding over the ground grew closer.

"But they won't see us in the dark," she said in a hushed tone.

At that point, the moon made another appearance, turning the landscape silver-gray. She could see Brandon clearly. He'd raised an eyebrow at her. "Right, let's get on." He stood and offered her his hand, then pulled her up into his arms again. They'd only gone another few yards when a dark shape ahead blocked their way.

"The boundary of the estate," he said. "If we can get over that wall, they are less likely to pursue us."

On reaching it, he put her down and wandered a few yards to survey it. The stone wall was too high for her to climb, even if her ankle wasn't wrenched.

"Perhaps there's a gate somewhere," she said when he came back, alarmed by the thought of him pushing and pulling her over it.

"At this rate, they'll be onto us before we find it." His grim voice made her gasp.

He drew her into the darker shadows caused by a fir tree. "Sit there and don't utter a sound. I'll go farther afield. See if I can find a way through."

She hated him leaving her, but knew she'd hold him back were she to come. Annoyed with herself, she sank down onto the cold hard ground again, a branch of the fir sticking into her arms. "Be careful," she whispered. But he had gone.

As Brandon sprinted along beside the wall, a yell came from somewhere in the park. The men were hunting them and closing in. Given enough time, they might lose heart and leave, but not before they'd made a thorough search for them in daylight. He and Letty could not be here then. The wind must have blown the storm out over the Channel, for the sky had turned a milky grey as dawn approached. Concerned for her, he was about to go back when he came to a wooden gate in the wall. It was bolted but not padlocked. "Perfect," he murmured, and swiftly retraced his steps. As he ran through the deep shadows cast by the shrubbery, it all looked the same, making it hard to work out where he'd left her. He was forced to slow to a walk, not daring to call out to her.

Suddenly, the clip clop of a horse's hooves was almost upon him. Brandon plunged into the bushes. One of them was checking the boundary wall. He prayed Letty would stay put. She might be impulsive on occasion, but he trusted her, she was smart. Fancy launching that cannon ball into the room and setting the men against each other. What a good spy she would make.

The horse whickered as it passed so close to him, it brushed the branches near his arm. He held his breath. A few meters farther on, the rider dismounted, his boots hitting the ground. Brandon heard the screech of the gate opening, and a moment later, the bang as he closed it. Brandon abandoned his hiding place and crept back to where he reasoned he'd left Letty. Forced to take a chance, he whispered her name.

"I'm here," came the quiet reply.

Greatly relieved, he stepped into the shadows. Letty's hand found his shoulder, and she whispered near his ear. "One of the men just rode past me."

He breathed in her hair's sweet scent. "I've found a gate. We have very little time before it grows light. We'll have to take a chance that he's ridden farther on."

"I can walk. My ankle feels better."

He didn't believe it but gripped her arm. "Let's move on."

There was no sign of the horseman as they followed the wall. At the gate, Brandon eased back the bolt and shoved it open. The loud shriek of rusty hinges would have been heard for miles. Cries went up and a thud of hooves shook the ground too close for comfort. He pushed her through the gate. "Go! Turn left and keep moving as fast as you can!"

"What about you? Aren't you coming?"

"In a minute, I'll catch you up."

"I don't like to…"

"For heaven's sake, Letty. I need you to go."

Without another word, she left him, limping down the lane close to the wall.

Brandon waited for the rider, praying the man didn't have a gun. But even if he did, he was unlikely to use it for fear of bringing the land guard who covered the inland areas while the excisemen dealt with the coast.

He barely had time to whirl around when the horse was almost on top of him.

"Got you, Cartwright!"

Brandon was glad it was Elford. He was too well bred to be a ruthless killer, and completely untrained in the arts.

Elford angled the horse to wedge him against the wall and brought his whip down painfully on Brandon's shoulder.

As the nervous horse shifted, Brandon grabbed the whip and pulled sharply, unseating Elford who crashed to the ground. The horse tossed its head and whinnied, backing away, then turned and galloped off.

With a cry of rage, Elford bounced to his feet and swivelled to face Brandon, holding up his fists. He bellowed for the others. An answering shout told Brandon they were only minutes away. With no time for the sort of fisticuffs Elford had been taught at Jackson's boxing salon, he stepped in and dealt the man a sharp blow to his throat. He went down without a murmur.

Brandon barreled his way through the gate and set out full pelt in pursuit of Letty.

He found her around a bend in the road. She hadn't gone far, she was limping badly.

"Step up on that rock and lean against my back," he said. "Faster that way."

Without a murmur of protest, she perched on the stone and pulled up her dress to reveal stocking tops and blue satin bows and a flash of rounded pale thigh. He turned from the beguiling sight and bent, allowing her to place her hands around his neck. Holding her legs against his waist, he set off at a good pace toward Hythe.

"This was how my father used to carry me," she said somewhat breathlessly in his ear.

"He sounds like a good man."

"Yes, he was." Her voice caught.

What happened to her father? He hoped to hear more about that later. He tried to harden himself against the fragility he heard in her voice. "You neglected to tell me you saw Marston and Lady Fraughton in the library."

"Would it have stopped you seducing her yourself?" she asked casually.

"I wasn't seducing her," he growled. "I wanted that letter and anything more she could tell me."

"What was in the letter?"

"It concerned the meeting at Ascot races," he said shortly, determined that any further interest in this affair was nipped in the bud.

"Is that all there was?" she murmured, her breath tickling his neck.

He declined to answer while he kept up the pace. The men would not be far behind them and moving faster unless finding Elford delayed them. Dawn had broken, casting a pink glow in the sky. Would the excisemen still be about? Or would he and Letty be left stranded? There was a church in the village, he remembered, if they must, they could hide there. But some of these churches sheltered smugglers and even stored their goods. How long could they hide before they were found?

The thunder of horsemen riding hard came from somewhere behind them.

CHAPTER FOURTEEN

T HE HORSEMEN WOULD soon be upon them.

Letty's arms almost strangling him, she cried out. "It's them, they're coming after us!"

"*Hush.* Too many." Brandon lowered her to the ground.

A squadron of dragoons in their blue and gold, swept around the corner and surrounded them; hard faces beneath elaborate helmets, their fierce swords swung at their hips. A customs officer rode at the head.

They looked so fearsome that Letty clutched hold of Brandon's sleeve.

"Cartwright, Captain." Brandon gently released her hand and stepped forward to address the officer. "We are very pleased to see you."

The captain dismounted. He offered his hand. "Captain Dogwood, sir. Are you in need of assistance?"

Brandon shook it. "You might say that. Miss Bromley and I have fallen foul of smugglers."

The officer's eyes widened. "Well, that is right up our alley, Mr. Cartwright. Where might they be hiding?"

Once Brandon had explained, the captain sent his dragoons to Elford Park with an order to begin a search and detain the inhabitants should any contraband be found.

"I shall require you to accompany me, Mr. Cartwright. We need a witness. Lord Elford might prove difficult."

"If you wouldn't mind one of your men taking Miss Bromley to a respectable inn," Brandon said. "She has hurt her ankle."

"I am perfectly all right," Letty protested, annoyed that Brandon dismissed her like a fragile china figurine. And after all they'd been through! Hadn't she proven herself capable?

"I know you are, but what will follow is something I would rather spare you," Brandon said.

At the captain's order, one of the soldiers dismounted. "Allow me to assist you onto my horse, Miss," the big soldier said. "I believe you will find the Star Inn in St. Mary's Bay comfortable. The proprietor is a good man."

"Please have a physician attend Miss Bromley's ankle," Brandon said with a sharp nod in her direction. He turned away to talk to the captain.

Letty could do nothing other than agree and permit the fellow to lift her onto his horse. That familiar light in Brandon's eyes told her she'd get nowhere with him if she argued. Denying her the satisfaction of witnessing the men's arrest didn't trouble him.

The soldier mounted behind her. One hand on his saber, and one on the reins, he rode silently with her along a road that took them through fields of sheep and grazing cows. Letty gripped the pommel as the earthy, dank smells of the marshes gave way to the fresh salty brine of the Channel, and the strong odor of fish. The dragoon put her down outside a two-story, whitewashed inn facing the shore. Courteously, he offered her his arm to escort her inside.

The innkeeper hurried out to greet them. After a rudimentary explanation of her falling foul of robbers, he offered his sympathy and observed that nowhere was safe anymore. Then to tidy herself, he directed her to a chamber with a maid to attend her. She removed the now filthy cloak, washed her face, and attempted to deal with her hair, which proved impossible because all the hair pins had disappeared, along with the flowers. The knot she twisted it into wouldn't hold, so she shrugged and left the room.

A servant led her to the inn's parlor where comfortable furniture was grouped around the fireplace beneath a low-beamed ceiling. The mullioned windows emitted little of the early morning light into the room from a pale blue sky. The innkeeper appeared and told her the apothecary who was a job of all trades with some of the skills of a physician, had been sent for to tend her ankle.

Letty gratefully settled in a chair by the big hearth, finding the crackle of the fire soothing. Well, she had wished for an adventure, hadn't she? And got rather more than she'd anticipated. Despite her bravado, which was mostly for Brandon's sake, her limbs still trembled. There had been an air of quiet menace in Elford's grand drawing room, incongruous amongst the antiques and priceless paintings, the trappings of a wealthy gentleman. She had thought that gentlemen operated under some sort of honor code, but those men made no secret that she and Brandon were to be disposed of without the blink of an eye.

She ruefully examined her lovely white gown, crumpled and soiled, the flowers hanging by a thread. No amount of careful laundering could restore it to its original beauty, and nothing could be done with her sandals. It was indeed remarkable they still remained on her feet.

A maid brought in a tray and unloaded a pot of tea, a plate of ham and cheese, bread, and a large slab of currant cake. Letty, her stomach rumbling in anticipation, thanked her. She poured herself a cup of tea and set about the serious business of eating. Every mouthful was bliss. As she poured a second cup, she wondered if Brandon would be long. He must be hungry, too. Consumed with guilt, she gave a moan of dismay. All she'd put him through! He must be very angry with her.

A shepherd dressed in a smock entered the parlor with a small, bleating black-faced lamb in his arms.

"Oh, he's beautiful." Letty suffered an inexplicable pang of home-sickness for Hawkeshead village, and her reassuring plain-speaking, no-nonsense, uncle and aunt. How horror-struck they would be to learn about this. She had no idea how to explain it to them, but she couldn't of course. Nor could she tell Jane or Geoffrey, which made her feel uncomfortable. One did not keep secrets from one's friends.

The young shepherd settled the small animal by the fire and fed it from a bottle. "He's lost his mother and been poorly, Miss. But a bit of food and warmth will set him to rights."

"How good of the innkeeper to allow you to bring the lamb here."

"It is a kind of tradition around these parts. The flocks are brought here regular like."

Letty's heart lightened. She had witnessed the worst devilry at work and feared for her life, but now with that behind her, and the meal and the tea warming the cold knot in her chest, her inner strength returned. Her thoughts settled on Brandon. What was occurring at Elford Park? She eagerly waited for him to arrive and tell her everything.

The shepherd stood, and with a tug of his forelock, scooped up the little lamb and left the room, leaving Letty to her thoughts.

Soon afterward, the apothecary, a kindly man with a ginger beard, came to examine her ankle. He diagnosed a sprain and advised her to rest it.

Her foot resting on a cushion, Letty watched the crackling flames turn the coal a hot orange-red, the smoke curling up the chimney. Brandon had proved himself to be a brave man, and very much involved in his work. He was unmarried, but might there be someone? It hardly mattered, for she was unlikely to see him again after they reached London. A throb in her chest near her heart forced her to admit she felt more for him than was wise. Of course, such a life-and-death experience would evoke such raw feelings. Naturally, when her life returned to normal, she reasoned, he, and the excitement sur-rounding him, would cease to have such an effect on her.

But things were not yet at an end. There was Arietta. Her patron-ess knew more than she'd given Letty to believe. Letty struggled not to think badly of her when she'd been so generous and kind. She recalled how they'd spent the evenings laughing together while discussing Letty's suitors. How they'd enjoyed shopping in Piccadilly and Bond Street, while Arietta's footman followed, his arms full of their parcels. Arietta had been so driven to discover the truth about her husband. But was it merely to clear his name? Or might she in some way be caught up in this web of intrigue? Whatever the reason, Letty was sure she would be most dreadfully worried about her.

Letty gloomily acknowledged that should she be unable to remain with Arietta, she could not make her curtsy to the queen. She would be forced to return to Cumbria, and much as she loved the small village and the people in it, she'd begun to enjoy the Season and would like to stay until the end.

Fifteen minutes later, Brandon entered the parlor. He raked his dark hair back from his forehead with his long fingers and smiled. She sighed. If only he wasn't so dashing!

BRANDON WRESTLED WITH his fury at the bruise on Letty's chin where Marston had hit her. Her thick dark locks hung down over her shoulders, stirring an inappropriate image of her in his arms and in his bed, which he quickly buried. To see her alive and relatively un-harmed squeezed his chest. He drew in a breath and strode forward to pull up a chair to be near her.

"How are you, sweetheart?"

She firmed her lips as if to stop them trembling. "I'm quite well."

"Are you?" He studied her with a smile, then shook his head. "Good lord, Letty, to see you sitting here more or less in one piece is a tremendous relief to me."

"I confess, I am a bit relieved myself," Letty said with a wobbly smile that made him want to hug her. "For a while, I feared we might not survive."

He had, too, but did not mention it. She needed to go back to London, and thence, to another place of safety as soon as possible, where he could stop worrying about her.

"I've arranged for a chaise to take us back to London. It will be here soon." He looked at her slender ankle which didn't appear to be badly swollen. "Has the physician examined your ankle?"

"Yes. It's only a strain and is already much better." Her wide brown eyes searched his. "Well? Are you going to tell me what happened? Don't leave anything out. Did the dragoons stab them with their sabers?"

He grinned at her. "You are a bloodthirsty young woman. They did not. But the dragoons were remarkably efficient. Elford was discovered unconscious where I left him and brought to the house."

She raised her eyebrows.

"I disabled him, Letty, I didn't wish to kill him."

"Pity," she murmured. "And the rest?"

"Descrier is demanding his lawyer. Says he was a houseguest and has no knowledge of the contraband found in the cellar."

"And Fraughton?"

"Fraughton is dead. Marston killed him."

She looked stricken. "Oh! Was that my fault? Because I told him about his wife's affair?"

"No, Letty. As if what you said could make a ha'penny's worth of difference. The men harbored a deep hatred of each other."

"And Marston?"

"He got away, I'm afraid. The dragoons are searching for him, but he has probably left the area."

"Where would he go?"

"He'd pack up and leave the country if he is wise." Brandon frowned. He was prepared to follow the devil to France. He wouldn't rest until the brutal man was dealt with.

"Why would such well-to-do gentlemen involve themselves in smuggling?"

"Same old story. Greed. But it's not a case of smuggling a few barrels of brandy, casks of wine, or bolts of silk. They were intent on setting up an empire. Bringing in opium through the Silk Road to Italy which was then under Napoleon's control, thence to France."

"Opium? That's a drug, isn't it? Don't they use it for medicines like laudanum?"

"Yes, and morphine, but in its pure form, it is very destructive. Many would become dependent on it, which would keep them in business."

"They *are* evil."

A clatter of carriage wheels sounded on the road outside the window. Then men's voices were raised in the entry.

"Our chaise has arrived."

"Have something to eat first."

"No time." He grabbed the cake she'd left uneaten, off the plate. Discovering it to be moist and tasty, it disappeared after a few hearty bites. He stood and offered her his arm.

As the chaise took them to London, Brandon sat back and ran a hand over his eyes.

"You must be dreadfully tired," Letty observed.

"You get used to going without sleep in this business."

"What made you get into it? Surely your father would have objected? Do your parents live in London?"

"They prefer to spend most of their time in the country. Father has never approved of me. But he knows nothing about the work I do."

"Why don't you tell him? Surely he would be proud of you."

He shook his head. "The work of agents is not considered to be particularly admirable."

Her eyes widened. "Not admirable? When you risk your life for your country? Why ever not?"

"Agents are seen to lack the nobility of soldiers. It involves some rather unsavory aspects which gentlefolk don't wish to acknowledge goes on."

"But for a good cause, surely?" She leaned forward. "What for instance?"

"We don't always fight fair, Letty. But I prefer not to go into it." He cocked an eyebrow. "I suspect you would find it far too interesting."

She grinned. "I might. But doesn't your father's unfair disapproval bother you?"

"It did once. I've grown used to it." This conversation was heading into dangerous territory. "Your parents are no longer with us?"

"No. A carriage accident when I was seven. My father's older brother, Sylvester, Baron Bromley, is a widower and suffers ill health, so I was sent to Uncle Alford, Father's younger brother. He's the vicar of Hawkshead."

He raised his eyebrows. "You were brought up by a vicar?"

"Do you find that surprising?

"He doesn't seem to have eradicated your adventurous spirit."

"It wasn't for lack of trying," she said, looking a little shamefaced. "I suspect I've inherited my great-great-aunt's sense of adventure. Lydia kept diaries in which she describes her incredible life in Africa, and her adventure on the high seas."

"The high seas?"

"Yes, she met a pirate and traveled with him on his ship."

"Remarkable!" Brandon's gaze lingered on her mouth, her lips curling up as she spoke of this adventurous great aunt. He would like to hear more of the story if only to enjoy her telling of it.

"Oh, she was, indeed, most remarkable," Letty said. "Her father was a botanist and a scientist." She yawned. "Geoffrey is always accusing me of being like her."

"Who is Geoffrey?"

"Geoffrey Verney is the squire's son. He taught me to ride."

There was a smudge on her cheek, her hair hung down in disarray, but a keen light still shone in her eyes. Luminous brown eyes a man could drown in. He shook his head with a slight grin. "And will you now settle down in Cumbria with a quiet, reliable husband? This Geoffrey, perhaps?"

A frown creased her smooth forehead. "No, Geoffrey is a friend." Letty put a hand to her mouth to hide another yawn. She looked nothing like the gently-reared niece of a vicar in that soiled gown. Would she return home and marry this friend of hers, Geoffrey? Certainly possible, despite her denial, but he found the idea not to his liking. "Perhaps a nap?"

"Yes." She nodded sleepily and settled back on the carriage seat opposite, tucking her legs up.

He stripped off his coat and covered her with it, then sat back and watched her, slightly amused at her abandoning any attempt at decorum, but also very much stirred and flattered by the trust she showed in him. Her disarray seemed to emphasize rather than diminish her fresh, youthful innocence. He would see her home, and once she'd moved out from under Lady Arietta's roof, that would be the end of their association. He found this very unappealing.

Two hours later, the streets of London appeared under a darkening sky. "Letty?" he said quietly. He leaned over and gently shook her shoulder.

She stirred and sat up. "Oh! Have we arrived?"

"We are just entering Mayfair."

"I've come to a decision about what we discussed, Brandon," she said, her hands busy at her hair. "I will stay with Arietta for the time being. Surely it's better I should try to find out what lies behind her curious behavior." She rushed on before he could interrupt. "Kendall might have been a French spy, but it doesn't mean that she is."

He frowned. "Either way, I don't want you living with her. It's not safe, Letty."

"Don't be ridiculous. Arietta would never hurt me."

"She hasn't cared too much for your safety until now, has she?"

"That isn't fair. It would never occur to her that I could be snatched away from a ball by a gang of murderers, now would it?" She scowled at him. "I suppose you'd prefer me to return to Cumbria?"

"Far be it from me to suggest you leave before your Season ends, but if there's no one suitable to chaperone you, it would be wise." He brushed away his own selfish motives, not having to worry about her, as well as removing her from the lure she held for him. Letty had got too far under his skin for his liking.

"Well, I appreciate your advice." She stiffened her shoulders. "But I shall decide what's best for me."

Frustrated, he frowned at her. "Well, don't say I didn't warn you!"

She shrugged and glanced away. "I shan't bother you again, have no fear."

"Letty, if you have need of me…"

She firmed her lips but said nothing.

He had made a hash of it and now it was too late. The carriage had pulled up outside Arietta's townhouse.

After he assisted her down, the butler opened the door.

Letty coolly curtsied. "It has been quite an adventure, Mr. Cartwright. Thank you for bringing me through it safely. I doubt we shall meet again. I am to be presented to Queen Charlotte in her drawing room next week. The following evening, we shall go to Almack's Assembly Rooms. One hears so much about it, one can't leave London without experiencing it," she added airily.

"The marriage mart? I hope you are not disappointed." he said, rising to the bait.

"Is that what it is called? Then I don't expect to see you there. I suspect it would find little favor with you."

He sighed, he could hardly argue with her here on the pavement with the butler watching on. Better to work behind the scenes to remove her from Arietta's influence. "It is my hope that you will enjoy the rest of your Season, Miss Bromley." He offered her his arm and escorted her to the front door. "Even if you do not see me, know I am never far away if you should need me."

Her gaze flew to his with an expression he found hard to interpret. "I foresee no reason to need you, but I am grateful, thank you."

They reached the porch. "Be happy, Letty," he murmured, bowed, and left her.

The front door closed behind her as he crossed the pavement, annoyed with himself for suffering some inexplicable sense of losing something precious. He would not drag Letty down into his world when she deserved so much better. Advising the driver of his home address, Brandon entered the chaise. He must bathe and change, then go to Whitehall to give Willard his news. No doubt he would be anxious to hear it.

CHAPTER FIFTEEN

HOLMES'S IMPERTURBABLE BUTLER'S manner faltered. His eyes wide, mouth ajar, he took in the state of her appearance. "Miss Bromley! Lady Arietta has been most dreadfully upset."

Letty swung around at a cry. Footsteps ran lightly down the marble staircase.

"Letitia!" Arietta gasped when she reached her. "I've been frantic. Where have you been?" Not waiting for an answer, she placed an arm around Letty's shoulders and drew her toward the stairs. "I feared you might have eloped."

Letty stared. "Eloped? Who with...?"

"Some catastrophe has befallen you. A carriage accident?" Arietta glanced at the footman who had just entered the hall. "You shall tell me all about it upstairs. Are you hungry?" A foot on the step, Arietta turned to the butler. "Poor Miss Bromley has suffered a carriage accident, Holmes. Order tea and sandwiches, and some of Cook's carrot cake. She will have it in her bedchamber."

Once the door closed behind them, Arietta burst into noisy tears. She fumbled for the lace handkerchief tucked into her sleeve and sobbed into it. "I was so worried, Letitia, you cannot imagine. I shall be patient until you've bathed and changed your gown and are more comfortable. And then you must tell me what happened from the moment you disappeared at the ball!"

On the long journey back to Mayfair, Letty had discussed with Brandon what to tell Arietta. She was to stick as close to the truth as possible while withholding what was said about her late husband.

When she had bathed and changed into a dressing gown, she joined Arietta on the sofa in her room.

"Lord Fraughton, Mr. Descrier, and Lord Elford were involved in smuggling?" Arietta exclaimed, after Letty had given a brief account of what had happened, omitting some of the more scandalous aspects of her and Brandon's experience. "Kendall and I knew them socially, but not this Marston."

"Did Sir Gareth mention anything about these men?" Letty swallowed the last of the ham and cress sandwiches and picked up a slice of iced cake.

"I doubt he would have even if he had heard something. He did seek to spare me anything unsavory. He thought of women as delicate beings. And dear Kendall would never become involved with smugglers."

"Mr. Cartwright can be of no further interest, surely."

Arietta frowned. "Perhaps not. It would appear he is working for the Home Office in this matter."

"Yes, and he looked after me. He was a gentleman."

"Well, that's to be applauded, Letitia, certainly," Arietta said thoughtfully. "One would expect him to say nothing about your involvement in this episode, for he might find himself compromised."

"Compromised?" Letty asked, surprise distracting her from Arietta's *volte-face* about Brandon.

"Well, you did spend the night together. It would be damaging to you both should it be put about." She raised her eyebrows. "Unless he wishes to marry you?"

"You don't understand!" Letty pulled back the sleeve of her dressing gown and showed Arietta the raised welts on her wrist. "We were both tied up!" She thought it prudent not to add they were tied together, it might give the wrong impression. Lying a foot away from Brandon, his handsome mouth at kissing distance. She wished now that he had kissed her. She might have something to remember. Frowning, she forced herself back on track.

"Oh, how horrible!" Arietta's eyes filled with tears again. "I shall send for a salve, and some arnica for your poor chin."

"Mr. Cartwright doesn't have the remotest desire to marry me," Letty said firmly. "Nor do I consider him a possible husband." *She could never allow herself to dwell on such a possibility, for it would surely result in heartache.*

"Well, that's to the good then." Arietta poured out another cup of tea from the pot. "If the business is hushed up, I'm sure nothing will come of it."

Letty had little fear that the *ton* would hear about it. Whitehall would surely draw a cloak of secrecy over it. She ate the last of the cake, sipped her tea, and watched Arietta blow her nose, wondering if she would give up her quest now to uncover the truth behind her husband's death. She seemed, thankfully, to have lost interest in Brandon.

"I'm sorry about the costume," Letty said.

"A trifling matter, my dear. Don't give it another thought. On a lighter note, your court gown has arrived. Adele has placed it in your wardrobe."

A surge of anxiety tightened Letty's stomach. Her curtsey to the queen was looming, and her uncle and aunt eager to hear of it. "Shouldn't I do more to prepare for my presentation, Arietta?"

"There is not much to do. I shall go through the details of the ceremony with you tomorrow, and if your ankle is better, you can practice until your entry and exit from the room, and your curtsy, are perfect."

"Thank you, Arietta." Letty's voice trembled. How on earth would she explain to Uncle Alford if she missed it? The suggestion of an ankle injury would bring him to London. "I'm so grateful for your generosity."

"Nonsense. It is my pleasure as I've told you." Arietta kissed Letty's cheek. "You must rest now, for you look quite drained. It's important you look your best, for I have accepted two engagements for this week." She stood. "Now, I shall order a light supper to be sent to you after you've had a nice long rest. Best to stay quietly in your room tonight."

"Yes, Arietta," Letty said meekly.

When Arietta had gone, Letty rushed to the wardrobe. The gown held no surprises, she had tried it on twice, but hoped somehow it would become something more pleasing. It had not. It was still an odd style with its wide hoop, flat at the front, the waist sitting just beneath the short low-cut bodice. It seemed to represent something to be endured rather than enjoyed. She could not think of it now and shut the wardrobe door.

With the intention of going over everything that had occurred after she was snatched from the masquerade, Letty crawled onto her bed. But once she rested her head on the pillow, her eyelids grew heavy and she drifted into sleep.

Letty woke at a knock on the door. "Come in."

The footman entered, carrying a tray. "I hope you are feeling better, Miss Bromley." He smiled at her and placed it on a table.

"I am. Thank you, Joseph." Letty breathed in the tasty aromas filling the room and discovered she was hungry again.

She sat at the table and sipped from a fortifying glass of red wine. Chicken soup, thinly sliced ham, salad, bread, and a slice of apple tart. She sighed, so relieved to be back in comfortable and safe surroundings.

Some hours later, filled with renewed energy, she glanced at the mantel clock. Eleven o'clock. Perhaps Arietta was still awake and might welcome some company.

Letty knocked on Arietta's bedchamber door but received no answer. Returning to her room, she quickly dressed in her blue cambric that buttoned down the front, donned her house slippers, tidied her hair, and descended the staircase. The marble foyer stood empty, the butler having retired and the footman who was to replace him, not in position.

The salon lay in darkness, but light rimmed the drawing room doors. The voices were too soft to guess who it might be. A dinner guest? Letty's hand hovered indecisively over the latch. It might not please Arietta should she interrupt them. As she turned away, the voices grew louder. Arietta raised her voice, and Letty distinctly heard her say the man's name. *Pierse.*

Startled, Letty backed away, turned, and hurried down the corridor. Pierse was the Frenchman who'd been with Fraughton in the library when she and Brandon hid in the closet.

The footman now at his station in the entry hall, stared at her.

Letty slowed her steps and forced a smile. "I wished for some chocolate," she said, a hand on the banister-rail. "I didn't want to disturb the staff, and was going to make it myself, as I often do in Cumbria."

"Might I fetch some for you, Miss Bromley?"

"No, thank you, Joseph. I've changed my mind." She yawned. bringing a hand to her mouth. "I find myself most awfully sleepy. Goodnight."

"Goodnight, Miss Bromley."

As she hurried up the stairs, she heard the door to the drawing room open.

Letty reached the landing as they entered the front hall.

"It was good of you to call, Monsieur Pierse." Arietta's voice floated up. "You must be fatigued having just arrived from France."

"A little perhaps," Pierse replied. "We shall meet again, soon, *oui?*"

The front door closed on him. Letty hovered on the landing while Arietta spoke to Joseph, wondering if the footman would give her away. She sagged with relief when he didn't. Arietta said goodnight and began to climb the stairs.

Her heart pounding, Letty ran lightly over the carpet to her bed-chamber. As she pulled her gown over her head, a seam ripped. She kicked off her slippers, then shoved the lot into her wardrobe. She snuffed out the candles, climbed into bed, and drew the covers up to her chin.

Moments later, the door opened. "Letitia?"

With a mumbled reply, Letty rolled over and blinked at the shape of Arietta outlined by the sconces in the corridor.

"Just making sure you are all right, my dear. Good night." The door shut again.

Letty lay staring into the dark. She wished she could have heard what they talked about. Her initial desire to warn Arietta, was quickly quashed. Arietta had made no mention of a visitor. Because he'd called so late, it appeared secretive, when it really might not be that at all. The Frenchman could be an old friend of Kendall's. Had he known that Fraughton was dead?

Whether his visit to Arietta was something concerning or not, Brandon must be warned. But she had no idea where he lived. She thumped her pillow which had turned into a rock. What to do? It was impossible to send a letter to Whitehall; all the post was dealt with by the butler. And Brandon may not appreciate it.

She might find Brandon at the card party they were to attend the following evening, or failing that, the soiree on Saturday. Her heart still thudded uncomfortably. Had Arietta lied to her? Did she, as Brandon had suggested, have some secret agenda? Letty could do nothing until she spoke to him, and only hoped it would be before her curtsey to the queen, for she was sure it would not go well with this weighing heavily upon her.

BRANDON SAT IN a leather chair in Fraser Willard's library nursing a brandy. He had revealed all that transpired and now waited in the charged atmosphere while his spymaster digested it.

"I still can't see Napoleon's connection to the opium smuggling. They fear this *Journal Noir* being discovered, however," Willard said. "That much is clear. And are determined it never sees the light of day. It is sure to prove of great interest to Whitehall."

"I'm informed Robert Marston has gone into hiding." Willard rose to top up their glasses. "He hasn't been seen in London. And as there's no record of him having fled to France, someone must be sheltering him."

With a nod of thanks, Brandon accepted the freshly filled glass. "Has the comtesse been in contact?"

"Yes. She received an unwelcome visitor. The porter was stabbed to death, and her Paris apartment turned upside down. Her country estate, too, although there was no staff except an aged caretaker—the house was closed, everything under holland covers, apparently. Nothing taken from either residence. The comtesse has been staying at a friend's apartment and assures us the journal remains in her possession."

"I'm relieved to hear she wasn't hurt."

"The bad news is that Comte de Lavalette's appeal has been dismissed, and the date of his execution set for Thursday."

Brandon released a breath. "We run out of time. We need to keep these men behind bars in case Lavalette reaches London. Is the escape plan still in place? Does she say?"

"She assures us everything is prepared for his rescue. It is to take place within days."

"Did she explain what she has in mind?"

"No, she prefers not to. She fears her letter may be intercepted."

"Then we must curb our curiosity and wait." Brandon rubbed the prickles on the back of his neck. He found the waiting excruciating.

"And in the meantime, see if you can sniff out Marston. Visit his old haunts. Bring him back alive if you can. We need to question him."

"I'll start at the Covent Garden brothel he favors," Brandon said, pleased to see some action. "Not a man of taste by all accounts."

CHAPTER SIXTEEN

AFTER BREAKFAST THE next day, Letty tried on the court dress the price of which had shocked her. She'd seen the bill from the dressmaker, before Arietta whisked it away saying it was a necessary expense. Such a lot of work had gone into the making of it, and understandably so, embroidered as it was with wreaths of silver leaves and decorated with rows of lace, ribbons, and bows. It was undeniably pretty. Unfortunately, it didn't flatter her. She looked rather like one of those balloons that carried people aloft in a basket. While she could not like the style, just stepping into it and having Adele do up the hooks brought a rush of excitement. She gathered up the skirts and the long train and carefully descended the stairs to the drawing room where Arietta waited.

"The magnolia white suits your complexion," Arietta said. "Debut court gowns are notoriously unflattering, we must lay the blame for that at the door of Queen Charlotte and the Prince of Wales who insist on employing last century's hoop but with the fashionable high waist. Do you like the headdress?"

Letty put a hand up to the bandeau of pearls with the five ostrich feathers. Shoulder-length lappets hung down from it. "I shall find it hard to see when I turn my head." She suffered another hot surge of anxiety.

"I'm sure you'll do well. I don't recall hearing of a debutante falling over before the queen although one or two might have stumbled."

This failed to fill Letty with confidence. She swallowed as her ankle gave a throb, reminding her of the weakness there.

"You will do nicely, Letitia," Arietta reassured her, at Letty's gasp of dismay. "What a pity your family are not here to see you." She gestured to the door. "I shall take the part of the queen. You must enter the room, walk toward me, make your curtsey, and back away again."

Letty slowly crossed the drawing room Axminister carpet to where Arietta waited on a sofa near the fireplace. She curtsied low as she'd been instructed.

Arietta nodded approvingly. "Your curtsey is graceful. Now, walk backward, but keep your eyes on me."

Gathering up the train, Letty retreated, the long lappets stirring oddly against her neck.

Arietta clapped her hands. "You did that very nicely. Do it a few more times, it will give you confidence. I am sure you will make me proud. Afterward, I shall write to your uncle and aunt and tell them how well you did."

After two more attempts, Letty did feel a little better.

"Go upstairs and have my maid help you out of the dress. You don't want it crushed."

Arietta's warmth and encouragement threw Letty into confusion. The late-night visit from Monsieur Pierse consumed her thoughts. She'd slept badly, and tired, struggled to act naturally while questions flooded her mind. How did they come to know each other? And how well? She tried to recall Pierse's conversation with Fraughton in the library while she and Brandon hid in the closet, and was fairly sure that neither Arietta nor her husband were mentioned. Surely Brandon would wish to hear of this. He would want to see this Frenchman, perhaps he was searching for him. Brandon might attend the card party tonight.

She bit her lip. Brandon had ordered her not to get mixed up in this affair again. It was plain that he'd prefer her to return to Cumbria. Conflicting emotions warred within her. It hurt that she was nothing to him but a nuisance. But what else could she do? She must tell him and would be greatly relieved for him to take this on his shoulders.

But that evening, Brandon did not appear amongst the guests. Letty searched the busy reception rooms and the card tables where whist and faro were played. She wandered through the townhouse without success. The thought struck her that as he was no longer following Fraughton, he might not come to many parties. Or indeed, he might have left London!

Her suspicion was confirmed when he failed to come to the Jameson's soiree. Letty became so fidgety, she drew a concerned comment from Arietta. But thankfully, she put it down to her coming presentation.

Letty was at a loss to know what to do next, but as her curtsey to the queen was to take place the following day, the matter would have to wait.

BRANDON HAD SPENT two days on the hunt for Robert Marston. He had not been seen at any of the haunts he favored in London, so he rode into Surrey to Marston's country house. Marston's servant informed him that his master had returned home, packed a portmanteau, and left again on horseback, planning to visit friends in Ireland. The fellow was believable, but whether Marston had told him the truth was another matter. The Irish Sea was a long way from Surrey, and Brandon reasoned that Marston would not have gone all the way to the ferry on horseback.

His frustrating search continued as he inquired at the coaching inns along the road and found no trace. Brandon's inquiries revealed Marston had a cousin living in the county. There was a chance that William Marston might have some idea of Robert's direction.

Brandon spent the night at an inn, and the next morning after a fortifying breakfast, rode past farms and water meadows along a road bordered by Windsor Forest toward the village of Addlestone.

It was close to noon when he sighted the famous *Crouch Oak*, believed to have existed in the time of Queen Elizabeth I. It was said the queen stopped beside it to have a picnic. At the village inn, The Red Lion, he was told the way to William Marston's property, and more information besides. The loquacious innkeeper expounded on the famous oak tree, which was a great symbol of the town. It had been around since the eleventh century and marked the boundary of Windsor Great Park.

"Haven't seen hide nor hair of Robert Marston in these parts for nigh on a year," the innkeeper informed him, placing a chicken pie and a tankard of ale before Brandon. "Not to say he hasn't visited his cousin, though. He resides at Cottleshield Manor, five miles north along this road. You'll come to Brown's Lane. Take that, it leads you right to his house."

William Marston's square, thatched-roof manor house sat amid a cottage garden. Brandon dismounted and knocked at the door. As he brushed the dirt from his boots, it was opened by William himself, smoking a pipe. There was no mistaking the tall man. He had similar features to Robert, but was of a narrower build and lacked the signs of dissipation which had begun to appear on his cousin's face.

"Cartwright, sir. I have come in search of your cousin, Robert."

"He is not here, Mr. Cartwright. But do come in."

"Will a servant see to my horse?"

William called his groom and gave the order. "May I offer you a glass of wine?"

Brandon accepted and was taken down a narrow hall into a

bookroom where tomes were stacked on every surface. One book lay open on an oak desk. A cheery fire burned in the hearth.

He handed Brandon a glass of claret. "Robert stayed last night with me." He shrugged. "We don't have much in common. He found it dull here, I suppose. He left only a few hours ago. What is your interest in him, may I ask?"

"He needs to return to London. An important matter. I'm afraid I can't say more."

"Trouble, no doubt." William nodded and sucked on his pipe. "Robert seems to attract it."

"Did he mention a trip to Ireland?"

William frowned. "No. He was going to visit friends as I understood it. Wanted to get away from London for a while. Things have not been going well for him of late."

"Where might this friend live?"

"Reading, I believe. Didn't say who it was, however." He frowned. "I thought him in very low spirits."

Brandon emptied his glass and rose. "Thank you for the wine."

"I hope the matter can be resolved." He looked doubtful as he escorted Brandon to the door.

He wished to quell the man's doubts, but unable to do so, could only thank him for the wine and leave. With a pat of his horse's neck, Brandon mounted and set out along the road toward Swindon. He glanced up at the sun. Past noon. While he wouldn't ride his horse into the ground, he hoped to catch up with Marston before nightfall.

Brandon had been riding for two hours when the terrain changed into the rolling verdant hills of Wessex Downs and its grazing sheep.

As he rode down a hill, he spotted a rider about a half mile ahead of him. Marston, at a slow trot. This was open country, with very few trees. Marston wouldn't hesitate to take a shot at Brandon, so he held back, steeling himself to be patient.

Dusk was a mere hour away. Brandon, waiting for better cover, kept Marston in view. If he noted Brandon's presence, he made no sign of it. Long shadows rippled across the hills as the day drew to a close. Brandon dismounted when his horse began to tire, and led him by the rein. He expected to lose sight of his quarry and would have to make up ground tomorrow. But rounding a bend in the road, he found Marston bent over his horse's hoof. The animal had lost a shoe. He swung around and saw Brandon approaching.

"I'm not here to kill you, Marston," Brandon called. "I witnessed Fraughton's attack on you. It was self-defense. I can vouch for that."

"Forget it, Cartwright." Marston shook his head. "Even if you do mean it, you can't help me."

When Marston raised his gun, Brandon threw himself to the side. The explosion ricocheted around the hills as the scorching heat of the bullet grazed his arm.

Marston threw down his gun and began to climb the rocky hill.

"Devil take it!" Brandon tied a handkerchief around his arm and went after him. It would be even more difficult now to overpower the big man. "Don't be a fool, Marston, there's nothing around here for miles!"

Marston ignored him. He must have been aware that Brandon could easily pick him off. As if he had some clear objective, he climbed strongly, while Brandon followed, his wounded arm sending a protest with each movement.

Marson stopped beside a large cluster of rocks. Fearing he had a knife, Brandon took cover behind a rock. "Give yourself up, Marston," he yelled.

"Go to hell," Marston cried. He climbed onto a large boulder that jutted out from the cliff and stared down at Brandon as if inviting him to shoot him.

Brandon warily emerged from his cover and continued up the incline, still hoping to take him alive.

With a shout, Marston suddenly leaped headlong into the air, his arms flailing. He came crashing down, limb over limb, sending dirt and rocks flying, then lay twisted and still at the bottom of the cliff.

Brandon, cursing loudly, descended as fast as he could. On reaching the inert man, he bent over him, aware of what he would find. Marston's blank gaze stared up at him.

Brandon's veins flooded with ice and he shivered. The awful moment when Freddie Maxwell fell from the church tower, flashed vividly into his mind's eye. Freddie laughing at Brandon, suddenly cold sober, urging him to give it up and come down.

Brandon sank to the ground and buried his head in his arms, deeply shaken.

CHAPTER SEVENTEEN

L ETTY FEARED SHE might faint. It had been a long time since she'd eaten. She'd barely touched her breakfast and was far too nervous to eat a bite of luncheon.

With Arietta beside her, she waited in the presentation drawing room of St. James's Palace for her name to be announced by the Lord Chamberlain. How did women in the last century manage these hoops every day? She placed a hand to the headdress of ostrich feathers, fearing it had not been secured well enough. She was *so* tired. She'd been made to stand for hours, for no one sat in the queen's presence.

When her turn came at last, Letty managed her deep curtsy to the queen without mishap. The queen deigned to speak to her, asking how Letty liked London, and was she enjoying the balls?

Letty answered her with a smile, and they chatted for several minutes. Heaven knew what the queen would think had she learned the truth. With a deep breath, Letty arranged her train over her arm and began to back away. She had gone a few steps when the ostrich feather headdress shifted alarmingly. It moved forward onto her forehead and would soon fall over her eyes. With a flood of warmth to her face, her smiled plastered on her lips, she continued her retreat, step by careful step, her breath shortening. Then, reaching the door, with a gasp of relief, she turned and entered the antechamber where she pushed the offending headdress back into place.

"That went extremely well," Arietta said with a smile. "The queen seemed to enjoy your conversation. I don't know why you were so worried. I told you it would!"

Still shaking, Letty stifled a giggle.

The next day, she accompanied Arietta to Hookhams Lending Library in Old Bond Street, to purchase tickets for the opera the following week.

"On Wednesday, we will attend a dance at Almack's," Arietta said as they partook of luncheon in Grillion's hotel dining room. "And tonight, we have a musicale. The Willard's niece is an aspiring soprano."

"How pleasant," Letty said, forcing enthusiasm into her voice. She doubted she'd find Brandon at a musicale.

BRANDON ARRANGED FOR Marston's body to be placed in the care of his saddened cousin. The local apothecary treated the powder burn on his arm with basilica powder and bound it up, then Brandon rode back to London. Willard was in his office in Whitehall.

"You look done in, my boy," Willard said, as Brandon took the chair opposite him. "I'll send for coffee. I am eager to hear more of your news. And I have some interesting news of my own to impart."

Brandon, his back stiff in the chair, related the facts about Marston's death. "I am sorry I could not bring him back to London as you wished," he said, his voice a low growl. The weight of the man's death still weighed heavily upon him. He put it down to his failure to carry out Willard's orders and bring Marston back alive.

"Not your fault that Marston chose to die the way he did. He was well aware of what would happen to him as a traitor." Willard studied him. "This has hit you hard, hasn't it?"

"It's somewhat inexplicable," Brandon admitted. "Not as though I liked the fellow. He was a brutal, unfeeling devil, who would have dispatched Miss Bromley and me without a second thought. I had nothing but contempt for him. And I've been involved in worst situations and seen many people die in one skirmish or another."

"But the manner of his death has some resemblance to your friend's, is that not so?" Willard, astute as ever, suggested. "I confess to being glad you do feel the weight of it, Brandon. That you are not hardened by the work you have performed for the Crown. Honorable though it is."

"Honorable? Some would not say so."

"Resign," Willard stated flatly. "Such work can strip a man of his values. Leave this business before it drags you down to a place you do not want to go."

Brandon noted Willard's furrowed brow. "You wish me to leave the service?"

"It is something I suggest with reluctance. You are one of my most reliable agents. But I have always felt some measure of responsibility for you, as you know, since I was instrumental in bringing you into the business."

Brandon was about to object, but the door opened, and their coffee was brought in.

"Don't make a decision now," Willard said. "Give the matter some thought."

"I will." Brandon picked up the coffee cup and took a sip as the prospect of a life without purpose struck him with force. "Now what have you to tell me?"

Willard opened a drawer and drew out a fat, black leather journal.

"Is that what I think it is?" Brandon leaned forward, excitement tightening his chest.

"Arrived by special courier this morning. I have much to tell you, but first read it." He pushed the journal over the desk to Brandon.

His heartbeat picking up, Brandon held the journal in his hands. He flicked through the pages. The four men were listed again and again over the course of several years. Beside each was an amount and a date. "Bullion." Brandon glanced up at Willard. "They sent Napoleon gold to finance his campaigns, and in return, he sanctioned their smuggling ventures."

Willard stirred his coffee. "Some quite sizeable amounts."

Brandon sat back with a grin. "Treason. We've got them."

"Indeed, we have. They are being rounded up as we speak."

"Ah, this is interesting," Brandon said, after going back a few pages. "Kendall is listed."

Willard nodded.

"What about that associate of Fraughton's by the name of Pierse? I don't find him here."

"No, the Frenchman was Napoleon's aide and his courier. These men would have continued to make use of Pierse after the war. We are searching London for him."

"So, does this mean that Lavalette has been freed?"

"Free as is the wind," Willard said, quoting Shakespeare.

"But by what means?"

"Best read this first." Willard pushed a letter across to him. "The account came with the journal."

Brandon scanned it. It explained how during the changing of the guard, the comtesse had been permitted to visit her husband. She entered the prison cell where they exchanged clothing. Lavalette had then left the prison dressed in his wife's clothes. "Audacious," he murmured, deeply impressed.

"Simple but ingenious, wouldn't you say?" Willard said. "The prison guards didn't discover he had gone until the next morning."

Brandon looked up. "But the comtesse expects to remain in prison?"

"Yes, for a period," Willard said.

147

"What an extraordinarily brave woman."

Willard leaned back in his chair. "Indeed. Her husband was furnished with a passport and has since crossed the border into Belgium. And so ends stage one."

"Elford and Decrier's lawyers won't get them off this," Brandon said. "And stage two?"

"To free the comtesse," Willard said.

Brandon nodded. "I am eager to see that done."

"Like to be involved in it?"

"Perhaps."

"But before we discuss that possibility, you should know that the Regent has taken special note of this treasonous affair. The prince likes to best Bonaparte in any way he can. Even if the general is beaten. His highness is most pleased."

"I can quite see he would be," Brandon observed. "The Regent hated that Bonaparte was a superb strategist and soldier, something he could never achieve himself."

"Now, a matter of lesser importance to us, but not Mrs. Willard. She is holding a musicale here this evening. My niece is to sing for us."

Brandon's eyes widened. "The niece who makes her debut this Season?"

"The same." Willard chuckled. "Never fear, Angela won't bite. At least I don't think she will."

Brandon grinned. It would be the perfect distraction. He'd stop wondering how Letty's presentation had gone, and if she was well and safe. He had an urgent desire to see her to banish his concerns, and also to tell her what had occurred since they parted. But he was unable to disclose much of it. To give in to the impulse to see her was unwise as his next mission would take him out of the country. Now that Lady Arietta was of interest to the Home Office, it was to be hoped that Letty would soon return to Cumbria. The fact that she might meet a possible husband before she did, was something he refused to contemplate.

CHAPTER EIGHTEEN

THE WILLARD'S DOUBLE-DRAWING room was filled with guests. Letty had little expectation of finding Brandon there and was surprised when he entered, handsome in midnight blue and crisp white evening clothes. He spied her and nodded before turning to talk to his host and hostess.

Letty bit her lip, dismayed by how much she cared for him. She'd caught the signs of strain around his eyes. It was all she could do not to rush over and ask him what had happened since she had last seen him. There was so much she wanted him to tell her, and although she felt in some way entitled to a few crumbs after all she'd been through with him, she couldn't expect him to reveal government secrets. She supposed she'd never learn from Brandon if Marston was imprisoned with the others, and certainly not here, where they would be overheard. But somehow, she must find a way to tell him about Pierse.

Arietta had taken one of the seats arranged around the pianoforte, and she was forced to join her. The elegant room decorated in burgundy wallpaper and gilt molding, was filled with the polite murmur of guests seating themselves and preparing to be entertained. Afterward, a supper was to be served, and tables set up in the salon for those who wished to play cards.

A hush came over the room as the pianist walked in and bowed to polite applause. He threw up the tails of his coat and sat before the pianoforte, massaging his hands. Mrs. Willard came to stand before them. "Miss Angela Willard, will this evening sing for you a lyric aria by Mozart."

Angela was close to Letty in age. In a white muslin gown, her hair caught up with pearl combs, she stood demurely but quite confidently before them whilst the pianist played the introduction. Then, her hands clasped at her waist, she began to sing. Her pure voice soared and sent prickles down Letty's spine. She sat transfixed as the beautiful music flowed over her. No one moved, no gentlemen's feet shuffled, even the ladies' fans stilled. When Miss Willard's voice died away, there was silence, and then the audience erupted to their feet. They clapped and demanded an encore.

Miss Willard, flushed but composed, sang another by Mozart which was just as wonderful.

After the concert had ended, everyone rushed to congratulate her before slowly gravitating to the next room where supper was served.

Letty, still very much moved by Angela's lovely voice, entered with Arietta. Her gaze, sweeping the room, failed to locate Brandon.

As they filled their plates with the sumptuous foods on offer, she spied him in the corridor outside. He talked to a blonde lady in black lace whose back was to Letty. She reached up a black glove to touch his cheek. He leaned over her, a strong emotion in his eyes, which Letty could not decipher, then he took the lady's hand and tucked it into his arm, leading her through the open double doors.

It was Lady Fraughton.

Letty dropped the piece of lobster patty she held on her fork, back onto her plate. It didn't help that she had no right to feel this sense of betrayal. Brandon owed her nothing. But somehow, it made her slightly sick to see him with her, while Fraughton was barely cold in his grave.

"Do you not care for the food, Letitia?" Arietta asked at her elbow.

Letty turned away from the unwelcome sight of Brandon and Lady

Fraughton together. "It's delicious, but I am still so moved by Miss Willard's singing, I can barely manage a bite."

"Why there's Mr. Cartwright, Letitia," Arietta murmured, gazing over her shoulder. "Don't you wish to speak to him? He may have some news."

Letty turned. Lady Fraughton had left him. Brandon now talked to Mr. Willard. Despite still deeply disapproving of Brandon's flirtation, she must speak to him. "I should not like to interrupt them. Perhaps, when he is free."

Arietta's suggestion raised the opportunity for them to have a private conversation. Letty fought to bring her disappointment under control. She would not forget her manners again, and certainly not amongst the Willard's elegant guests.

The chance arose after supper when many guests had gone into the salon to play cards. By accident or design, Brandon had wandered out onto the wrought-iron balcony to smoke a cheroot. With a glance to make sure Arietta was not within earshot, Letty slipped out to join him. She might not have long before others appeared with the same aim, which would make even a discreet conversation impossible on the narrow balcony.

"Miss Bromley. How nice to see you again," he said politely, his blue eyes searching her face. "Are you fully recovered from your...ordeal?"

"Yes, Mr. Cartwright, but..."

"And your presentation went well?"

"Yes, thank you," she said impatiently. "What has happened since I last saw you? Has Marston been found?"

"No need to worry about Marston anymore," he said in a tone that invited no questions. "If you are planning to attempt to draw more information from me, you should go back inside."

"There is something I must tell you."

His gaze flickered to the lighted room visible through the French doors. "Yes?"

"Pierse came to see Arietta."

He frowned, straightening his shoulders. "Right, that's it, Miss Bromley. I want you out of there. I'll find somewhere for you to stay."

"I don't see the need," she said edgily, determined he not try his high-handed tactics on her. "I wasn't able to hear what was said, but should he come again, I could try..."

"Let me stop you there, Miss Bromley." Brandon flicked his cheroot into the garden below. "While I'm grateful for this information, I prefer you not to be there if he visits again."

"I have nowhere to go," Letty said, frustrated. "And I am perfectly safe where I am."

"Has anyone told you that you are exceedingly stubborn?" He sighed and gazed at her. "If the Frenchman should show up before I am able to remove you, you are to leave the house, come directly here to Willard's. They will take you in."

"But nothing has happened to alarm me. I don't see why..."

"Pierse could be dangerous, that's why."

Her face heated. "I expected you to be more grateful."

"Letty, *please!*" He sighed. "Pierse will be dealt with. But I don't want you involved. In fact, I insist that you stay out of it."

"But what about Arietta?" She frowned. "She may be entirely innocent. I don't wish her to be caught up unfairly in this. I consider myself in the best position to learn what their association might be."

A couple wandered across the drawing room toward the French doors. "Haven't you had enough excitement?" he asked in an undertone. "Must you place yourself in danger again? Do nothing, do you hear me? Find someone to take you in. It would be best if you go back to Cumbria should there be no alternative," he added sharply. The couple stepped through the doors onto the balcony. "I must agree, Miss Willard's performance was certainly a tour de force," he said, and took her arm in his firm grip. "The night grows cool. Shall we go inside?"

As soon as she was able, Letty stepped away from him. "Please, don't let me keep you from Lady Fraughton."

He turned to look at her, his blue eyes hot with anger or frustration. She thought he might speak again, but he strode away.

WHEN LETTY GAZED up at him, her plump bottom lip trembling, her enormous brown eyes flashing an accusation he could hardly stand there and deny, it almost brought him undone. He wanted to whisk her out of the room and kiss some sense into her. Fool that he was! The thought that she might be in danger again was intolerable. He went in search of Willard, but he was caught up with his niece within an enthusiastic circle of guests.

"That must have been an interesting conversation you just had with Miss Bromley," Susan Fraughton said beside him.

"We discussed music. An interest of hers. She was much moved by Willard's niece's performance."

Susan fluttered her lashes. "Did she offer to play or sing for you? A private performance? I would be wary, Cartwright. It could be an excuse to trap you, although a novel one I grant you."

"Haven't we said everything that needs to be said, Lady Fraughton?" Not trusting her in this state, he drew her into a corner, aware she was unhappy and looking for someone to blame.

"I want to know what happened to Marston. He has not been seen in London since... Since Fraughton died. I expected him to come to see me. Did he kill Fraughton?"

"If you think he dispatched your husband so you and he might be together, you are mistaken."

She narrowed her eyes. "As you refuse to furnish me with the facts, I must come to my own conclusions."

"As there is nothing further I can tell you, you must excuse me." He made to move around her.

"Cartwright?" Her eyes were pools of misery. "Did that letter I gave you lead to Fraughton's death?"

Concerned she was not dealing with this well, Brandon gazed around at those who stood closest to them. No one appeared to be interested in their conversation. "That letter was of no use. You had nothing to do with any of this, but I'm profoundly sorry you've been hurt by it."

He bowed, and as he left her side, caught sight of Letty watching him from the other end of the room. He hated the thought of her mixed up in this. Rejected it totally. He must find the means to get her away. Should Pierse pay another visit to Lady Arietta, they would be lying in wait for him. What were those two schemers planning? He'd find it easier to deal with twenty men than that young lady in her demure primrose muslin! He shrugged his tight shoulders as he made his way toward Willard who was now free, determined to persuade him to have Letty removed from the house.

Brandon considered writing to Letty's uncle. But then dismissed it. It would take too long to get a response, and she would hate him for it. Short of kidnapping her, another way of removing Letty from that house must be found, and quickly.

Willard beckoned. "I could do with a brandy. Come to the library?" he asked when Brandon reached his side.

Brandon seated himself in one of the leather chairs. "I was surprised to find Arietta Kendall here."

"She is well-liked and is a friend of my wife's."

"Your niece has a fine voice." Brandon accepted a snifter of brandy with a nod of thanks. "Remarkable young woman. So poised for her age."

"Angela avows that her interests lie with performing and not matrimony, but she has expressed a desire to meet you."

Brandon smiled. "I relish the opportunity to praise her remarkable performance."

"If you can tear yourself away from the two other ladies seeking your attention," Willard said with a raised eyebrow.

"Susan Fraughton demands to know where Marston is."

"But you told her nothing?"

"I thought it better not to. The news of his death will reach London by tomorrow. I doubt learning the manner in which he died would help her."

"She expressed a wish to rid herself of Fraughton, didn't she?"

Brandon eyed him with a frown. "Talk is cheap. The lady is troubled, Willard."

Willard sighed. "Yes, of course she is. One gets hardened. That is why I want you to leave the spying game. It's difficult to hang onto your integrity and even your sanity in this business."

"You haven't lost either, my friend."

"I am not in the field, but even so...."

Brandon took a sip of brandy. "Miss Bromley has advised me that Pierse made a late-night visit to Lady Arietta."

"Did he indeed? Slippery fellow, haven't been able to find him. We'll put a watch on her house and pick him up. Her, too."

Brandon leaned forward. "I want to remove Miss Bromley before any action is taken."

"That will alert Pierse that the house is watched. We'll take care to see she is safe, move in as soon as he arrives. Is there somewhere she can go as soon as this business is over?"

"She says not," Brandon said. "Her only relatives live in Cumbria."

"Leave it with me. I'll ask Mrs. Willard. Some of her friends are bringing out daughters this Season. I am sure someone will take her in."

"Thank you. I'd be relieved. Miss Bromley suspects Lady Arietta has been duped. Removing the young lady will be as difficult as prying an oyster from its shell."

Willard nodded sympathetically. "And perhaps you are not the one to do it, my good fellow."

Brandon looked up from placing his empty glass on the table. "Meaning?"

"You have formed a tender for the young lady."

"She is remarkable, I grant you. But I am not about to involve her in my disorderly life."

"Then change your life." Willard rose. "I must return to my guests or risk Veronica's wrath."

Brandon stood. "We men are greatly put upon."

"You have experienced nothing yet. Wait until you have a wife and daughters."

Brandon couldn't conceive of such a life, but conceded it might be pleasant to have a family. As they left the room, he reminded himself of his father's opinion of him as the family's black sheep. He would do well to remember it.

CHAPTER NINETEEN

At breakfast the next morning, Letty was forced to admit that her distaste at seeing Brandon with Lady Fraughton was not entirely due to the couple's past association. She was jealous. When she'd seen others struggle with jealousy, she'd been a little contemptuous of them, sure that she would never succumb to such a lowly emotion herself.

And her heated response to seeing them standing close, and appearing so familiar with each other, disturbed her more than she liked to admit. She'd dismissed Brandon's advice out of hand, when he expressed a genuine concern for her safety. She should have been grateful. Her parting comment was unforgiveable. If only she could have been more reasonable. If only he hadn't been so...bossy.

But thinking on it now, she doubted it would have made a penny's worth of difference. He wanted nothing from her but her promise to leave Arietta's house. So, they had reached an impasse. He wanted her gone while she had no intention of abandoning her kind patroness until she was sure there was proof that Arietta was guilty of some crime.

"Did Cartwright tell you anything of interest?" Arietta inquired on the way home in the carriage.

"No, we only had a moment before some people came out onto the balcony. It's unlikely he would have," she said. "I doubt our paths will cross again." This seemed to sustain Arietta for she'd lapsed into a thoughtful silence for the rest of the journey.

The next day, an article about Robert Marston's untimely death while rock climbing, an apparent favorite sport of his, appeared in *The Gazette,* beneath an article about the corruption and the shady dealings plaguing London and the need for better policing.

Letty would love to know what involvement Brandon had in his death, but perhaps it was better not to know. The whole sordid business should be relegated to the past. Were they being watched? She rose from the table and walked to the breakfast room window which overlooked the small kitchen garden and the mews in the back lane. She could see no one about, except the groom she knew was one of Arietta's washing the carriage. Annoyed with herself, she turned away. Brandon might well have told her if she'd kept a cool head and asked him. It would have been comforting to know that the house was being watched.

Arietta came into the room in her dressing gown. "What shall we do today? You decide. We might go to see the Egyptian artifacts at the British museum, or an exhibition at the art gallery."

"I've always wanted to see the museum," Letty said. "If you care to? I'm sure you have already been there."

"There is always something new to see in the museum. So, we shall," Arietta said with her genial smile. "I have a few letters to dispatch beforehand. Shall we go at eleven?"

Some hours later at the museum, they studied the mysterious hieroglyphic languages of the Rosetta Stone, which was discovered during Napoleon's Egypt Campaign, before being brought to England. And displays of Egyptian friezes, ancient pottery, and stuffed wild animals.

The displays, as fascinating as they were, failed to prevent Letty's thoughts from returning to Brandon. Surely, she was not being overly romantic to believe that from that first unfortunate beginning, there had been a strong link between them. And while she told herself it was Arietta's demands that sent her after him, it was also a desire to know him, to understand him, and then, to be close to him.

His dictatorial manner, which made her wish to give him a good set down on more than one occasion, failed to dampen her desire for his company. It perplexed her, that despite what they'd been through, she felt safe when with him. Her heart beat faster when he came near, and when he smiled at her, she felt somehow special. It didn't matter what he had done in his life. She instinctively knew him to be a good man. Had sensed it in their first meeting. She sighed as she stood sightlessly before a glass display filled with grotesque ceramic masks. It appeared she was a sad case. She admitted that she had tumbled into love with him and could gloomily foresee returning to Cumbria with a heavy heart after their last meeting had ended badly.

"You are in a brown study, today, my pet," Arietta said. "Shall we have afternoon tea at the Piazza? It might brighten you up."

Letty smiled. "Am I being tedious? I am sorry, and suppose I'm a little tired. I should like tea."

"Early to bed tonight, Letitia. You have been through a lot. I don't wish to see dark shadows beneath your eyes. We have yet to find a suitor you approve of, and I am determined not to send you back to Cumbria at the end of the Season without you becoming engaged. There's Mrs. Royston's picnic at Richmond Park, tomorrow, perhaps some charming gentleman will attend."

This declaration failed to excite any enthusiasm in Letty. Arietta had set herself an impossible task, for no man would measure up to Brandon in her eyes. But she smiled and thanked her, opening her umbrella and holding it over Arietta's head, her arm tucked in hers as they left the museum. The weather was as dreary as her spirits. It had so far proved to be a cold spring with dull skies, said to be caused by a violent volcanic eruption somewhere else in the world.

As if she'd come down with some malaise, Arietta fussed over

Letty that evening, even escorting her up to her bedchamber, and later coming to say goodnight. She turned to smile at the door. "Sleep well, my dear."

When the door closed, Letty lay in the dark, her mind too busy for sleep. She slipped from the bed. There was no movement in the street below. Had what she told Brandon been of no importance? She'd half expected someone to call during the afternoon to question Arietta, and indeed had been on tenterhooks, fearing they would give her away, but no one had come.

Letty settled back into bed, determined to sleep. She managed to drift off, but woke again some time later. She stared into the dark, unsure what had awakened her. She started up at a muffled cry, threw back the bedclothes and lit her candle. Outside her room, the corridor was empty. Over the banister rail, the hall downstairs was a well of darkness. She crept to Arietta's bedchamber, fearing it might have been her. Candlelight flicked under the door. She put her ear to it to listen.

Another soft cry.

Letty put her candle down on the hall table, opened the door, and stepped inside. With only a small candle lit, most of the room lay in shadow, and for a moment, Letty couldn't make out the two bodies writhing on the bed. They were caught up in their passion, both naked, Arietta's pale body entwined with that of a swarthy, dark-haired man.

With a gasp, Letty fumbled for the door latch behind her as the couple broke apart. She opened the door and was about to dart out into the corridor when the man demanded she stop.

Letty froze.

Pierse rose naked from the bed and stalked to his clothes, pulling on his breeches. "*Mon Dieu!* You said she was asleep, Arietta!"

"I thought she was." Arietta reached for her dressing gown.

"I am dreadfully sorry." Letty's heart beat in her throat, her face burning. She wanted to look away from him, but couldn't. The Frenchman stood before her, bare-chested, his hands on his hips. "I thought Arietta was in trouble," she managed to croak out.

"This complicates matters, Arietta," he said coolly.

Tying her belt, Arietta scuttled over to Letty. She placed an arm around her shoulders. "It doesn't need to, Pierse. Letitia is my friend and confidante." Her bright blue eyes both implored and warned, sending a shaft of cold fear through Letty. "She would never say a word to hurt me, would you, my pet?"

Before Letty could affirm or deny this, the man stalked over to them. He took hold of Letty's arm and shoved her roughly into a chair. "A silly young debutante." He gazed at Letty dismissively. "She will spill it all as soon as someone says boo to her."

Letty opened her mouth to refute it, but closed it again, as a wave of terror rushed through her. The man, his mouth a thin line, his eyes as cold and hard as stone, had curled his hands into fists, and she feared he would hurt her.

Arietta pushed her way in between them. "Darling, I tell you she won't. Letitia is wise beyond her years. Has she not done a marvelous job of spying for us?"

He shook his head. "We'll have to deal with her."

Arietta burst into tears.

He paused. "It has grown too hot for me in London, *mon amour.* I'm leaving by boat at the first morning tide. They will throw you in Newgate if you stay. Come with me!"

Arietta wiped her eyes with her handkerchief. "You promise not to hurt her. *Pierse?*"

With a trail of French curses, he stalked to the window and pulled down the silken cords. "Pack your valise while I tie her up."

Arietta dressed and then flew around selecting items to pack while Pierse secured Letty to the chair with sharp hurtful tugs at her wrist and ankles.

"Go outside," Pierse ordered Arietta, when she had done up her valise. "Wait for me in the rear lane while I dress."

Arietta eyed him fearfully, but she finally left the room, leaving Letty chilled and afraid for her life.

Pierse strolled over to where he had thrown the rest of his clothes in a jumble on the chair. His expressionless black eyes on Letty, he dressed.

After he'd donned his shoes, he still studied her meditatively, then stood and pulled a knife from his pocket.

Letty's blood froze. "I'll scream the house down if you come anywhere near me."

He took a step closer. "One peep out of you and I'll cut your throat."

Arietta ran into the room. "No Pierse!" She rushed at him, and in her haste, stumbled against him.

She crumpled to the floor with a moan.

With an inhuman growl, Pierse fell to his knees beside Arietta's still form, the knife lodged in her chest. Blood gushed from the wound, staining the carpet. Shocked, Letty's throat closed over. With a strangled gasp, she struggled against her bonds.

Noise erupted downstairs. It sounded as if a hundred people stampeded into the house. Pierse straightened. He shoved Letty's chair out of the way, made a dash for the door, and was gone.

It was clear that Arietta was dead. Tears flooded down Letty's cheeks. She sagged against the chair, fighting for breath. Would he change his mind and come back to kill her? Footsteps ran along the corridor.

Brandon rushed inside. "Good God! Letty!" He knelt beside Arietta's limp form, then sadly shook his head. "Are you hurt?"

"No! Hurry! Pierse will have gone down the servant's stairs."

"He won't get far."

Brandon walked over to the bed. He picked up the quilt and placed it carefully over Arietta's body.

"She put herself between Pierse and me, Brandon. She saved my life."

"Did she, sweetheart? Perhaps your faith in her wasn't entirely misplaced."

"I was wrong about her association with that man, but she *was* fond of me, Brandon. Perhaps she loved him." She took a shuddering breath. "Why are so many people I come to care for taken from me?"

"Not everyone, sweetheart," he said soothingly as he untied the curtain cords which bound her to the chair. "I can easily predict your future filled with people who care very much for you."

Her whole body had begun to shudder. "Can...you?"

Free of her bonds, he gently rubbed her wrists. "You are eminently loveable, sweetheart." He took out his handkerchief and handed it to her.

Letty wiped her eyes and blew her nose. Her wrists, still sore from the earlier assault on them, stung, her throat too tight with emotion to talk anymore.

She held the handkerchief out to him. She hiccupped, and gazing down, realized she was still in her thin-lawn nightgown.

"No, keep it, sweetheart. Let's go and get your dressing gown, then I'll take you away from here."

A hand around her waist, Brandon helped her to her bedchamber. "I'll have the maid pack a bag for you," he said.

THERE WAS A commotion in the street. Candlelight flickered in the surrounding houses. Front doors opened. Men in blue coats ran past. The staff had emerged and were milling about, looking stunned. One of the Bow Street runners came to tell him they had captured Pierse.

"You have nothing to fear now, Letty, we've got him." He drew her to her feet from the chair in the front hall. She wobbled, and he wrapped his arms around her slim body in the thin silk dressing gown, as the awful fear he'd had of finding her dead faded, and his racing pulse slowed.

"We needed to catch them together. I was coming to find you," he said. "I thought you'd be asleep," he said almost accusingly.

"I was, but a noise woke me." She dropped her chin, a flush coloring her pale cheeks. "They were…"

"No need to explain." He ran a soothing hand over her back. "We have somewhere for you to stay tonight. Let's find your maid. Her voluble French has mystified the Bow Street runner."

"You won't leave me?"

"No, I won't leave." He smiled down at her as relief gripped him again. He placed his arm around her to reassure himself as much as her. The hurt this evening had caused her would take some time to heal, and he wished she could have been spared this frightening business. Their agent watching the house had taken too long to alert them of Pierse's presence. "Ah, here she is," he said as Adele appeared from the servant's stairs, gasping and crying. "She will help you dress. I'll be right outside the bedchamber."

When Letty emerged again, she was pale, but composed, her hair in a smooth topknot. She was dressed in a lavender pelisse and gloves and carried a shawl and a portmanteau. "Adele wants to stay here, she says her brother will come for her."

Brandon nodded. "She may do so."

He escorted Letty down the stairs and out into the street. She gazed around at the confusion, the wagon trundling off with Pierse inside, but said nothing as he led her to the carriage.

In the minute when he'd burst into that room fearing the worst, the depth of his feelings for Letty struck with force. He cared for her deeply. Such an emotion rocked him, it made him want something from life he'd refused to believe he could have. That he didn't believe he could have without causing some hurt to her.

"I want to go home, Brandon," she murmured.

"Yes, of course you do, sweetheart. And so you shall," he said, his breath catching.

CHAPTER TWENTY

B RANDON ASSISTED LETTY into the carriage. Once seated, he took her hands in his, while he explained that Mrs. Willard had expressed some confidence in finding a sponsor for her, to allow her to remain in London for the rest of the Season. "If you wish to stay," he added, studying her in the faint glow of the carriage lamps. "You did express a desire to go home, which might be best."

Letty looked away from him. He wanted her gone. She watched the shadowy quiet streets pass by, and the halos cast by the gas lamps. "How very kind of her," she murmured, aware that she sounded flat, dismissive, and profoundly weary.

It was barely halfway through the Season. That meant many weeks living with a new family. She feared she would make a dreadful companion. She and Arietta had shared such good times together, giggling at nonsensical things whilst browsing amongst the jewelry and furs at the Pantheon Bazaar, or the perfumery and millinery at Harding Howell & Co in Pall Mall. To contemplate joining another household, trying to fit in with a new family, with the possible resentment of their daughter who would hardly care to share her come-out, did nothing to lessen the sensation of being cut adrift.

Letty kept revisiting the frightening scene in Arietta's bedchamber in her mind. Pierse, as he held up a vicious-looking knife and moved toward her, having made up his mind to kill her. Then, Arietta rushing in to save her, only to be impaled on the blade. It all happened so fast and left Pierse as stunned and shattered as Letty. She shuddered. She would never forget the almost inhuman sound of his heartbroken cry.

As if in response, Brandon's arm came round her shoulders. "But I can't arrive at the Willard's door in the middle of the night," she murmured.

"Mrs. Willard is more than happy to take you in. She is a pleasant woman, is she not?"

"I met her only briefly. I hate to impose."

"None of this is your fault."

"I've had the most dreadful Season," Letty said almost to herself. "I wouldn't want another like it."

"Another? Then you might stay in London?" Brandon's voice began to sound strangely hollow as if he was far away.

"I don't know..." Warm beneath the rug he'd tucked around her, Letty gratefully leaned her head against his chest and closed her eyes, while the juddering carriage took them away from the dreadful carnage.

"Letty?" Brandon's soft voice reached her. It was too soon. She wanted to go on like this for hours.

"Yes?" She opened her eyes. They'd stopped in front of a townhouse she recognized as the Willard's. A lady in evening dress waited on the porch. "There's Mrs. Willard," she said, surprised. She had not expected to see the lady until the morning.

"She will look after you," Brandon said again.

"I'm such a nuisance," she said. "Will you come in, Brandon?"

"No. I'll return tomorrow to see how you fare."

After the footman put down the step, Brandon lifted Letty down. They stood on the pavement as his concerned, blue eyes met hers. "You need rest, sweetheart."

Letty nodded numbly.

The elegantly dressed Mrs. Willard greeted Brandon informally like an old friend.

"I'll leave you in Mrs. Willard's capable care, Letty," he said.

Strangely bereft, Letty watched the horses pull away from the curb.

"Come, my child. You are all done in." Mrs. Willard's soothing voice eased Letty's discomfiture as she placed an arm around her and drew her into the house.

"I am most dreadfully sorry to have disturbed you," Letty said.

"Nonsense. No one goes to bed until very late in Town. We are not long returned from a party and prior to that, the opera."

"We had tickets for the opera, Arietta and I." Letty gulped, and tears ran down her cheeks.

Mrs. Willard offered her a scented handkerchief. "More will come out about this, I imagine, although we may not get to hear the whole. We women do not. It's not a world we are often exposed to, because our brave, honorable, gentlemen work hard to protect us from it. I am so very sorry indeed, my dear, that you have been hurt. You liked Lady Arietta, didn't you? So did I. But I'm afraid our loyalty to her was sadly misplaced. Now, up to bed with a hot drink and a bedwarmer at your feet. You'll feel ever so much better tomorrow."

She tried to save me, Letty wanted to say as a need to defend Arietta tightened her chest, the words hovering on her tongue. But what good would it do? She wiped her tears and followed Mrs. Willard up the stairs. "I must write to my uncle and Aunt Edith. They will be distressed at the news. My aunt especially. She placed me in Arietta's care after she became too ill to sponsor me. And because she's in Cumbria, she won't be able to attend the funeral. But I shall go."

"Women do not attend funerals, and certainly not young women. You need to rest, my dear. We'll talk tomorrow," Mrs. Willard said, her firm hand on Letty's arm guiding her into a bedchamber.

BRANDON WEARILY ENTERED his townhouse, his relief so profound he could almost taste it. Letty, safe at last with the Willards. It was possible that she might decide to stay for the rest of the Season should her uncle allow it. But the horrible experience she'd witnessed tonight had left her badly shaken. He now knew her well enough to be confident the spirited young woman would rally, given time, but Lady Arietta's betrayal, and how she had died would leave its mark.

With a deep regretful sigh, he acknowledged his involvement in Letty's life must end. An agent had no business dallying with a debutante. A wife weakened a man's resolve. All his thoughts were channeled into protecting her. And there would be children, even worse. At least he'd managed to keep his head and not gone with his rampant emotions. She must be left to find her feet, and enjoy a lighthearted time in London, if she chose. And perhaps meet the man she would marry. He ran up the stairs as his mind skittered away from that possibility. It would be a lucky man who married Letty. The fellow better be worthy of her.

The next day, Brandon met Willard in his office where they discussed the events of the previous night, and how matters now stood.

"So, Lady Arietta was working for the French?" Brandon asked.

"She was enamored of Pierse, but we've discovered nothing to suggest she passed secrets to the French. The fire's gone out of Pierse. He is talking. We've determined that he first met the lady through her husband. Pierse must have subsequently pursued her after Kendall died. He used her for his own ends while he worked for Fraughton, who was perhaps the only member of the gang of four who had political leanings with a view to incite revolution. Pierse is merely an opportunist who offers his services for hire. A violent man, and is suspected of being behind Kendall's death and that porter's death in

France."

Willard ran a hand over his eyes. "Descrier and Elford are businessmen, Marston, too, to a lesser degree. Descrier lost money after the decline of slavery, and Lord Elford after a storm razed his cotton plantation in the West Indies. Marston was a gambler who went through his family's money. They all looked to fill their coffers by any means available to them. When the opportunity arose to engage in opium smuggling, they grabbed it." He leaned back in his chair. "The Home Office is satisfied with the outcome. The *Journal Noir* proves these men were contributing money to Napoleon's cause, aided by Pierse. A clear case of treason. They will stand trial, as Fraughton and Marston would have, had they survived to face justice. That is why the journal frightened them. Napoleon had advised them of it, perhaps with a view to keep them under his control, who knows? But knowing their names were in it made them all too aware of the consequences should the journal ever fall into British hands."

Brandon folded his arms. "The mystery of the journal is at last solved. How was Miss Bromley this morning?"

Willard lifted his bushy eyebrows. "She was breakfasting with my wife when I left home. I gather you will call and see the young lady today?"

"This afternoon. Did Miss Bromley mention whether she planned to remain in London?"

Willard shook his head. "The offer is there should she wish to do so. My wife is so taken with her, she might sponsor Miss Bromley, herself."

Brandon smiled. "That is good of her."

"With Lavalette freed, the journal in our hands, and the three remaining culprits awaiting trial, the matter is now at an end." Willard steepled his fingers and eyed Brandon. "Might you be interested in getting your teeth into something new? Or are you planning to take my advice and resign?"

"What's the mission?" Brandon asked idly.

"What we discussed earlier. It's a matter of diplomacy. You may, however, need to apply a little pressure in some quarters to facilitate the comtesse's release from prison. We owe her a debt since she delivered the journal into our hands. It's the least we can do for her."

Brandon waited for that spark of excitement to kick in that familiar tightening of the belly. But he felt nothing. He expected he was tired. And perhaps he did want something more from life than this. "I'll give it some thought."

At two o'clock, he called at the Willard's home. Letty entered the parlor looking pale and subdued in one of her demure white muslin gowns. Concerned, he took her hand and raised it to his lips.

She smiled slightly at the old-fashioned gesture and sat opposite him on the sofa. "Would you care for wine, or coffee?"

"No thank you. I only wish to hear how you are."

"I'm quite well," she said, not sounding at all like herself. "It was decent of you not to mention you were right about Arietta, for you were, weren't you?"

"There's not much I can tell you about all this, Letty, except that her motives might have come more from a matter of the heart, than any desire to betray her country."

"Yes, I thought that, too," she said with a heavy sigh. "I'm glad it's over, but I will miss her." She glanced up at him. "I believe Pierse loved her, too. Why did he wish to spy on the others?"

"He was covering his back, I imagine. Not much trust among thieves. You have written to your uncle?"

She nodded. "I sent him a brief letter in this morning's post. Mr. Willard told me to say little about Arietta, only that she had died."

"He will be advised of the details later. Did you ask him to let you remain in London?"

"I saw no point. Even not knowing the truth, he will insist I come home. He already believed London to be a den of thieves." She bit her lip. "And when he learns what happened to Arietta, he will be certain of it."

"Bow Street will notify him of the true facts of her death, of course, being a relative. But a rumor will be put about that Lady Arietta was taken suddenly by a catastrophic illness. I'm sorry you will miss the rest of the Season."

Letty dropped her chin, hiding her expression. "It doesn't matter. I'm so very tired, you see."

"Yes, but you won't always be tired."

She raised her head. He almost gasped. Gone from her beautiful brown eyes was her vivacity and optimism, to be replaced by a sad awareness of the world's darker underbelly. He would have spared her that if he could. It crushed him that she had come to London seeking romance and adventure and now seemed bowed down by what life had thrown at her.

"I will miss you, Letty," he found himself saying.

Her eyes flew to his. "Will you, Brandon?"

"Yes." He gave a brief smile. "We have been through quite a lot together, haven't we?"

"What will you do now?"

"There's a chance I'll be sent to Paris." He hadn't decided to accept, rather he'd almost decided not to take Willard up on it. But suspected he used it now as a way to stop himself from reaching out to her.

She nodded. "Paris? I hope it's not a dangerous mission, Brandon."

"No, merely a diplomatic posting."

"I'm glad. Paris. My, I would love to visit Paris one day." She rose briskly and smoothed her skirts. "You must excuse me. I believe I'll return to my room. I have a headache."

He stood. "I'm sorry, Letty," he repeated, frustrated, and constrained by how little he could say.

"Goodbye, Brandon. Thank you, for taking care of me."

"Not goodbye," he said, not ready to say it. "It will be days before you receive your uncle's reply. I'll call tomorrow afternoon. You might care for a drive in the park if the weather is fine."

Letty stood at the door. "I should like that. I fear I might become a nuisance for the Willards if I'm always underfoot. Mrs. Willard insists I accompany her to Almack's tomorrow evening. She has procured a voucher for me from her good friend, Lady Sefton." Letty smoothed her skirts with anxious hands. "Mrs. Willard refuses to accept that I'm in mourning. She believes I should not allow this tragedy to spoil my life. She said that..." Letty swallowed. "That... Arietta was certain to have suffered a sad end because of the path she chose."

Brandon moved closer to her. "Mrs. Willard is quite right, Letty."

"I suppose you are both right," she said with a faint smile. She offered her hand to him as if he was a new acquaintance.

Wanting to hold her, Brandon took her small hand in his. He continued to hold it while searching her eyes. "Tomorrow, Letty."

He quitted the house, reminding himself of how much her association with him had hurt her. His world should not and would never be hers. But if he were to give up that life...he quickly dismissed the improbability of suddenly becoming a man worthy of marriage. It seemed well beyond his reach, but yet, he couldn't get her out of his thoughts as he strode toward his carriage more conflicted than ever.

When Brandon arrived home, his father awaited him in his parlor.

He stood up from the sofa with a gesture, Brandon recognized, thrusting out his chest as if to emphasize his still strong and upright carriage. He had not come for a friendly chat. Something was on his mind. And he wasn't in the mood to take no for an answer.

Brandon steeled himself for an argument. "Sherry, Father?"

"Thank you."

His father strolled over to the fireplace. A hand on the mantel, he gazed down at the empty grate. "Can't imagine what you do in London. Is it an endless supply of *ton* parties or do the opera dancers at Covent Garden still hold some appeal?" He turned to face him, irritation flickering across his face. "You aren't gambling away your inheritance, are you?"

Brandon turned back to the crystal decanter and concentrated on pouring a whiskey for himself without his shaking hand spilling it. His father was well aware he rarely gambled, he was gearing up for an argument that Brandon had no energy for.

"I have something I wish to discuss with you." He took the sherry glass from Brandon and returned to the sofa.

"Oh?" Brandon sat in a wing chair and took a good long pull at the whiskey.

"You will be aware that our neighbor, Colonel Smythe-Jones has a daughter, Juliette. She's been out for a Season or two. You might have come across her at a ball or some such. She has changed considerably since you last saw her. She was a child then, she's a pretty young woman now. I believe it would be an excellent match for you. She seems a sensible young woman, or so her mother tells me."

Brandon tried to swallow his anger at his father's interference, along with the last of his whiskey. He put the glass down on the occasional table. "I'm afraid I shall have to decline such an appealing offer, Father. I am about to sail for France. I'll be in Paris, should you have need of me, you can reach me at the Hotel Westminster 13 Rue De La Paix."

His father's glass was replaced on the table less gently. "Continuing with your rakish ways, eh!" he said, standing up. "Well, I suppose I didn't really expect to find any desire in you to settle down, or to make your mother happy."

"I apologize for never having made either of you happy, Father."

"No." His father nodded. "Well, I am having luncheon with the prime minister. I'll see myself out."

Brandon stared at the closed door. Would his father feel any differently if he knew the truth? He somehow doubted it. His father had expressed a poor opinion of some of the actions of Whitehall on more than one occasion when a politician. Well, at least his parent had made up his mind for him. He would go to Paris.

THE NEXT AFTERNOON, Brandon advised Willard of his decision to accept the Paris mission. Confident that his promise to his spymaster was now set in stone, and could not be changed, he went to join Letty.

She awaited him in the parlor, rising to greet him in a lavender-colored dress and white spencer jacket. Her bonnet, lined with silk the color of bluebells, reminded him of the flowers growing in the woods at Fernborough Park. She carried a pink parasol in her lacy, white-gloved hands. He thought her pretty as a portrait, but didn't miss the faint shadows beneath her dark eyes.

"Thank you for taking me out, Brandon," she said in a strangely formal tone, as he assisted her into his curricle. "I had begun to hate being indoors. I seemed unable to escape my thoughts."

He tooled the horses through the streets, and they entered the park gates. It was early for the *ton,* and few carriages drove down the South Carriage Drive. "I should love to have ridden in Rotten Row," Letty said with a regretful sigh. "There are so many things I wished to do and see while in London."

"You'll come back one day," he said, hating to see her so subdued.

"No, I doubt my uncle would permit it." Beneath her parasol, she shook her head, her dusky curls stirring against her cheek. Her big brown eyes regarded him seriously. He suffered a foolish urge to kiss her, to awaken her again to that vibrant young woman he had known. Letty was no sleeping beauty, she would rally, he told himself. And he was no prince. He looped the reins in a hand, turning his attention to his horses.

He was about to suggest her future husband might bring her to London, but the words stuck in his throat. He couldn't voice them, for some illogical fear that it might come true. Surely, he wished her to find happiness? He didn't understand himself. Once he left for Paris, perhaps he would think more clearly. But not here with Letty, not as he breathed in the scent of her violet soap, and was so patently aware of her slender body so close to his on the seat. He rested a boot on the footboard and pulled up the horses. Letty gazed at him in inquiry, her lips parted in surprise. He was unsure what he would say, what ridiculous promises he'd make that he might not be able to keep…

"I say, Cartwright!" Frederick Delridge hailed him, and rode his neat roan over to the curricle. "Haven't seen you in an age." He turned with a smile to Letty. "Please introduce me to this delightful young lady."

Brandon clamped his teeth at the keen light in Delridge's eye. He issued the introductions, all the while wishing Delridge to Jericho, who was now asking Letty to save him a dance at Almack's. Brandon frowned. He had no right to act like a lover. And by the time Delridge had ridden off, he had himself under control. Taking up the reins, he moved the horses on, with a smile at Letty. "Bit of a bore, old Delridge."

Letty cantered her head. "He seemed quite nice."

Not trusting himself to comment, Brandon urged the horses into a trot.

When they arrived back at the Willard's, he leapt down and held up his arms for her. He swung her lightly down to the pavement, while all the time despairing that he might not see her again.

"Save me a dance at Almack's," he said finally.

"I thought you disliked the place." Letty raised her eyebrows. "Didn't you say it was a detestable marriage mart?"

"And so it is, but nevertheless, I shall be there," he said shortly, and raised his beaver hat in farewell. He ran down the steps and climbed smartly back into the curricle. He wasn't about to let the fortune hunters and rakes move in on Letty. Nor Delridge, who was quite the wrong man for her. Not when she was in such a vulnerable state.

CHAPTER TWENTY-ONE

"MY GOODNESS, ALMACK'S is crowded tonight," Mrs. Willard observed as they entered the elegant rooms in King Street.

Guests roamed from the card rooms to the supper rooms, the gentlemen uniformly dressed in black breeches, white stockings, and black pumps. Sparkling crystal chandeliers lit the ballroom where couples performed their steps, the younger ladies' white gowns reflected like dainty moths in the huge, gilt-framed mirrors around the walls. Above in the gallery, the orchestra played Haydn.

The Willards were soon surrounded by friends. Mrs. Willard immediately introduced Letty to a young gentleman who requested a dance.

An hour later, while Letty danced with Mr. Delridge, she saw Brandon enter the ballroom, so handsome in black and white, a chapeau bras in his hand, and her heart set up that strange pit-a-patter. She smiled when his searching gaze found her among the dancers, but thought his returning smile restrained. He made his way over to the Willards. Perhaps Brandon didn't approve of Mr. Delridge, but after all, what did it matter? In a few days, she would leave London.

"You are enjoying your stay in the metropolis, Miss Bromley?" Mr. Delridge asked. She did not think him handsome, but every man suffered in comparison to Brandon.

"Oh yes, but regretfully, I am returning to Cumbria in a few days,"

Letty explained.

"Then might you take pity on me and indulge me in another dance, later in the evening?"

"I am not sure if I have one to spare, sir," Letty murmured, trying not to watch Brandon's progress through the crowd.

It seemed like years ago when she and Brandon waltzed. They were strangers then who did not trust each other. She longed to waltz with him tonight, now they were on more intimate terms. She would hug that memory close when she returned to Cumbria.

After Mr. Delridge led her back to her seat and departed, Brandon approached her. He bowed to Mrs. Willard whose gaze roamed over him approvingly.

"Good evening, Mrs. Willard." He turned to Letty. "Miss Bromley, I wonder if I might have the waltz?"

"Indeed you may, Mr. Cartwright. Miss Bromley has the waltz free," Mrs. Willard said, answering for Letty, who raised her fan to hide her smile.

When the waltz was called, Brandon came to her side. Slightly breathless, she rested a hand on his silk sleeve as he led her onto the dance floor. When the musicians struck up, he took her in his arms. His smile was so familiar and warm, it reached right to her toes. "So, old Delridge is here tonight," he said in a conversational tone.

"Yes. He has asked for another dance."

"Has he indeed? Impudent fellow," he said with deceptive calm, his eyes narrowing.

Pleased to find him jealous, Letty tried not to smile. "I find him quite personable."

He settled her closer, a glint in his blue eyes. "You do?"

"I must say, I'm surprised to find you here," Letty observed, while a coil of pleasure wrapped itself around her heart. She pushed away the thought that she must not put too much store by his behavior. That it did not matter if he cared a little for her, he was determined to see her return to Cumbria.

"What do you think of Almack's?" he asked.

"It's very elegant."

He grinned. "But not the food, I fear, stale bread and dry cake, and only tea and lemonade to drink."

"One does not come to Almack's for the food," she scolded.

He raised an eyebrow. "Oh? What does one come for?"

"To see, and be seen."

"By whom? Men like Delridge?"

"And other handsome gentlemen," she said, beginning to enjoy herself. "To dance," she added breathlessly as he reversed her swiftly, his hand tightening at her waist.

"I agree, the dancing makes it well worth it," Brandon said, his voice low and seductive. His gaze took her in from head to foot.

Against all reason, she was filled with a strange inner excitement, her pulse racing. She ran a tongue over her lips, and found him watching her. Only he could tease her senses in this way. Whenever she was with him, she wanted to draw closer, to rest her head against his shoulder, to breathe in his familiar, reassuring male smell. She longed to throw her arms around his neck and press her lips to his.

But Brandon appeared to have mastered his emotions, for he now held her at a polite distance and guided her over the floor at a more sedate pace. She must content herself, it seemed, with the warmth of his hands through the gloves he wore. His hand at her waist seemed to burn through her muslin dress. Could he not sense what she felt, what she longed for him to say? She raised her chin and met his smoldering blue eyes, willing him to beg her to stay in London. He did not. He had accepted their paths would take them in different directions.

While the expression in his eyes revealed some deep emotion, he talked of pleasantries, and when the dance ended, he escorted her back to Mrs. Willard.

"My, Mr. Cartwright, you and Miss Bromley dance very well together, I must say," Mrs. Willard wickedly observed. She had expressed the view at breakfast that Letty and Brandon were perfectly suited, and tossed her head at Mr. Willard when he scolded her for making mischief.

Brandon's lips rose in a wry smile. "If I trod on Miss Bromley's toes, she is far too nice to mention it."

It was nonsense. He was far too good a dancer for that. Letty bit her lip. Why was he being so formal? But she knew the answer. He was seeking to protect her reputation, and perhaps his own? Didn't Arietta once say that Brandon would take care not to become compromised? And with his mission in France soon to begin, he would be eager to depart.

He stayed for a few moments in conversation and then took his leave, promising to call on them before she left London.

She watched him shoulder his way politely through the crowd, and all her pleasure and enjoyment of the evening went with him.

A DAY LATER, Letty received her summons from Uncle Alford. A prompt letter by special post ordering her home. In a few lines, her uncle had managed to convey his fear that Letty was at the mercy of the scoundrels who inhabited that immoral city. He would not take a calm breath until she was again under his roof and in his care.

Brandon, calling that afternoon to see how she fared, insisted on escorting her to the mail coach the following day.

It was a cool day, the weather insistently overcast, which matched Letty's mood, as they stood together outside the Peacock Inn in the busy Islington street while the mail coach was loaded up for the journey north.

Brandon's eyes darkened. "I'm sorry it's worked out like this. You should have enjoyed your time in London, and I regret the part I played in ruining it."

"I can hardly blame you for that," she said with a forced smile. She'd been cheerful on the way here in his curricle, having decided whilst lying awake during the night to hide the awful hollowness she suffered at leaving him. "Please thank the Willards again for me, especially Mrs. Willard who was such a dear."

While emotional farewells went on in the crowd all around them, he slipped his arms around her waist, which quite destroyed her plan to leave him composed and seemingly unmoved. The very thought that she would never see him again sent a bolt of ice straight to her heart. Hot tears scaled her eyes, and she blinked them away.

His hand moved softly over her back. "After all we've been through together, let us not part as polite strangers," he murmured. He kissed her cheek, then, with a sharp intake of breath, his lips found hers, soft, and firm, sending fire dancing along her veins. She feared she would crumple in his arms, but he drew away, his eyes betraying his emotion, if his words did not. "I wish you a wonderful life, Letty."

"Don't be too brave in Paris," she said urgently.

"I won't." His eyes darkened. "I'll be dueling with words, Letty, not swords."

"Yes," she whispered, not believing him. "You did say it was a diplomatic posting."

"Don't compromise on your dreams, Letty. Remember Aunt Lydia," he urged.

Before more could be said, she was called to the coach by the driver.

As she took her seat beside an elderly gentleman, she turned to the window for a last glimpse of Brandon where he stood on the pavement with a hand raised in farewell. The imprint of Brandon's mouth lingered on her lips long after the coach had turned a corner. She ran a tongue over her bottom lip. Brandon cared for her, maybe even loved her. But not enough to give up his way of life. And had he asked her to marry him, she would have feared for their future together. The pain of losing her father and mother had never left her, and to suffer the loss of a beloved husband would destroy her peace forever. She tamped down a sigh, becoming aware of the scrutiny of the three people sharing the coach.

As she was carried back to Hawkshead village, she thought over her time in London, from her first experience with Aunt Edith right to the distressing conclusion. She was not looking forward to facing her uncle and aunt with what had occurred. She would struggle to find words to explain it when there was so much she couldn't say. Although a blatant lie did not sit well with her, she finally decided on the brief account of Arietta's sad end that Mr. Willard had instructed her to say.

As the miles passed by, it was the vision of Arietta's pale body entwined with that of the swarthy Frenchman's, which seemed to stay with her, the bedchamber filled with their moans and murmured declarations of love. She hadn't had much idea of what occurred between men and women, although growing up in the country, you were familiar with the mating of animals. The passion expressed by the two lovers was so sensual and exciting, and when she thought of the act in terms of her own possible future, it was Brandon taking her in his arms; Brandon sending her pulse racing. She couldn't imagine any other man being on such intimate terms with her. She only hoped that time would lessen her memory of the warmth of his blue eyes, the sound of his voice, and the way his very presence seemed embedded in her soul.

But he didn't want her. He would soon forget her as he sailed for France, his mind on the Paris assignment. Could she believe him when he'd said it was not dangerous? She simply must for her sanity's sake.

"Are you returning home, miss?" The middle-aged lady opposite smiled at her as she took out her knitting.

"Yes." Letty gave an answering smile. *Home?* There was some comfort in the thought of their quiet village where one could be fairly confident that each day passed like another.

"I hope you're not too sad," the woman said, her fingers flying over the needles as she settled in for a chat.

"Perhaps a little." Her distress must be obvious. Writ large on her face, she supposed. Letty didn't have the strength to pretend otherwise. She didn't want to talk, she'd rather have a good cry before she reached home. But the lady's bright eyes observed her, and it appeared Letty would be denied the opportunity.

"Leaving your young man behind?" The lady nudged the cleric seated beside her. "Such a good-looking, robust fellow he was, too." She cast Letty a hopeful glance. "Will he be coming after you, miss?"

The elderly gentleman sitting next to Letty gave an impatient rattle of his newspaper.

Letty smiled and shook her head. She must not allow herself to dream of such a possibility, not for a moment.

BRANDON WATCHED THE mail coach until it was out of sight. So, she was gone. Home to marry some fellow, he supposed. While he found it hard to accept that she would marry, he fervently hoped it wasn't Geoffrey, Letty should have passion in her life, not settle for friendship. Nor Delridge, who was probably too fond of London to travel all the way to Cumbria. Brandon groaned softly. Shouldn't have hugged her, certainly shouldn't have kissed her, but he needed to hold on to some memory of her. Her slim body in his arms, how her soft lips opened beneath his, drawing a response from him that he struggled to dismiss. He walked down the street to where his curricle awaited, the horses held by his groom, while admitting that London had soured for him. He'd be glad to get away for a time.

Hove awaited his instructions. The packing of Brandon's trunk had become a matter of great importance since his valet learned he was to accompany him to Paris. He was enveloped in a fever of organization, which Brandon would prefer to avoid if he could. While Hove considered Paris to be deplorably overflowing with the French, a voluble lot who had no sense of decorum, the gentlemen were well-dressed. And as Brandon's valet, he expressed the view that he would see to it that his master was turned out in the epitome of good taste.

His valet fussed about the bedchamber and dressing room seeking direction from Brandon who attempted to read the newspaper in the adjoining sitting room, his unsettled mind refusing to take in either Hove or the news articles. Instead, he could only think of Letty, her face at the window as the mail coach took her away.

"Does sir wish to take his undercover gear? Might two dozen neck cloths suffice? Who knows what the laundry service is like in those hotels? Have they heard of starch? Does sir want the carmelite brown coat? Sir has never expressed much fondness for it. But if left behind, it would mean abandoning the bronze silk waistcoat, which didn't look well with the blue coat. Might the gray greatcoat with the four capes be too warm for a French summer?" And so on, until Brandon ordered him to surprise him, folded his newspaper, and quit the room, taking his thoughts of Letty with him.

The next day, they sailed for France.

CHAPTER TWENTY-TWO

Hawkshead Village, Cumbria
Six weeks later

GEOFFREY SHEPHERDED LETTY from the dance floor. "Shall I fetch you a glass of ratafia?"

"No, lemonade please. It is dreadfully hot." Letty employed her fan vigorously, the assembly rooms were crammed with guests tonight, all of whom she knew. How unlike London. One could depend on these people to behave more or less in the same manner from day to day, week to week, and month to month. She should be grateful for that, but found perversely that she wasn't.

Mrs. Crosby passed her with a knowing nod. Everyone anticipated she and Geoffrey would soon marry because one did not often surprise the village by doing something completely unexpected. Not since Mrs. Downer, the banker's wife, ran away with the young man who worked in accounts. That happened some years ago and was still spoken of.

Brandon's life in Paris must be so different to hers. Her thoughts turned unwillingly to him again, along with that hollow sense of yearning. She tried to be patient, to wait until the memories of her time in London, the thrilling and the glamorous, along with the dangerous, and the eventual wretchedness, had lost its hold over her.

But it took far too long. She smiled at Geoffrey, while struggling with the guilty knowledge that she was unworthy of him, and any other suitor. She wanted Geoffrey to be happy, and she feared he wouldn't be if married to her.

Letty waved to the widow, Anne Wilson, as she walked past in a pretty lavender dress. "Mrs. Wilson has cast off her mourning clothes," Letty said to Geoffrey. "She looks quite lovely tonight, doesn't she?"

Geoffrey handed Letty the glass of lemonade. "Eh?" His eyes narrowed. "What are you suggesting? That Anne Wilson and I should be more than acquaintances?"

"No, for I know you won't allow it. I suspect she would like it to be so, however." Anne had been widowed after Timothy Wilson died in a wagon accident two years ago. "Anne is too young to be a widow. She is the same age as you."

"There is nothing between Anne and me. If you are trying to dissuade me from declaring myself, I should like to know why."

"No, but you wished to marry her, until your parents expressed their disapproval because her father owned the haberdashery," Letty persisted. "Anne accused you of not fighting for her. And then she gave you up and married Timothy."

Geoffrey glared at her over the top of his wine glass. "You are accusing me of being spineless."

"It's hard to oppose one's parents when we are young. We wish to please them. But broken hearts are not easily mended."

"Broken hearts? You have not lost your sense of romance, I see."

Letty sighed. "I just don't believe you really want to marry me," she said, lowering her voice. "My uncle and your father are behind this. They've put their heads together."

"Perhaps they have, but I'm well past my majority. They cannot tell me what to do if I don't wish to do it. Not anymore, Letty."

He sat beside her. "Don't you want to marry me? When you came home without a beau, I hoped you might prefer me to one of those cynical, aimless London fellows who choose to do nothing but gamble and visit their tailor." He eyed her. "You have been acting strangely. Not at all like yourself. Was there someone down south you came to care for?"

"I suppose my time in London has changed me," Letty admitted. She *was* different, of course. No longer the eager, uncomplicated country girl who went to London.

"What did happen there? You've told me little, apart from being forced to return because you lost your chaperone to illness."

"I could hardly remain in London after Lady Arietta died," she said, horrified by the lies she'd been forced to tell. After a summons from Whitehall, Uncle Alford had left on the mail coach, returning later in the week shocked to learn of Lady Arietta's alliance with the French. His lips were sealed. He declared he had been sworn to secrecy and kept rigidly to it although Aunt Edith did try to discover more from Letty when he was gone from the room.

"We'll enjoy a good life together," Geoffrey said, breaking into her thoughts. "You were restless before you left, and I didn't think I had a chance. But you're more settled now. We'll work together, we both share a love of the land and horses. Both Mama and the squire would be delighted with the match. They are both fond of you."

"Yes, and I'm fond of them. Aunt Edith is forever urging me to marry you."

"Well? What prevents you? Can you tell me? It doesn't matter if you don't love me, Letty. That isn't always a good basis for marriage."

"You sound like my uncle," she said.

"A man of considerable wisdom," Geoffrey said with a smile.

His similarity to her uncle failed to fill her with confidence. Did Geoffrey love her? He hadn't said the words. Surely one of them should feel love for the other? Letty suddenly feared she would cry. She could not go on like this. Was she to become a melancholy old maid? Better, surely to marry her best friend, instead. Although the idea of marriage to Geoffrey failed to make her heart beat fast, it began to seem right, because it gave her a sense of purpose. A future. She was interested in the same things as he was. Might she make him a good wife?

"I'll give you your answer soon, Geoffrey."

"I'll call tomorrow. A reel is about to be announced, Mr. Yardley is on the dais and clearing his voice." Geoffrey stood and offered her his arm. "Shall we join the set?"

Letty wished Jane was here, she was an excellent sounding board. But Jane was away visiting a sick relative. Unable to find a sympathetic ear, Letty spent a restless night trying to come to terms with her future. Geoffrey was a decent man, gentle with animals. That always said a lot. They had shared a warm friendship. But he did not feel any passion for her. She was as sure of this as she was of her own feelings. Did it matter? Would love grow after they'd tied the knot? She wished she could be sure of it. And she wished another man didn't keep entering her dreams. But even if Brandon had asked for her hand, she would have been sorely conflicted, because of what marriage to him would mean. Waiting for him to return from perilous journeys undertaken for the Crown, always with the constant fear of him never coming home.

The next afternoon, Geoffrey called, having forgone his usual riding clothes for a neat coat and breeches, his fair hair slicked back. Aunt Edith welcomed him in with a warm smile, and even Uncle Alford emerged from his study to greet him.

When they were afforded some privacy with her aunt's promise of afternoon tea taking her from the room, and her uncle retiring to write his sermon, Geoffrey relaxed in a chair and smiled at her. "Your uncle has given his blessing. What have you decided, Letty?"

Was it unreasonable to want him to be more romantic? She might have been considering a new curricle.

"Yes, Geoffrey, I will marry you."

He smiled and came to kiss her.

BRANDON STEPPED OFF the gangplank onto the wharf. London skies were a familiar gray, the air humid with the promise of rain. While Hove fussed over the luggage, Brandon hailed a hackney.

It was good to be back in England. Paris had proved to be a triumph with the comtesse released from prison. He hadn't enjoyed the ensuing soirees and dinners which followed, longing inexplicably for home, his thoughts often returning to Letty. What was happening in her world? He had not expected that short period they'd spent together to hold such sway over him. While admitting it would be unfair to her to marry her, he'd bought a ring from a Paris jeweler. Even after he removed the small velvet box from his pocket and flipped open the lid to gaze at the twinkling diamond, he was still unsure.

"It's a fine ring," Hove observed. "Am I to be told the lady's name?"

"Not yet, Hove." Brandon was not prepared to tempt fate.

As the carriage took him and Hove to Mayfair, he realized that although glad to be in London, this city held no particular joy for him either. This peculiar restlessness had even dampened the pleasure of receiving notice of the Regent's intention to honor him with an award for services rendered during the capture of French traitors. Descrier, Elford, and Pierse had been found guilty and hanged, and the matter at an end.

This evening, the Willard's were holding a dinner. Tomorrow, at Carlton House, Brandon would be among those the Regent awarded. A party was to follow to which his parents were invited.

Brandon had received a fulsome letter from his father expressing his surprise and joy to learn that his son, over the last five years, had performed exemplary service for king and country. Apparently, all was forgiven. But he still hoped, with increased enthusiasm, Brandon would marry the colonel's daughter.

Brandon buried his cynicism. If he ever had a son, there would be no restrictions placed on his love, whatever the boy amounted to.

While the circumstances of Marston's death were in no way similar to Freddie's, Brandon admitted that something had changed him, that whatever had caused him to seek this dangerous work no longer drove him, and he'd come to accept that Willard was right. He should change his life. But not to set up a nursery with the colonel's daughter.

Willard and his wife, Veronica, greeted him in their drawing room. "Welcome back, Brandon. Your time in Paris has been well served!" Willard said with unusual insouciance. "London has failed to turn on its best summer weather for you."

Still strangely out of sorts, Brandon glanced at the rain lashing the windows. "No, but it is reliably unreliable."

"You must enjoy the rest of the Season, before everyone retires to the country to escape the heat," Mrs. Willard said. "My niece, Angela, has been asking where you'd got to. She is to perform again tonight."

"I look forward to hearing her lovely voice again." Brandon's smile hid dismay. He enjoyed Miss Willard's superb performance last time, and would again, but he wearied of society, after endless Paris soirees filled with clever repartee and flirtations which hadn't captivated him like they once had. He had met several charming, beautiful women, but resisted any involvement. Perhaps he did need a change of scene. Cumbria must be nice this time of year. The thought of seeing Letty brought him alive.

"Shall we adjourn to the library?" Willard led the way to the door. "You can fill me in on the details. One learns so little from dispatches.

"The comtesse was in good health despite spending time in that wretched prison?" Willard asked as he poured the drinks.

"I encountered few difficulties. Nothing, should it be discovered, that would cause a diplomatic upset. The comtesse appeared to have been treated well by the guards who greatly respected her. She is soon to join her husband in Vienna."

"What are your plans?" Willard rose to replenish their glasses after they'd covered the events on the Continent. He settled back in his chair.

"Sleep, ride, read some books, drink the best claret from my father's cellars, and try to avoid my mother's endless parade of young debutantes."

"And then?"

"Not entirely sure, Fraser. I've given it some thought over the last few weeks. Buy a country property and become a farmer, perhaps."

Willard's eyes widened. "Sounds...bucolic."

Brandon laughed. "Well, for part of the year, perhaps. But don't ask me about the rest."

Willard rose and picked up *The Gazette* on the desk. He folded the newspaper and handed it to Brandon. "I wonder if you're aware of this?"

A small article circled in the Births, Deaths, and Weddings: *Mr. Geoffrey John Verney, son of Squire Verney of Hawkshead Village, Cumbria, and Miss Letitia Eliza Lydia Bromley, daughter of Mr. Aubrey Charles Bromley, deceased, and Eliza Mary Bromley, deceased, and niece of Sylvester, Baron Bromley, have announced their engagement.*

The force of his reaction shocked him. It almost brought him up from his chair. Aware that Willard watched him, he shrugged and drank more of the fine burgundy, its superior qualities failing to register. "I wish them happy. Letitia is a wonderful young woman." He managed to sound casual, while his mind was in turmoil. He had feared this would happen, that a lovely girl like Letty would meet a man she wished to marry. But not so soon! To see the evidence stark and vivid in black and white newsprint caused his stomach to tighten.

"Yes, we thought so," Willard said. "An exceptional young lady."

He brushed lint from his sleeve. "So, shall you be living alone in this country idyll? Or do you seek to find a wife to share this rustic life of yours?"

"No idea," Brandon said, narrowing his eyes. Willard was going too far. "What makes you ask?"

"Miss Bromley's uncle came to London a few weeks ago. It was necessary for him to be briefed about what occurred, although nothing more was revealed to him beyond Lady Arietta's involvement. Decent fellow, a bit straight-laced as country parsons are, but he dropped a couple of things in conversation, which alerted me to Miss Bromley's state of mind."

"Oh?"

"Said she was depressed and unsettled. Both he and her aunt were concerned about her. The uncle doesn't believe in modern ideas of marriage. He expressed the wish that she marry the squire's son—and as you can see, she is about to. As the vicar pointed out, friendship forms the best basis for marriage. And they have been close friends since she came to Hawkeshead Village as a child. Although he did admit to being a little uneasy about her going off to London and showing no obvious signs of reluctance to leave Geoffrey."

Brandon made no reply. He knew in his heart that Letty didn't love this man. He remembered how dismissive she'd been when he'd asked her if she might marry Geoffrey. Nor had he forgotten their passionate farewell kiss. Was he clutching at straws to believe she was about to make a mistake? To settle for something she had not wanted.

There was no need to inquire the reason Willard revealed this to him. He suspected Mrs. Willard to be the driving force. Women loved a romance. "Perhaps the uncle is right, friendship is better than love, which can tread a rocky path," Brandon said, preparing himself for the inevitable heartbreak.

"Dash it all, he isn't right," Willard protested. "For either of you. I don't profess to know what went on between you two during that time you spent together unchaperoned, but I have eyes in my head. As does Veronica. Are you going to let the chance of love pass you by?"

Surprised, Brandon stared at his impassioned spymaster. He was usually so cool whilst dealing with matters of life and death. "My father is urging me to marry our neighbor, Colonel Smythe-Jones's daughter."

"I shouldn't worry about Sir Richard. He will be content with Miss Bromley. A baron's niece trumps a colonel's daughter."

"I can see you intend to press your argument. You won't be happy until you see me settled. If it arises from some misplaced guilt, I beg you to give it up. Don't think I've regretted the life I've lived since meeting you, Fraser. Have I not come out of it relatively unscathed?" At Willard's scowl, Brandon shook his head with a smile. "Don't look doubtful! To prove it to you, and prevent any further nudges from you or your charming wife, I shall visit Cumbria and discover for myself how Miss Bromley goes on."

"Don't leave it too long." Willard ran a hand through his grey-streaked fair hair. "That announcement is two days old."

"I shall go and wish her happy. Straight after the award ceremony, I'll head north."

Willard laughed. "I've trained you well, Brandon. You are first rate at hiding your feelings. You won't admit to loving the girl, but I caught the excitement in your eyes. Haven't seen that for a while. And never for a lady. I wish you luck!"

"Thank you, Willard," Brandon said with a grin. "And please, thank Mrs. Willard for her concern." If he got the chance to confess his love, Letty would be the first to hear it. *If he wasn't too late.*

Brandon walked to his carriage with a heavy heart. Despite his outward insouciance, he admitted he was deeply in love with Letty. He tried to tamp down his raging impatience. If only he could leave immediately for Cumbria, but to insult the Regent by not appearing to receive his medal, would also permanently injure his relationship with his father. He was forced to face the unpalatable fact that his future happiness must remain uncertain.

CHAPTER TWENTY-THREE

I F LETTY HAD thought accepting Geoffrey's proposal of marriage would bring her peace, she was wrong. She had not had a moment's peace since. Now that the matter was settled with everyone busily discussing the ceremony and the wedding breakfast, her unease only grew. They weren't often alone, but she must talk to him away from his parents and her uncle and aunt whose enthusiasm made it impossible for her to think clearly.

A week had passed, and she'd hardly slept, and knew she was not in her best looks as she set out for the squire's, where Geoffrey was breaking in a new horse. Squire Verney organized the hunt for the local gentry and supplied many of the horses. He now left most of the work to his son, and Geoffrey was perfectly content with the arrangement.

While it would be wrong of her to be critical of his disinterest in the world beyond their village, she did not share his view. It upset her to realize she would never return to London. She'd just begun to find her feet in society and make some friends when she was forced to leave it.

Geoffrey would no more attend a London Season, than honeymoon in Paris, another city he'd expressed an abhorrence for. If she had changed, Geoffrey had not. He was like an immoveable rock. And the differences between them seemed to widen while her fears grew.

She found him in the paddock, holding a rope which was looped around the colt's neck as the horse circled. He gently guided the animal which was young and unsure, but exhibited no fear of him. There was no violence in Geoffrey, she admired that about him. But he also lacked something that she felt she needed in a husband, the ability to laugh, and be a little outrageous, and not care so much what others thought of him. Because Geoffrey did. He cared very much for his parents' approval. A fine thing, but taken to extreme she considered it a sign of weakness. An inability to take life by the throat and live it according to one's own lights, and not others. He should have told his parents to go to the devil and married Anne Wilson years ago. He should now.

Letty sighed. She knew why she felt this way. It was Brandon. He had chosen his own path in life against much opposition. She smiled, recalling his wry humor in the face of trouble. He could be gentle, too. He'd protected her, cared for her. Her chest tightened, she really must stop thinking of him. It was unfair to Geoffrey to compare the two men, when they were so different, and both exceptional in their way. Brandon's final words came back to her. *Don't make compromises, remember your great Aunt Lydia's adventurous life.*

She rested her arms on the rail as the awful realization struck her like a lightning bolt, making her tremble with distress. Even though she would never see Brandon again, she could not marry Geoffrey.

AFTER TRAVELING THROUGH barren moorland bordered by stone walls that seemed to march for miles, the landscape changed to mist-shrouded dells, and fells falling away to large bodies of water, while above in the mist, the mountains rose majestically. It was very beautiful, but all Brandon could think of was Letty. Was he too late?

Would he have to offer his felicitations to the bride and groom?

Brandon arrived in Hawkshead Village in the late afternoon. A small pretty place of higgledy-piggledy houses and narrow lanes and squares, surrounded by green pastures dotted with cattle and sheep, known to be the childhood home of the poet, William Wordsworth.

He put up at the King's Arms, a tidy, whitewashed two-story building with a slate roof and well run by the look of the patrons. Drawing the innkeeper into conversation, he was told that as there was to be a full moon this evening, a dance would be held at the church hall. People came from miles around to attend it. Brandon thought it likely that Letty would be there.

After he washed and changed into his blue coat and buff breeches, he partook of a good supper in the dining parlor, then walked up the hill toward the church spire rising above the trees. In the summer twilight, the air was crisper than London, fragrant with flowers and greenery. The church hall was alight with candles, chatter and laughter drifting out.

A foot on the step, Brandon paused. Might this be a ceremony of some kind, a celebration? The innkeeper would surely have warned him when he expressed his intention to attend it. He would hate to appear in the middle of a wedding breakfast or a pre-wedding celebration. Might it be preferable to wait until he could visit Letty at home? With an impatient shake of his head, he mounted the steps and strolled through the door.

It seemed as if every person in the long hall turned to observe him.

A fiddler and a pianist played a lively piece, a country dance in progress. A gentleman stared at him, lost his place, and trod on his partner's foot. The lady was vociferous in her condemnation, but the man merely grinned and someone dancing past them chuckled.

Struck by how informal it was and how different to London, Brandon searched the room until he spied Letty where she sat talking to an older woman on one of the benches. She looked up, startled, and said something to the woman who peered at him curiously. Letty rose and made her way over to him, her cheeks pink, a question in her lovely brown eyes he was eager to answer.

He bowed, taking note of her dress, one he remembered she wore in London, and unlike a wedding gown, although he couldn't be sure, because country weddings would be a different affair. "I came to offer you and your fiancé my best wishes," he said, smiling down at her.

"That was very good of you." Her gaze roamed his face as if learning every feature. "Such a long way to come."

"Yes. Quite a tedious journey in fact," he said with a smile. "Charming place though, once you get here." He looked around. "Which one is Geoffrey? I must congratulate him."

"Over there, the fair man in a brown coat. He is dancing with Miss Ann Wilson."

"Oh? Why isn't he dancing with his bride-to-be?"

Letty smiled and shrugged. "He might be, who knows?"

His breath quickened. Unfamiliar with the force of the emotion which gripped him, he struggled to retain his composure. "You and Geoffrey are not to be married?"

"No. We decided against it. I've behaved foolishly. Everyone thinks so."

He took her hand. "Then we need to talk."

He drew her toward the door.

"Mr. Cartwright, Brandon, you can't just drag me off," she said, half startled, half laughing. "Really, I am already the subject of much gossip."

"I suspect you will always be the subject of gossip, Miss Bromley." He led her down the steps.

Drawing her back out of sight of the window, he placed a hand on the wall on each side of her, in case she should choose to escape him. She made no attempt to, however.

"Let me look at you." His gaze wandered from her shiny dark hair to her lovely eyes and soft lips.

She lowered her brows. "I look tired, I haven't slept well since…"

"Since?"

"Since London."

"Ah. Why is that?"

"You are not going to learn anything more from me, Brandon, until you tell me why you are here."

"I think you know why I'm here."

She flushed, and her eyes slid away from his. "How was Paris?"

"I will tell you about it…later."

A troubled look crossed her face, which he feared might herald a crushing refusal.

"Before you're sent on another mission?"

"No more missions. I've retired." He searched her lovely brown eyes, watching them change from disbelief to hope to joy. "Do you want me, Letty?" He held his breath.

She gasped. "Oh, Brandon. I do, of course I do."

"Then please say you will marry me."

She breathed in sharply. "Yes, oh yes, my darling, of course I will marry you." She smiled, tears in her eyes. "Even though you have not asked me properly."

He grinned and eyed the muddy ground. "I could go down on one knee, but I shall present a sorry picture when I approach your uncle and ask for your hand with dirty breeches."

Letty laughed. He remembered that laugh and felt as if he'd come home. His troubled world seemed to right itself. Willard was right, he'd been extraordinarily slow witted.

He pulled the small jeweler's box from his coat pocket and flipped it open with his thumb. The diamond sparkled in the light from the window above them. She gasped as he took her hand and threaded the ring onto her finger, pleased that he'd accurately guessed the size.

"It's beautiful!" she murmured, holding it up before her. Her eyes met his warm and loving, sending heat rushing through his veins. "Is it a family piece?"

"No. Bought it in Paris. You see, this has not been a hasty decision, Letty." Gazing down at her lovely face, he yearned to hold her tightly, to carry her off. Now, wouldn't that be talked about in the village for years? Aware that her uncle might still disapprove of him, he restrained himself. Framing her face with his hands, he lowered his head to capture her lips. He drew away and gazed at her. "I love you, Letty." *The deuce!* He had to kiss her again. He sighed and gathered her into his arms, lowering his head to kiss her deeply.

A rousing cheer came from above. Brandon looked up. Several faces were pressed to the window overhead, and more people peered out the door. "Kiss her again," some fellow yelled.

"My goodness," Letty murmured with a startled laugh, turning to look up.

"No objections there at least," Brandon said with a grin.

"Perhaps not, but I'm more worried about what my uncle will say."

"I remain hopeful he will agree to marry us."

"Married here in his church? I would love that, but the bans must be read for three whole weeks."

He cupped her chin with a thumb and forefinger. "I won't wait that long," he said huskily. He put a hand in his pocket and drew out the document. "Which is why I brought this with me."

"What is it?"

"A special license. We can marry as soon as we wish, with your uncle's blessing, I trust."

"I've never heard of such a thing. How did you come by it?"

"Fraser Willard."

He took her hand to lead her inside, but stopped before they reached the steps, reluctant to share her with the whole village just yet. "Willard is on good terms with His Grace, the Archbishop of

Canterbury, who furnished me with this extremely useful document. Despite the notice of your engagement to Geoffrey in the newspaper, he and Mrs. Willard remained hopeful of our marriage. I think Willard expected me to fight your fiancé for your hand. Fortunately, I shan't have to. Geoffrey looks quite fit," he added with a laugh.

Letty grinned and shook her head. "Geoffrey is a peaceful fellow and perfectly content not to marry me."

"I am glad he suffers from a disorder of the mind," Brandon said.

"No, he's just sensible." She laughed and shook her head. "I would not have made him a good wife."

"You'd run the poor fellow ragged. Which no doubt you will do to me."

A smile tugged at her lips, and she raised a hand to trace over his chin. "Then perhaps you should not marry me."

He caught her hand and pressed a kiss to her palm. "I suspect I am made of sterner stuff than Geoffrey. I won't let you get away."

She sighed. "Oh Brandon, I do love you."

He kissed her again.

Finally remembering where they were, he released her. "The Willards intend to hold a party for us when we return to London. That is, if you would enjoy it?"

"Oh yes. I would. I like them both, very much."

"Good. My digs aren't suitable for us. I plan to purchase a house in a better street. Near the park perhaps. There will be furnishings to purchase, the staff to hire. You'll be busy, Letty."

Her eyes widened with delight and disbelief. "We are to live in London?"

"Yes. But first we will pay a visit to my parents."

"Oh, Brandon, are you now on good terms with them?"

"A lot has happened that I must tell you about. I'm sure they will be pleased, my mother particularly, who has been trying to marry me off for years."

She giggled, and then her eyes grew worried. "Shall we go in? I do want you to meet Geoffrey. I think you'll like him."

"I believe I like him already. But will he like me?"

She held his hand tightly in hers. "How could he not?"

Brandon looked up at the smiling faces of several young women clustered around the doorway. The musicians struck up, and they disappeared inside. Another dance had begun, feet marching over the floorboards. "Very well, let us face the music."

CHAPTER TWENTY-FOUR

"OH LETTY, MR. Cartwright is so handsome," Jane said. She had come straight to the vicarage as soon as she arrived back in the village and heard the news. "I am so happy for you! I expected you to marry Geoffrey, and then I come home to this! It's like a dream." She glanced half-accusingly at Letty, her eyes alight with warmth. "You only mentioned Mr. Cartwright once in your letters."

Letty threw her arms around her. "I didn't dare hope he would ever want to marry me."

"Well, of course he would! Why ever not?" Jane said staunchly.

Letty grinned at her loyal friend. She'd pushed aside her fears that Brandon would one day accept another dangerous mission with the joy of being with him again. The very sight of him had stolen her breath away. She would have married him, anyway. Life was to be lived after all, she had only to read Lydia's diaries to reinforce that view.

After the shock had passed, and Uncle Alford learned that Brandon's father was the esteemed Sir Richard Cartwright, a politician of some note, he accepted the inevitable, and before long, he and Brandon were on good terms, most particularly because Brandon proved to be well read and could speak knowledgeably on almost any subject.

"Didn't you tell me you were sent down from Oxford?" Letty

asked when they were alone. "You certainly managed to amass a considerable amount of knowledge before you left."

"Most acquired after Oxford, I'm afraid. And now your uncle has kindly offered me several interesting tomes from his extensive library on Greek and Roman history," he said with his teasing smile. "A panacea for those long, lonely nights."

Fighting a grin, she shook her head at him.

After giving his permission to Brandon for their marriage, Uncle Alford had called her into his study. He'd told her to sit down and then cleared his throat. Letty expected some salutary advice and was surprised when he apologized. "Despite that unfortunate business with Arietta, which was your aunt's doing, I see now that I was wrong in my reluctance to send you to London." He shifted in his seat. "I feared after your father left you rather more than a comfortable competence, you would become the subject of fortune hunters. And as I couldn't be there to protect you." He cast her an anxious glance.

If he knew the whole of what happened in London and Kent, he might feel justified in his reticence. Letty smiled warmly at him. She didn't like to see him uncomfortable when he'd been so good to her. It was natural for him to want her to marry Geoffrey and remain here in the village. "I can quite understand your fears, Uncle," she said. "But 'all's well that ends well', as Shakespeare wrote, is that not so?"

"Indeed." Uncle Alford leaned back in his chair with an approving smile. Letty smiled back, pleased to have hit on her uncle's favorite playwright to help ease his conscience.

Aunt Edith awaited her in her bedchamber.

"I am happy with your choice. Mr. Cartwright will take you to London. The countryside, as pleasant as it is, does become rather dull after a time. I quite intend to return to Town myself when I'm completely well again. And we shall see more of each other," she said, with more warmth than Letty would have anticipated.

Her aunt's eyes filled with tears, and she withdrew her handkerchief to blow her nose. "I did not have great expectations for you, not after poor Arietta passed and then, you and Geoffrey…well, let us say no more about that." While Letty considered whether she would welcome a hug, her aunt tucked her handkerchief into her pocket and straightened her shoulders. "There are more important things to discuss, your wedding gown most particularly. Now, what about that lovely ball gown Mrs. Crotchet made for you? You've barely had a chance to wear it."

Letty bit her lip on a gasp of dismay. "I'm sorry, Aunt, the skirt never hung properly after the hem was torn, so I gave it to Arietta's maid."

"Oh, what a shame." She cast a suspicious glance at Letty as she fiddled with her lorgnette. "With the wedding Sunday next, we are short of time. Shall we go through your clothes and see if something can be altered?"

"I have a dress that requires no alteration," Letty said hastily, visualizing another horrid gown stitched up to her neck. "One Lady Arietta chose for me."

"A very nice thought, my dear. Wear it in memory of her." Her aunt nodded approval in happy ignorance of the truth of Arietta's death. When Uncle Alford had told his sister that Arietta had been struck down by a seizure, Letty was quite surprised at how comfortable he seemed with the lie. She supposed that some lies were necessary to spare others. She had told quite a few herself. "I shall wear your pearls, Aunt."

Aunt Edith nodded, somewhat appeased.

After several days of rain, Sunday dawned fine. Aware that many in the village would turn out to witness their wedding, Letty fidgeted with nerves. Her friends were happy for her and considered it to be very romantic, but some older folk had been set on Geoffrey.

Geoffrey had accepted it all without a qualm. It made her wonder if he was relieved. It could not have made him happy to marry a hesitant bride. When Brandon and Geoffrey appeared to get on so well, riding together over the countryside, and partaking of ale at the inn, much of the gossip died away. After only a few days, Brandon was hailed in the street and greeted as if an old friend. Letty put it down to his open, friendly manner, because usually one had to live here for years before they were accepted into the community. She only hoped this was a sign the ceremony would go off without a hitch and be a special day for them to remember.

In the late morning, wearing her net and white satin gown with the pink sash, and carrying a poesy of blush-colored roses, Letty walked down the aisle on the arm of Jane's husband, Gordon. Jane, in her best sprig muslin, with flowers in her red hair, had arranged Letty's short veil which floated from a circlet of pink rosebuds, then walked ahead, taking her place at the side of the altar as Letty's matron of honor. Every pew was filled, and more crammed in to stand at the back of the church.

Handsome in a dark coat with silver buttons, Brandon turned to smile at her from the head of the altar. Geoffrey, causing a stir among the guests, stood beside him as his best man.

Gordon stepped away. Letty's heart gave a skip when she reached Brandon's side. She smiled into his loving blue eyes.

Her uncle cleared his throat and began. When he came to the words "Who giveth this woman," he paused. "Well that would be me," he said, displaying an unusual penchant for humor. Laughter broke out around the church, then silence fell as the ceremony progressed.

And then it was over, Brandon pressed a brief kiss on her lips, shook Geoffrey's hand, and they left to sign the register.

A group of villagers hovering around the entrance tossed flower petals over them.

"Give her a proper kiss," a man called.

Brandon obliged, as they all cheered.

Laughing and holding hands, she and Brandon walked to the church hall for the wedding breakfast.

IN A CHAISE Brandon hired, they reached Royal Oak in Keswick by nightfall. He'd expressed the desire to spend some days exploring the beauty of the area and staying at wayward inns on route, before heading down to Surrey to visit his family. He had received a surprisingly conciliatory letter from his father, who had given up gracefully on his hopes for the colonel's daughter, and an impassioned one from his mother, who expressed her eagerness to meet Letty. He looked forward to introducing her to them. They would love her as he did.

He and Letty were directed to a private parlor Brandon had engaged for supper. In the small cozy room, Letty untied the fetching cherry-red bow beneath her chin and pulled off her straw hat. Seated, he smiled at Letty across the table. "Happy, my sweet?"

"So very happy." She cast him a loving glance, as a waiter entered with a tray, and the tasty aromas of hot soup, broiled chicken, and mushrooms, filled the air.

As they ate, they talked about the wedding and the breakfast.

"Geoffrey danced three times with Ann Wilson," Letty said as a trifle and coffee were brought in.

"You'd like to see him married?" He wasn't in the mood to discuss Geoffrey, good fellow that he was.

"To Ann. Yes. There's a history there, I'll tell you about it sometime."

He nodded, in no hurry to hear it. His gaze roamed over her from her glossy dark hair to her sweet mouth, and the exciting glimpse of décolletage making a mockery of the demure muslin dress. How pretty was his bride, and how much he looked forward to making love to her.

When the coffee and cake were removed and the door closed, Brandon poured more champagne into their glasses. "I think we should make a toast to our future, Mrs. Cartwright."

"Indeed, yes."

"It requires you to sit on my lap."

Letty glanced at the door. "The waiter might come in."

"He won't."

"How can you be sure?"

"I slipped him a few coins to stay away after serving the meal."

"I didn't see you. When was that?"

"While the boots was seeing to the luggage, and a maid was assisting you out of your pelisse."

She attempted to frown but her eyes filled with laughter. "You spies are not to be trusted."

He lowered his lids to half-mast and studied her. "Are you coming over here, or do I go over there?"

She rose. "I'm coming." She perched on his knee, an arm around his neck and took the champagne flute from him. They clinked their glasses together. "To a blissful life," he said solemnly. "And the hope you will not lead me into any more scrapes."

Letty's eyes widened. "Oh, that's unfair, Brandon."

He chuckled.

She repeated the words with great seriousness and drank deeply.

With an approving grin, Brandon removed the glass and placed it beside his on the table. He cupped her chin and lifted her face to his, kissing her. Her mouth tasted of sweet champagne. When the urge to deepen the kiss grew too demanding, he drew away. From their first meeting, Letty had stirred something in him that he'd tried to dismiss. And, fool that he was, he could have lost her. What a decent chap Geoffrey was. He'd become quite fond of the fellow.

Letty sighed and rested her head on his shoulder.

Her soft body pressed against his, and the emotion and profound relief he felt that she was his at last, swelled in his chest. "You make sense of my world, Letty," he murmured.

She gazed up at him, the merest hint of tears in her eyes. "When I fell head over heels in love with you, I tried to convince myself it was foolish. A mistake. That what Arietta said about you might be true. But I never believed it," she said passionately. "Looking back on it now, I suspect I agreed to follow you just to disprove it."

"*Sweetheart.*" He kissed her again, yearning to make her his own. He set her on her feet and rose. "Shall we retire, my love?"

Her ardent gaze told him all he needed to know.

CHAPTER TWENTY-FIVE

I N THE INN bedchamber, Letty washed and changed into her night attire. During the trip, Brandon had been amusing and lighthearted, but when their eyes met, his had caressed hers with an unspoken promise. Her body responded with a surging tide of emotion. He had gone downstairs to order a fire to be lit as the evening was cool. The servant had appeared, and soon a bright, crackling fire of applewood burned in the hearth, the perfumed smoke scenting the air. Brandon had not yet returned. Letty suspected he was giving her some time to herself.

She removed the pins from her hair and was brushing her long tresses when he entered. A little nervous, Letty smiled at him in the mirror. His large masculine presence changed the atmosphere in the room; it became charged with expectation. It made her catch her breath. She understood now that passionate love was beautiful and exciting, and she was eager to experience it with the man she loved.

He came to stand behind her and lifted a lock of her hair to breathe it in. "You have such pretty hair, Letty."

"It's deplorably straight. I always wanted curly blonde hair like my mother." She stood and faced him, filled with such longing to be one with him, her knees were weak.

"No, my love. You are perfect the way you are." He lowered his mouth to hers as his arms drew her close. When his hands on her derriere pulled her against him, the evidence of his desire sent heat rushing to her belly and set up a strange throbbing. A passionate kiss left them both breathless.

He untied the ribbons of her negligee and eased it off her shoulders, leaving the thin silk nightgown which hid little from his gaze.

"*My sweet love!*" Brandon cradled her breast. He brought his mouth down on her nipple, his tongue teasing it through the fabric. She wobbled on her feet and clung on to him as unfamiliar and intense sensations rocked through her.

He hefted her into his arms and crossed to the bed where he laid her down. Seated beside her, his blue eyes gleamed as he poked at the mattress with his hand. "Comfortable, with just enough bounce, I must thank the innkeeper."

Letty's eyes widened. "You wouldn't."

Brandon' laughed and pushed her gently back, leaning over her. "Wouldn't I?"

She giggled and traced his lips with a finger. "You are wicked, Mr. Cartwright!"

"My thoughts are very wicked at this moment, Mrs. Cartwright," he said huskily. He paused to kiss her again before rising to strip off his clothes.

He threw his coat onto a chair. "I can imagine what my valet, Hove, will think of this shabby treatment." He turned, pulling off his cravat. "You said you didn't require a lady's maid, but we can find you one, Letty."

She fought to order her thoughts, all her nerve endings alive as his body was revealed to her, his broad muscled chest with a dusting of dark hair as he pulled off his shirt. He unbuttoned his breeches.

"I'm used to doing for myself," she said, fighting to sound casual, and failing apparently, because he glanced at her with an amused smile.

"You'll need a good lady's maid in London."

"Yes, I'll find one there." She hardly knew what she said. She swallowed as her handsome husband advanced toward her, naked, erect, and alarmingly well-endowed.

He joined her on the bed, his hard, warm body pressed against hers, and she threw her arms around him with a moan of delight.

"Shall we remove this?" he asked.

She nodded, suddenly shy.

He drew her nightgown off and tossed it down. Then his gaze roamed over her. "My, but I have a beautiful wife," he said huskily, as she lay there blushing and resisting the urge to cover herself.

Brandon ravished her mouth, then began to explore her body slowly, moving down to kiss places she had no idea were so sensitive. As his mouth lavished attention on her tender, peaked nipples, his hand slid between her thighs while desire settled low in her belly. She was hot, her body slick with desire. With a mew of pleasure, she arched to meet him as he teased her, the quiet room filled with their labored breathing.

The warmth of his insistent touch caused ripples, shudders, and waves of sensation, her body pulsing beneath his clever fingers. The exquisite sensation built while she sought something maddingly beyond her reach. When he finally drew away, he left her panting, floating on a crest which slowly deposited her back in reality. She opened her eyes to find him watching her with tenderness and passion. "*Letty*," he murmured. A fission of desire rushed through her. She wanted him inside her desperately.

But when he parted her thighs and mounted her, and his erection pushed against her entrance, she tensed suddenly, fearful that it would hurt.

At her anxious whimper, Brandon stilled; his eyes sought hers. "Relax, sweetheart. It might hurt a bit, but not for long."

Brandon was an experienced lover. Letty tried not to think of all the women he had made love to. She would learn to please him and banish them all from his mind forever.

With a thrust, he pushed inside her. The jolt of pain and heat banished any thoughts as she clung to his shoulders with a gasp of surprise. Letty moaned. Brandon cradled her head and kissed her, his tongue tracing the interior of her mouth as he moved slowly within her. He filled her. The overwhelming emotion of being one with him brought a sob to her lips, the effect so explosive, the discomfort vanished. She moaned and reined kisses on his neck and shoulder and anywhere she could reach while her hands traced a path over his muscled back down to his slim waist and powerful buttocks. How lithe and strong he was. He began to thrust into her, hard and fast, stirring excitement to fever pitch, making her dig her fingers into his shoulders.

He groaned, and with a final thrust stilled, then withdrew. He rolled off her. "Did I hurt you, sweetheart?"

"Only a little." Letty trembled, limp, and profoundly moved. She licked her sore lip, which she might have bitten, and smiled at him.

"It will get better, I promise." He rested his head on her breast, his hand gently caressing her body.

His silky dark hair played through her fingers as she stroked his head. She smiled to herself. She was truly a woman now and felt so replete. So sleepy. Her eyelids grew heavy. She was vaguely aware of him pulling up the covers and kissing her gently before sleep claimed her.

BRANDON WOKE AS the sun rimmed the curtains, he gazed with tenderness down on his beautiful bride, curled up beside him, one hand on his chest. She had been wonderful last night. Well she'd been his Letty. Brave, passionate, and beguiling. He wanted to wake her and make love to her again, but steeled himself to let her sleep, to allow her body to heal. He threw back the covers and left the bed. He would dress and take coffee and read the newspaper in the parlor.

"Brandon?" A sleepy voice came from the bed.

He spun around, his breeches in his hand. "Yes, sweetheart?"

"Are you leaving me?"

He laughed and came over to sit beside her. "I was planning to let you sleep for a while."

She sat up, and the sheet fell away, giving him a delightful view of her beautiful, full breasts, the pert brown nipples begging to be kissed. His body hardened at the sight.

She patted the mattress beside her. "Come back to bed."

He sighed as he took in the sensual picture his wife made, her tousled hair and her lips plump from his kisses. "If I do, we'll make love again, Letty. You may not welcome it; your body will be sore."

She rewarded him with a temptress' smile. "Allow me to be the judge of that!"

CHAPTER TWENTY-SIX

B RANDON GUIDED THE chaise through a pair of tall gates. "Welcome to Fernborough Park, my boyhood home."

She could visualize him here as a young lad, climbing trees and tossing a ball to a dog.

The horses trotted down a long avenue of trees to an imposing brick mansion built in the style of the last century. Suddenly nervous, Letty drew in a breath as she looked about. Somehow, she had not expected him to come from such an impressive family. He was undoubtedly the son of a gentleman, attending Harrow and Oxford, but he'd never led her to believe his father was a wealthy man, although her uncle had mentioned Sir Richard Cartwright's parliamentary career in revered tones.

As the chaise approached the house, doubts assailed her. What if they disapproved of his marriage? While no one could criticize her family, of which she was proud, her upbringing had been that of a country girl, and not a society miss who attended finishing school and learned to become an accomplished lady. Letty did not excel at the pianoforte, having been indifferent to it, and although she'd been told her voice was sweet, it was not exceptional, and hardly a rival to Miss Willard's soprano. The thought of performing for a room full of guests terrified her. While she quite liked to sew, she had a hearty dislike for embroidery, drawing, and painting. She preferred to be outdoors, riding, tending the horses, picking vegetables for Cook, and feeding the chickens. Those things that country girls did, which young, well-brought up ladies might wonder at and never indulge in.

The mansion loomed before them. "Does your father keep riding hacks?" she asked in a strained voice trying to quell her fears.

He glanced at her with an amused smile. "There's a good stable. Shall we ride this afternoon?"

"I should like that." She would be glad to escape the house for a while. "The woods are beautiful, and countryside different to Cumbria."

"Sadly, the best of the bluebells have gone. I should've enjoyed making love to you amongst them, Mrs. Cartwright."

She quite believed he would. Her husband had proven to be an unpredictable and passionate lover. Letty blushed as she conjured up an image of their morning in bed. She hushed him as if those in the house could hear them.

Brandon turned to laugh at her. He pulled up the horses before the soaring front of the house as a groom rushed from the stables. Tossing the reins to him, Brandon lifted her down.

He took her hand, and they climbed the porch to the front door which had been opened by a formidable looking butler in black. The butler's craggy face broke into a smile. "Mr. Brandon, how good to see you, sir."

"Letty, this is Barnstable." Brandon laid his hat and gloves on the hall table. "Barnstable, I should like to introduce my bride, Mrs. Letitia Cartwright."

"How do you do, Mrs. Cartwright," the butler said. "We have been looking forward to meeting you." He took Letty's coat and bonnet. "You will find Sir Richard in the library, Mr. Brandon, and Lady Cartwright, I believe, is in the conservatory. Shall I send afternoon tea to the blue salon?"

"Thank you. Ask Cook for some of those Chelsea buns I like."

"Mrs. Fry set about making them as soon as she heard you were coming, sir."

The hall was two stories high, a huge echoing space with a marble tiled floor and a marble staircase sweeping up to the upper stories. It took Letty back to visits to Bromley Hall when she was a child. Brandon took her arm and walked with her down a lengthy corridor.

After passing through an elegant reception room, they emerged into a glass-walled conservatory filled with greenery. The air was dense with the scents of flowers, foliage, and earthy smells. A lady, her dark hair streaked with white, turned from where she was potting a flowering plant. "Brandon!" She stripped off her gloves and rushed over to embrace him. She kissed his cheek, then turned with a smile to greet Letty. "I beg your pardon, I have not seen my son for some time."

"Mama, this is Letty," Brandon said.

"How do you do, my dear!" She enveloped Letty in a scented hug. "I have been looking forward to meeting my son's bride."

"It is so good to meet you, Lady Cartwright," Letty said. "You have a splendid variety of orchids."

"Yes, I am fond of the flower." Lady Cartwright smiled. "You must call me Mama, dear child. I am your mama-in-law, after all. Let us go and find your father, Brandon, he has finally settled in the library. He has been pacing about all morning waiting for your arrival!"

Sir Richard raised his head from a chessboard he was contemplating as they entered. He stood and came across to greet them. "At last, someone to play with, Brandon, your mother shows no interest. And this is Letitia. How do you do?"

Letty came shyly forward. Up on tiptoes, for he was as tall as Brandon, she kissed his cheek.

He held her at arm's length and nodded approvingly. "Baron Bromley and I are old acquaintances, Letitia. Never met your father, however. I'm sorry such a tragedy befell you at such a tender age."

As they walked upstairs to the blue salon, Brandon put his head close to hers. "I told you they would approve of you." He called to his mother who walked a little ahead. "Which chamber have you put us in, Mama? I hope it's the yellow."

"It is, my dear. I've had your things moved there. It's the largest and has a nice view of the lake."

"It's also far away in the corner of the east wing," he whispered to Letty with a wink, as his parents disappeared into the salon.

"*Brandon!*" she hissed.

"You can be a bit noisy on occasion, Mrs. Cartwright," he said in an undertone.

She hit him on the arm with an embarrassed giggle.

He laughed and tucked her hand through his elbow. "Shall we go in, Mrs. Cartwright?"

After dinner, Letty roamed the drawing room, gazing at the fine oil paintings adorning the walls. She studied an oval-shaped gold medal in pride of place on the mantel. It was surrounded by a laurel wreath and attached to a blue and gold velvet ribbon. It bore Brandon's name.

"That was presented to Brandon by the Prince Regent," his mother said with a proud smile.

Letty turned to Brandon who was seated across the chess table from his father. "When did the Regent award you this, Brandon?"

"Three weeks ago. It was for his bravery and service to the Crown," his father said, looking up from the chessboard. "Brandon isn't much for awards. He sent it to us at his mother's request."

Letty suspected the award and his father's obvious pleasure in it had a lot to do with Brandon's lightness of spirit. She wondered if he would have told her about it as she came back to sit beside his mother again. "You must be very proud of him, Sir Richard."

"Indeed, most proud," Sir Richard said. He frowned at Brandon who was smiling at Letty. "It's your move, son."

AFTER HE'D LOST one chess game to his father, and won another, while Letty chatted quite knowledgeably to his mother about gardening of all things, they retired to their bedchamber.

In the four-poster bed hung with yellow chintz, Letty voiced a fear that he would return one day to his dangerous work. "I hate to ask you not to, but I lost my father and mother, Brandon," she explained, her big eyes imploring him. "And I won't lose you."

"When I told you I resigned, I meant it, my love." Deeply touched, he eased back her hair from her bare shoulder and placed a kiss on her satiny skin. "I shan't be tempted to change my mind."

She pleated the lacy edge of the linen sheet. "But I fear it won't suit you to give it up. It's not in your nature to live without some purpose."

"Well, I won't involve myself in politics." He had no intention of following his father's path in life. "I'll prefer to purchase that country house. We'll spend part of the year there. I have a fancy to be a gentleman farmer. There's my inheritance from Great Aunt Lawson, which I came into a couple of years ago. I hadn't thought much about what I would do with it. Would you care to be a farmer's wife, Letty?"

She leaned over his chest, toying with the dark hair, following the line down to his navel and distracting him. "I should enjoy being the wife of a gentleman farmer. I believe my talents lie in that direction. But might we spend the Seasons in London, Brandon? I did make some good friends, and should like to see them again."

"Then we shall. But first we must visit Paris. I seem to remember you expressing the view you'd like that." At her squeal of delight, he rolled over, taking her with him. "I am happy to do whatever my love desires," he declared huskily, as her soft body lay atop his, stirring all kinds of sensations. "Within reason," he added cautiously, reminded of Letty's own penchant for adventure. With a smile, he kissed her.

EPILOGUE

The Foster's ball, London
Six Months Later

HOW DIFFERENT LONDON was for a married lady. Letty smiled at her acquaintances who danced by on their partners' arms. As Lord Bakewell whisked her energetically around the floor, she thought over the changes the last few months had brought. Furnishing their new Mayfair townhouse in Curzon Street. Hiring staff. She had taken on Adele who had come to her seeking employment.

Every day and most nights were filled with engagements. She and Brandon dined with the Willards, attended breakfasts, picnics, and soirees, and dances at Almack's where they were greeted by Lady Sefton and Lady Jersey, and the other strict patronesses of the Assembly Rooms. When the weather was fine, Letty rode her new mare, or drove in her shiny new blue barouche in Hyde Park with friends.

Brandon visited his club, Whites, and argued with his father on matters of government policy over their frequent chess games. Letty could see Brandon was slowly being drawn into the political sphere and suspected he would become a fine politician one day like his father.

Aunt Edith had returned to London and inveigled Letty into joining her literary group. To her surprise, Letty found she thoroughly enjoyed their heated discussions of the latest novels and poetry.

When she left the dance floor and curtsied to her partner, Lord Bakewell, she glanced over with sympathy at the three debutantes clustered together, appearing awkward and painfully shy. That had been her not so long ago.

Her husband emerged from the crush. The sight of him never failed to send a thrill rushing through her. To her mind, he was the most handsome man in the ballroom. While she trusted him never to betray her, liaisons and infidelity among the *ton* were commonplace. Some men saw marriage as no barrier and flirted with her outrageously. They changed their lovers as often as they did a tailcoat, and *Ton* gossip was rife with intrigue. She had taken note of the ladies' eyes following Brandon, how they discussed him behind their fans. Letty admitted to being a jealous woman. A good thing when Lady Fraughton announced she was to marry again.

Brandon smiled down at her. "Are you free for the waltz, madam?"

"Yes, I've kept it specially for you, darling. Lord Bakewell has asked for the supper dance, and will take me into supper."

Brandon scowled. "The devil he will."

"You are overreacting. He is a flirt but quite harmless." She glanced around to see if anyone overheard them. It was bad *ton* to argue with a spouse in public, as it was to show too much affection.

"No man is harmless," Brandon said. "I know, I am one."

With several gentlemen claiming her hand for the last four dances, Letty sought to change the subject. "I haven't had a chance to tell you. I received a letter from Jane this morning while you were out riding. Geoffrey and Ann have become engaged!"

"That is good news." He nodded approvingly. "We must visit them before the weather makes the trip impossible. Your uncle, too. Poor chap is alone now that your aunt is back in London."

"Uncle Alford is very self-reliant. I believe he took me in under sufferance all those years ago."

Brandon chuckled. "Perhaps, but he came to care for you."

"And I, him." She raised her fan to hide her words. "Jane writes that she is enceinte," she whispered.

"Is she, by Jove! Gordon must be over the moon."

"Jane complains that he is quite indiscreet. Everyone in the village had learnt of it."

Letty glanced over at the forlorn wallflowers. "Those poor debutantes look marooned. I wonder if I might help ease their way into the Season? Their chaperones are quite ignoring them." She eyed Brandon. "They will feel more the thing if a charming man dances with them."

"I hope that doesn't mean you want me to dance with all of them?" he said with a quick glance to where three young ladies sat primly, hands clasped in their laps, their chaperones chatting together nearby.

She grinned behind her fan. "Well, perhaps asking one of them to dance wouldn't hurt. It's so difficult, you see, to be thrust into London society and not know how one is meant to go on."

"I'll mention them to Harold Reilly. He's looking for a wife." Brandon slipped a finger into the top of his cravat. "But really, Letty, I can't demand it of my friends. Gentlemen will seek them out soon enough."

"Yes, I'm sure you're right. But I can still offer them my support. I remember how awful it was for me at first."

He gazed down at her. "Your Come-out was a little different from the norm though, was it not, my love?" His blue eyes lit up with a wry smile. "Ah, the dreaded dress."

She tapped him on the arm with a fan. "I just knew you would mention it."

"You would look enticing in a sack. Or without it," he added huskily, raising her chin with his thumb and forefinger and planting a light kiss on her mouth.

Letty glanced around. There would be comments. Bad *ton*, the Cartwrights were flirting again. "Oh, dear. The Duchess of Malvern is glaring at us."

"No she's not. Her Grace suffers from astigmatism."

Letty laughed. "I shall ask Maria Foster to introduce me to the young ladies before I'm to dance again."

"Excellent notion," Brandon said, clearly relieved not to be inveigled into dancing with them. "There's Fraser Willard. I need a word with him about a matter I read about in the newspaper this morning. I shall return for the waltz."

Letty raised her eyebrows.

"Don't give me that look, madam," he said in a mock stern manner. "I'm not about to involve myself in anything untoward. If Willard wants me for some mission, I will tell him I already have one. To make you happy."

"How nicely put, darling. But if there's a mission you're tempted to take, be aware you have an accomplice."

Brandon chuckled. "And would that be you, madam?"

"I had no one else in mind."

Brandon arched an eyebrow. With a smile, he raised her hand, his lips grazing her gloved fingers. "There will be no mission, Mrs. Cartwright, but if there was, I would consider no other accomplice but you."

Letty smiled as she watched him walk over to Willard and clap him on the back. Then, she rose and crossed the floor to introduce herself to the debutantes.

The End

Printed in Great Britain
by Amazon

16695507R00132